SHE

WORE

A

PRETTY

MASK

SHE WORE A PRETTY MASK

J.W. BOUCHARD

To learn more about J.W. Bouchard visit:
http://www.jwbouchard.com

For Tom Piccirilli

prologue

SHE WAS RUNNING.

The girl didn't know where she was, lost in the woods, exhausted, but somehow finding it in her to keep running. She kept glancing over her shoulder, seeing nothing but the darkness and the trees, but there was something out there, chasing her.

Her heart was thudding against her chest, beating in her throat, and she couldn't remember how she had gotten here because she remembered undressing, showering, putting on a fresh set of panties and an over-sized t-shirt, taking two sleeping pills because she had trouble getting to sleep at night, and then she had slid into bed, closed her eyes, and after some tossing and turning, she had fallen asleep.

But she was lost now. Still running. Looking over her shoulder because something terrible was chasing her. She couldn't see it, couldn't hear it, but she could *sense* it.

All she could do was to keep running.

To her left, she could see the lake. There was a steep embankment, muddy and dangerous where the trees ended, sloping down sharply to a rocky beach far below. Then the lake, still but menacing, bisected by an uneven white line of reflected moonlight.

It felt like there wasn't enough air in the world to fill her burning lungs. She sucked at it in large gasping breaths, felt like she was trying to breathe through a straw. Her bare feet crunched over the terrain, mud oozing between her toes, rocks slashing at them like a maniac coming at her with a dull knife.

Where was she?

The woods.

That was all she knew, all she could be certain of. She had never been a hiker or a hunter or the outdoorsy type. She wasn't familiar with the woods, but she knew from growing up in the small town that they went on for miles and a person could get lost if they weren't careful, the way she was lost now.

How had she gotten here?

She tried to think, but her brain was focused on a singular concern. *Survival.*

Behind her, she heard a twig snap. It was close. *Too* close.

She thought she might vomit, the exhaustion was that bad. Her legs were on fire, white hot pokers jabbing themselves into her calf muscles, and her feet were wet and skinned raw.

Still, she continued to run, thinking she would die like this rather than risk facing the thing that chased her.

You went to bed, she thought. *Remember? You took the pills because if you didn't, you would never get to sleep, and you had to be up at six-thirty to get ready for work. You fell asleep with the TV on. What was it?* Criminal Minds *or* Law & Order: SVU. *Some cop show anyway. That's right. That means you can't be out here, lost in the woods. Because you're dreaming. It's the sleeping pills. They always do a number on you. Make you have the weirdest dreams. And that's what you're doing now. Dreaming. None of this is real. All you have to do is make yourself wake up.*

And for a moment she believed it. Believed that this was all a horrible dream, a nightmare. You don't just go to sleep in your own bed, in the safety of your own home, and then suddenly wake up in the middle of the woods, running from a wild animal. That was the stuff that happened in dreams.

But then she heard the sound of another twig snapping and it didn't seem like a dream anymore. It felt *real*, which was how nightmares could be, but the fishy smell of the lake invaded her nostrils, the sting of the rocks biting into her feet, the fire raging in her lungs and her legs, the sound of her own heartbeat in her ears like violent waves crashing against a sandy beach – those sensations were real, just like the thing chasing her was real.

It was closer now.

She forced herself to keep going.

Her foot came down on a rock, a big one this time, and she screamed. She lost her balance, twisted her ankle, fell to the ground. Her hands sank into the mud.

She screamed, picked herself up, got going again, limping now because at best she had sprained her ankle, at worst had maybe fractured something. She hobbled along, too slow, but refused to let herself quit.

She was caked in mud, decorated in dead leaves, limping along, and she knew in her mind that the thing was closer now, but she didn't dare look over her shoulder.

Wake up! Wake the hell up!

The command went unheeded.

Another twig snapped, this one so close, right behind her, and she screamed again but all that came out was a hoarse gasp.

Something fell on her shoulder, grabbed her. It was a hand, she knew that, but she imagined it had the long curving claws of a beast, incredibly powerful, digging into the meat of her shoulder until she could feel the wet warmth of her own blood.

She stumbled to the ground, felt the weight of the beast on her.

Something touched the back of her neck, followed by a brief stabbing pain that was quickly replaced by something else, something pleasant, almost soothing, and it stayed there, like a long gentle kiss.

Her terror subsided. There wasn't any pain now. It didn't hurt anymore. She had been wrong. It wasn't so bad.

Her vision swam, her mind went foggy.

But none of that mattered now.

She felt safe again, almost enjoying herself, the lips pressed softly against the nape of her neck, continuing to kiss her.

Why were you running? Were you really afraid of this, *silly?*

Yes, silly, that's what it was.

Because this was just what she needed. She felt herself relax completely, exploring the sensation, wishing it would last forever.

Only a dream, she thought. *And it's a nice one.*

part

I

body count

1

the girl
in the mask

NATHAN WATCHED AS they dragged the body from the water. He had been with the Chickasaw County Sheriff's Department for going on six years now, had been Sheriff for all of two minutes of that time, and had seen more than his share of gruesome acts, but nothing that had left him scarred, nothing that had given him nightmares.

Something told him all of that was about to change.

It was early yet, a little before six. The sun hadn't risen, but the sky was bright enough that he could make out the girl's body with perfect clarity.

"Female," Deputy Neal said.

"I can see that."

"What do ya think? Sixteen, maybe. Seventeen, *tops*."

"I'd say that's a fair guess."

"I was judging it by her tits. See how perky they are? They start to get much older than that, they start to sag."

"For Christ's sake, Carl, keep your voice down."

"I'm just saying, on account she's wearing a fucking *mask* and all. Besides, who the fuck cares?"

Nathan made his way down the steep embankment, the soft mud making squishing sounds under his boots. Carl rolled his eyes, followed after him.

Nathan stared at the body. The woman – no, not old enough to be considered a woman yet, just a girl, a teenager probably – was nude. Clammy white skin, hair hanging in thick wet clumps, small breasts, thin and fit like an athlete, muscular shoulders, a swimmer maybe.

He took in all the details, but his eyes kept going back to the mask that covered her face.

"Give it to me," he said.

"Couple of locals out fishing caught sight of the body floating in the lake about an hour ago. Towed it in, called dispatch."

"Where are they now?"

"I cut 'em loose right before you pulled up."

"Question them?"

"Course I did. It's not my first day on the job. They were pretty shook up. Can't say I blame them."

"Call the M.E.?"

"Gene Mathers is on his way over. Should be here any minute now. He wasn't thrilled about being dragged out of bed this early. Shit, Nate. I'm starting to sense a real lack of confidence here. I've been doing this for as long as you have, so what gives?"

"It's our first murder. I don't want to go fucking it all up."

"Your first murder since you made Sheriff, you mean."

"Don't start with that."

"I'm just saying, I know you're holding a grudge. I just want you to remember that nobody twisted your arm or anything like that. You can't blame me because you ran on a dare."

"I wasn't supposed to win."

"No. I guess you weren't. And I'm fucking baffled as to how you pulled it off, but the facts are the facts. Abe Talley never saw it coming. He got lazy. After a while, people started to notice. So here we are."

"I'm not holding onto a grudge."

"Could've fooled me."

Nathan let his eyes wander from the body, out to the lake, past it, to the woods beyond.

"You going to do it?" Carl asked.

"Do what?"

Carl pointed at the body. "Take the mask off."

Nathan's eyes went back to the dead girl. He was curious. What did she look like under the mask?

The mask was unlike anything he had seen before. Shaped in the form of a face, a young face, female, a young girl, which made it fitting that it was on this girl who probably hadn't even been old enough to vote when she died.

Murdered, his mind corrected. Her body was mostly unmarked, slightly bloated, stiff, meaning she hadn't been in the water all that long, not much longer than twenty-four hours he guessed since *rigor mortis* had set in. But the area around her throat was dotted with purple splotches, and his next educated guess was that she had been strangled. The bruises weren't pronounced enough to have been committed with a weapon, with the electrical cord of a lamp or a length of rope.

He did it with his hands.

And Nathan was already thinking they wouldn't find any prints. The man (and Nathan thought it was most certainly a *man*) had worn gloves. He didn't know how he knew this, but he could see an image of it in his mind and knew that it was true.

"Sheriff?"

"Let's wait for Mathers," Nathan said. "He can do the honors. I want you to call Des Moines and get them to send some divers out. We'll search the lake. See if there's anything else down there."

"You think there's more than one?"

"No. But they might have dumped evidence in the lake."

"Look at her. Doesn't look like we're going to find a murder weapon. No bullet or stab wounds."

"I want to play it safe. And after you do that, run a check with missing persons, see if there's anybody that fits the description. She didn't materialize out of thin air. Get going."

Carl lingered.

"Yeah?"

"This is going to be bad, isn't it?" Carl asked.

Nathan nodded. "Yeah, something tells me it is."

Gene Mathers arrived around half past six. He was in his early sixties. He was wearing plaid pants and a pullover sweater, meaning, Nathan thought, that he had been getting ready for an early morning round of golf at the Chickasaw Country Club before he had been so rudely interrupted by Deputy Neal's phone call.

Nathan watched him make his way down the embankment, his loafers sinking in the mud, cursing loudly as he navigated the slippery terrain.

"Morning, Gene."

"Like hell it is. Tee off is at seven. And now this," Mathers said, waving his arm at the dead girl that lay on the beach.

"It's a shame," Nathan said.

"It's too early for sarcasm, Sheriff. Congratulations, by the way."

"Thanks."

"Don't thank me. I didn't vote for you."

Mathers crouched down next to the body, stared at it for a while before he moved closer, inspecting it. Finally, he said, "Well, she's dead."

"Is that your professional opinion?"

Mathers glanced up at him, then back to the body.

"The forensic pathologist will do the autopsy once she's back at the morgue, but I'd say cause of death is strangulation." He pointed at the bruises around the girl's neck. "Help me get this mask off."

"Strange, isn't it. I've never seen anything like it."

"*L 'Inconnue de la Seine*," Mathers said.

"What's that? French?"

"It means 'Unknown Woman of the Seine.'"

"You've seen it before?"

"I spent a year in Paris. I saw a version of it when I was there. *La Belle Italienne*, they call it. Back in the late 1800s, they pulled a young girl out of the Seine River. Never identified."

"Murdered?"

Mathers shrugged. "Don't think so. Suicide maybe. Rumor has it, the pathologist at the Paris morgue became so infatuated by her beauty that he had a plaster cast of her face made. It caught on. So much so that it was used as the head of Resusci Anne."

"Who?"

"Not a who. A *what*. She was a first aid mannequin. That's why they consider it the most kissed face of all time."

"Learn something new every day," Nathan said, squatting down, putting on a pair of latex gloves. He gripped the face of the mask, tilted the girl's head to the side. A single elastic strap held the mask in place. Mathers lifted the girl's head as Nathan pulled back on the strap and gently brought it over her head.

She had a narrow face that was slightly bloated now. Her eyes were open, vacant, blue as the sky they stared up into.

"Recognize her?"

"No."

"Petechiae around the eyes. See how the eyes are blood red? That's an indication of subconjunctival hemorrhaging."

"Meaning?"

"Strangulation."

Mathers stood up, peeled off his latex gloves.

Nathan heard the ambulance pull up.

"I'll have her taken to the morgue in Alton," Mathers said. "I'll call you after the autopsy is finished, but I'm confident that strangulation was the cause of death."

"Thanks Gene."

They shook hands. Mathers started back up the embankment, paused, turned to Nathan and said, "Hell of a way to kick off your term, Sheriff Murphy."

2

jess

BY THE TIME he pulled into his driveway it was after 8 o'clock and the dull ache in his left testicle was back again.

He killed the cruiser's engine and sat there for a moment, trying to clear his mind, trying to get the dead girl out of his head. It was his first murder. Six years, and she was the first. He had seen fatalities, car wreck victims, overdoses, the occasional suicide. Never a murder. Not in Crater Lake.

You could make the hour's drive west to Omaha, and these days, in a city like that, people were killing each other on a daily basis. Murder was a plague that spread until it left nothing untouched, except for the small towns, where people were superstitious, stuck in the old ways, but still managed to hold onto their sanity when the rest of the world threatened to fall apart.

It wasn't the girl's body that was stuck in his head. It wasn't the nakedness, the innocent face, the bright blue eyes that had seemed to stare up at him.

The mask. That was what had glued itself to his memory, the darkness that lingered in his brain.

L 'Inconnue de la Seine, Mathers had called it. The Unknown Girl of the Seine. And wasn't that what they had here? An unidentified girl, so pretty, so innocent, Nathan unable to fathom how a girl like that wouldn't be missed. Somewhere out there, there was a concerned mother, worried sick, pacing the house, making frantic calls, wondering where her daughter was.

Carl hadn't gotten back to him yet, but it was still early. He wanted to put a name to the face, identify the girl, at least that would mean they were getting somewhere.

Nathan exited the vehicle, made his way slowly into the house. The dull ache in his testicle had started several days ago, and seemed to come and go spontaneously, not exactly painful, but it was uncomfortable, nagged at him.

He found Jess in what had once been the unused spare bedroom. Nathan had spent a weekend not too long ago painting it a bright shade of yellow. Jess was coming up on eight-and-a-half months, looked ready to pop any minute, and she had devoted most of her time to putting the finishing touches on the baby's room. She had chosen yellow for the room's color because it was supposed to be gender neutral. They didn't know the sex of the baby. Nathan wanted it to be a surprise. Jess was dying to know. She was a planner, and the not knowing bugged the hell out of her, but Nathan had stuck to his guns. The trade-off was that Jess got to decorate the room; got to choose the colors, pick out the crib, had final say on the arrangement. It kept her occupied. Now that Nathan had been elected Sheriff, the plan was for Jess to quit the bank and go full-time stay-at-home-mommy, but he didn't think she could do it. She had already cut down her hours to part-time, but the only thing keeping her sane was the knowledge that the baby would be coming any day now. That, and the countless hours she spent online shopping, searching for the perfect crib, the perfect sleeper, the perfect changing table.

Jess was leaned forward in the rocker, staring out the open window, a laptop open in her lap.

"Hard at work?"

"I'm taking a breather. It was a workout just to get my shoes on," she said. "I'm winded. This child can't come soon enough."

"You still look beautiful."

"I'm fat. That's all there is to it. And you're a liar, but that's why I love you."

"As Sheriff, I would never lie."

"Your authority stops the moment you step foot into this house."

"Don't I know it."

"I didn't expect you home so early."

"I can't stay. Just thought I'd check in."

He couldn't say exactly what compelled him to stop home that morning. Maybe it was seeing the dead girl, reminding him that bad things happened in the world, that there were monsters out there. Whoever had killed the girl was *still* out there, maybe close, and Nathan didn't believe for a second that he was a one-and-done kind of guy. So here he was now, checking to make sure Jess was all right, ready to check under the bed and in the closets if he had to.

"I didn't hear you leave."

"Official business."

"Bad?"

"You could say that."

"Spill it. *Wait.* Do I even want to know?"

"Probably not."

"Okay, tell me."

"It's bad, Jess."

"How bad?"

Watching her rock slowly back and forth in the chair, the sun streaming in through the window, the birds chirping, Nathan had a hard time believing that the dead girl was his reality.

"Remember a few years back when Dave Bates got creamed by a semi while he was riding his motorcycle?"

"That bad?"

Nathan nodded. "Yeah. Worse maybe."

Her hands rested gently on the beach ball that was her stomach as she stared at him, waiting for him to go on.

"It's a murder. We pulled the body of a young girl out of the lake."

Jess cupped a hand over her mouth.

"Who is it?"

"She's still unidentified. Nobody we know, I don't think."

"And you're sure she was murdered?"

"Gene Mathers thinks she was strangled."

"Oh my God."

"That's not the worst part. Whoever did it covered her face with a mask."

"A mask?"

"Weirdest thing I've ever seen," Nathan said, seeing the mask in his mind again, the girl's open eyes after he had pried it off of her.

"What kind of mask was it?"

"Huh?"

"What did the mask look like?"

"Does it matter? You really want all the gory details?"

She took her time answering. Finally, she nodded. "I think so, yes. Otherwise, I'll just keep thinking about it, imagining what it looked like. And that's worse."

"The mask was of a young girl's face. Some girl they pulled out of a river in France back in the 1800s. Nobody figured out who she was."

"Was that girl murdered, too?"

"Mathers said he recognized it from when he lived in Paris. He wasn't sure, but he didn't remember it being a murder. At the time, they labeled it a suicide. That was a long time ago, they didn't have the forensic capabilities we have now, so who knows."

"Why the mask?"

"Your guess is as good as mine. I'm thinking it must be symbolic somehow. The killer murdered a young girl, covers her face with a mask that looks like a young girl. Doubtful it's a coincidence. It must mean something to the killer, we just don't know what. Maybe he's taunting us."

"A murder in Crater Lake," Jess said, mostly to herself. "I can't believe it. When was our last murder? I've lived here all my life, I don't ever remember hearing about one."

"Sooner or later, the odds tip that way. A long time ago, an asteroid crashed into the Earth and killed off all the dinosaurs. They're always talking about asteroids on the news, about how close some of them are to hitting us. Someday our luck will run out and one of them will hit the Earth again, and we'll end up just like the dinosaurs."

"But a serial killer running around town killing people?"

"Jesus, Jess, don't say stuff like that out loud. Don't even think it. We've got one dead girl. No one's talking about a serial killer."

"Word gets around."

"Yeah, but that's no reason to cause a panic."

The pain in his testicle flared suddenly. He winced, hand going down to his crotch, staying there.

"What's wrong?"

"Nothing."

"You just now looked like someone kicked you in the junk," Jess said.

"It's nothing." He looked at her, saw she wasn't going to let it go at that, and said, "I've got this ache in my nut."

"You better make an appointment."

"It's nothing, Jess. It comes and goes. I'm not like you. I don't go to the doctor every time I have a sniffle. We don't need to rack up a two hundred dollar medical bill just so Cock-a-bashi can spend ten seconds feeling up my balls."

"It's Kobayashi. And you need to go. What if it's something serious?"

"And I'm telling you, it's not."

"Nathan."

"Let's just give it a few days. If it doesn't go away, I'll make an appointment."

"Two days," Jess said. "If it isn't better in two days, I'm getting you in to see Kobayashi, and you will let him feel your balls up for as long as he pleases."

"Fine."

He stood in the doorway to the room for another minute before saying, "I better get going. I love you. You too," he said, moving closer to her, placing a hand on her stomach. "Whatever you are."

"Funny. I love you. Catch him. Okay? I won't be able to sleep at night knowing there's a maniac on the loose out there."

"I've got my top men working on it."

She smiled at him and then went back to focusing on the laptop.

The reason he didn't want to see Kobayashi was simple: more than anything, he feared bad news, especially when it concerned his health. More specifically, he was afraid of cancer. He wasn't a hypochondriac, but whenever he started to get sick, he got worried that maybe he had cancer. There was no rhyme or reason to this fear, this paranoia, but it had started a long time ago, as far back as he could remember, and the older he got, the greater that fear became.

A few years ago, he'd noticed a lump in his lower back. A hard bump that hurt a little when he pushed on it. He had made the mistake of telling Jess about it, and she had harassed him until he had gone to see Kobayashi. Nathan had been certain it was a tumor, but Kobayashi had examined him, diagnosed it as a muscle knot, also known as a stress lump, had prescribed a list of stretching techniques, increased water intake, and educated him on maintaining proper posture. When Nathan had asked how one came to be blessed with such an ailment, Kobayashi had explained there were a variety of reasons, but that one known cause was sitting for too long. A light had gone off in Nathan's head then. He spent eight hours a day sitting in his patrol car. It seemed to fit. It wasn't cancer. Kobayashi was a brilliant man. Problem solved.

But here he was again, with something new, and already his mind was busy preparing him for the worst. Cancer. Had to be. What other reason could there be for inexplicable pain of the testicle. He had been performing self-examinations in the shower since the problem first started, and had determined that one testicle was noticeably larger than the other. He hadn't presented his findings to Jess. Her response would be to schedule an appointment with Kobayashi, and at this point that was the last thing he wanted to do. He didn't need to see the man just to find out he had testicular cancer. Nathan had come to that diagnosis on his own. Hell, by now it had probably spread through his entire body like a raging wildfire; probably past the point where surgery or chemo could save him. Worse yet, he had heard the horror stories before, of people that went in for a simple check up, been diagnosed with the "C" word, and had died a few months later. And that's how it worked. Once you knew, you weren't long for the world. Nathan realized this and had determined that staying in the dark was his best chance of survival.

Only now he had made the mistake of giving it away, had spilled the beans to Jess, and now he was on a timeline, the clock was ticking, counting down to the inevitable.

The pain was growing in intensity. He pulled into a parking space in front of Larry's diner, reached over to the glove compartment, pulled out a bottle of ibuprofen, selected two, dry swallowed them, and then headed into the diner.

Once he was inside, he took a corner booth, his back to the wall, ordered two coffees when the waitress came, and waited.

Carl arrived five minutes later, sliding into the booth across from Nathan, dumping two packets of sugar into his cup of coffee, stirring it, and then he leaned back and said, "The guys from Des Moines should arrive within the next hour or so."

Nathan nodded. The pain had started to subside, thank God for small favors.

"How you holding up?" Carl asked.

"Well enough, under the circumstances. You?"

"Can't get her out of my head."

"I know the feeling."

"You know me. I'm not squeamish. She wasn't half as bad as that guy we pulled from the wreck south of I-80 a few months ago. That guy was mangled all to shit. But you know what it is, don't you? It's that fucking mask, man. Gives me the heebie-jeebies."

Nathan nodded again, sipped his coffee, tried not to think about the mask the unidentified girl had been wearing. "Any luck with missing persons?"

"*Nada.* Nothing fitting the description of our girl. Which doesn't mean much. Depending on the timeline, she might not have been reported yet."

"Keep on it."

Carl nodded, sipped more coffee.

Nathan scanned the room, taking in the faces. It was a little after nine, meaning Sunday Mass would let out in the next half hour or so, and a lot of the old-timers wandered over to Larry's Diner after church on Sundays to get the senior discount on breakfast. The place would be packed soon. Nathan didn't want to be there for that.

"We're going to have to break the news sometime," Carl said.

"I know. But I'd like to put it off as long as we can. At least until we have more information. All it's going to do is cause a panic."

"This how you pictured it?"

Behind his cup of coffee, Carl was smiling.

"You know it isn't."

"Talley'd probably take the job back in a heartbeat."

"Under the circumstances, I'm almost entertaining the idea. Stuff like this isn't supposed to happen here."

"It isn't supposed to, but it is. There's a killer out there now. Maybe he's blown town, maybe he hasn't."

"If you're trying to inspire confidence, you're doing a lousy job of it."

"I tell you what we should do," Carl said. "We should put in a call to the FBI. They've got those behavioral guys that could look at things and give us a profile. Might give us a place to start."

"We've only got the one murder."

"*So far.* Just trying to be proactive, Sheriff. Besides, it's a weird enough one, isn't it, with that mask and all."

"Let's hold off on that. News of a murder is going to cause a panic. No getting around it. But if people got word that the FBI has been called in…that would make it ten times worse."

"Maybe when murder two comes around, you'll change your mind."

"Don't say shit like that."

"Hey, I'm just trying to lighten the mood. You're the guy that has to deal with the shit."

"Yeah, and you know what they say about shit, don't you?"

Carl cocked his head. "What's that?"

"It rolls downhill."

3

fading daylight

THE RESCUE DIVERS out of Des Moines finished searching the lake around seven that evening. Nathan met them as they were leaving and wasn't surprised to find out they had come up empty-handed. No murder weapons, no clues, nothing. He thanked them, watched them leave as he sat in his patrol car by the dirt path that wound its way around the lake.

Daylight was starting to fade. Nathan stepped out of his vehicle, wandered up the path, not really sure of what his intentions were. He trudged through the mud, glancing to his right at the steep embankment, toward the top where the trees started. To his left, the lake; placid, seeming to go on forever, its murky surface unwilling to give up whatever secrets lay beneath.

A perimeter had been erected earlier that morning. Stakes had been driven into the soft ground, yellow caution tape formed a large misshapen rectangle. Nathan made his way over to it, ducked under the tape, stood at the center of the crime scene. There was an amorphous impression in the mud where the girl's body had been, a mess of shoeprints circling it.

Nathan squatted down, touched his fingers to the mud, let them sink in, pulled them away, glanced at them and then out at the lake.

It was quiet and peaceful. He came here every now and then, not to this exact spot, but to the lake, when he wanted to be alone, when he needed to clear the cobwebs from the attic of his mind.

He had hoped that maybe they had missed something. That he could come out here now and stumble, almost serendipitously, on a piece of evidence that they hadn't found the first time around. But it had been a fool's errand. Perhaps he had known that all along, but he was restless, knew if he didn't do something that he would lay awake that night wishing he had, wouldn't be able to sleep until he had checked it out, and by then it would be dark, and he didn't like the thought of being out at the lake, near the woods, all alone in that endless dark.

When he got home, Jess had already showered. She was in her pajamas, sitting in the recliner, reading one of the many parenting books she had checked out from the local library.

"Home already?" she said without glancing up from her book.

"It's after nine."

"Isn't tonight poker night with the boys?"

Nathan had forgotten about that already. Carl had asked him if he was coming when they were back at the diner, but Nathan had excused himself, saying that Jess was ready to pop any minute, and he wanted to be around when that happened.

In truth, he hadn't been in the mood to talk to anybody. He knew sooner or later the topic of conversation would land on the dead girl. The rest of his and Carl's poker buddies consisted of retired law enforcement and military men. All of them were guys that knew how to keep their mouths shut, Nathan wasn't worried about them spreading gossip, but he didn't want to deal with questions. He had spent most of the day trying to get rid of his memory of the dead girl and the mask she wore. Carl was a social butterfly, and could be as garrulous as any of the grandmas that got together on bingo night. Let him handle it; let him field the questions.

"I'm playing hooky," Nathan said.

He deposited his muddy boots onto the plastic entrance mat, and then proceeded into the kitchen, where he shed his duty belt and slung it over the back of one of the kitchen chairs.

"Dinner's in the fridge," Jess called from the living room.

After seeing the girl's body, Nathan would have bet money that his appetite would be AWOL for a few days, but that wasn't the case now.

He went over to the fridge, removed a plate covered in tin toil, carried it over to the counter next to the sink. He stripped away the foil, revealing a slab of ketchup-slathered meatloaf and a generous dollop of instant mashed potatoes. He popped the plate into the microwave, took a cold bottle of Bud Light from the fridge as he waited for the meatloaf to finish warming up, screwed off the cap, took a long swallow. It tasted right, cold and smooth, warm by the time it reached his stomach. He removed the plate from the microwave, grabbed a fork from the drawer, carried everything back to the living room and sank down onto the couch.

He shoveled the food into his mouth, chased it with the beer. "Reading anything good?"

Jess glanced up from the book. "Did you know that at thirty-two weeks, a mother may experience heartburn, the baby may move around, waking you up at night. By now, fingernails, toenails, and real hair have already formed. And *maybe* a penis. I say 'maybe' because someone is hardheaded and won't let me find out the sex of my own child."

"*Our* child."

"You don't know how this works, do you?"

"What?"

"It's *my* child because, unlike you, I carry her around inside me for nine and a half months. Also, whenever she is being a little angel, she shall be referred to as *my* child. She only becomes *your* child when she is a.) being naughty or b.) when you aren't holding up your end of the bargain. For example, I might say something like, '*your* child has a poopy diaper, it's your turn to change it.'"

"Was that in one of your books?"

"No. But it should be."

"Well, you're wrong. Because *our* child is going to be a boy."

"Is that so?"

"Call it a father's intuition."

"Care to make a wager on that, Daddy-O?"

"I'm game. What do I get if I win?"

"Doesn't matter. Because you aren't going to."

"Okay. What do you get if you win?"

"Free foot rubs for life."

"You didn't say this was high stakes."

"Speaking of which, Mommy could use a foot rub right about now."

"I'm eating."

"This takes precedence. And let this be a lesson to you. I *don't* need a babysitter."

"You think that's why I skipped out on poker night?"

Jess nodded, shoved her body down the recliner, leg out, until her foot was inches from Nathan. She held it there, waiting.

"I think that's exactly the reason."

"You're only partially right," Nathan said, wolfing down another bite of meatloaf before placing the plate on the coffee table and taking Jess's foot between his hands. "It's true, part of the reason I didn't want to go is because I've got a feeling your dam is about to burst any day now, and I don't want to be halfway across the county when it does. But the rest of it is that I didn't feel like talking about a dead girl. For a little while, tonight at least, I'd like to pretend it never happened and just forget."

She stared at him as he began massaging her foot, as he moved his fingers under the arch, applied pressure there, his thumb making gentle circles over the top.

Nathan saw the concern on her face. He also saw that she had questions, lots of them, but if he had ever needed proof of her love he had it now, because she didn't ask them. She took her foot back, slid out of the recliner awkwardly, and sat down next to him, her face close to his. "Something else the book said," Jess said, "it's still safe to have sex."

"Oh," he said.

She nodded. "So what do you say I help you forget?"

4

autopsy

GENE MATHERS PHONED him at the Sheriff's Office on Monday morning saying that the forensic pathologist had completed the autopsy.

The town wasn't large enough to have its own morgue, so Crater Lake and its neighboring communities shared the one at Chickasaw County Memorial Hospital, which was located in Alton, the county seat.

Nathan and Carl made the twenty minute drive to the hospital.

The silence was disrupted intermittently by Carl, who fidgeted in the passenger seat as he sipped a tepid latte from a to-go cup.

"I'd be lying if I said I wasn't nervous," Carl said. "I don't like it, not one little bit. That girl…she was in my dreams last night, only I don't remember what her face looked like. Can you believe that? Our first murder vic, and I can't remember her face. I can still see her body though. I think she was a runner, track and field maybe."

"She was a swimmer," Nathan said, his hands tight on the steering wheel as they headed east on Highway 6. This wasn't what he wanted to be talking about. He didn't want to be discussing the dead girl, trying to give her a back story, didn't want to be thinking about her washboard stomach, or the perky breasts with the hardened nipples.

"What makes you say that?"

"Her shoulders. You don't get them to look that way by running track and field. That's from spending time in a pool, swimming laps."

"You might have something there. She was pretty in real life, I'll bet you that. Only I can't see her face. All I see is the mask. We're dealin' with a real sicko."

Carl went on, but after a while Nathan stopped listening, continuing to nod in the right places, staring straight ahead, through the windshield, at a desolate highway flanked by fields of corn and soy beans that had been planted back in late April. It was going to be a hot summer. He felt it in his gut. It was only late May and the temperature had hit the nineties a few times already. The humidity wasn't bad, not unbearable yet, but that was coming anytime now.

He hoped they would have this ordeal wrapped up in a fancy little package by then. He doubted it. His gut was big on telling him things these days, and one of the things it had been telling him for the last twenty-four hours was that this wasn't going to be open and shut, not by a country mile. Nathan didn't know how he knew this, maybe because anybody could have abducted the girl, overpowered her, strangled her, dragged her out into the water and left her there. She had been attractive, maybe a swimmer, could have been a cheerleader easy, a girl that probably turned all the boys' heads.

Who would have wanted to kill her?

Nathan thought the list was a mile long.

An ex-boyfriend? That was a logical assumption.

Or someone in her class, the reject, the kid that eyed her from afar, knowing he didn't stand a chance in hell of having her. Maybe he had tried engaging her, talking to her, but she had blown him off, spurned him even, and somewhere along the line he had decided that he was going to have her regardless of whether the feeling was mutual or not.

Nathan could picture it in his mind: the nerdy kid, the social outcast with the classic crush on the cool girl, the head cheerleader, the girl that would forever be out of reach. And most kids would have left it at that, would have dealt with the heartache, thought about the girl when they masturbated late in the night in the privacy of their own bedrooms, but would have still had a firm enough grasp on reality to know when to move on. Only this kid had been different. He hadn't moved on. He had become fixated, obsessed, watched her, stalked her, maybe would have gone so far as to mill around outside her house when no one was watching. If he was particularly inventive, perhaps he had snuck into the girl's house and stolen a pair of her underwear. Something he could use later in whatever fantasy his mind had concocted. That might have satiated him for a little while, but over time it wouldn't be enough to fulfill his desire. His fantasy would become more and more elaborate, until an object wouldn't do and the only way to fulfill the fantasy would be to have her.

He would have followed her, a predator stalking its prey, waited for her to be alone, for the perfect opportunity, and then he would have taken her, and when she resisted he would realize he had progressed past the point of no return, no turning back now, and the only thing that mattered would be bringing his fantasy to fruition by any means necessary. The girl had been athletic, could have put up a good fight. But if he had brought her to the woods, she could have screamed her lungs out and no one would have heard, especially if he had cut those screams off by using his hands, gloved hands that he had wrapped around her throat, choking the life out of her, tentatively at first, but discovering he liked it, enjoyed it, and when she had ceased flailing, when her chest had stopped moving up and down, when her eyes had opened and stayed open, maybe he would have gotten off then.

Or...

What if she had been a babysitter? Spent her weekends watching rugrats, and maybe the husband drove her home a few times, only what if it was more than that...what if they were having an affair, her under the legal age of consent, him with a wife and kids, and maybe the girl falls in love with him and tells him as much, and he tells her that he has a wife and kids, a family, and he could never leave them. Now she's the woman scorned, rejected, and so she wants revenge, says she'll squeal, ready to blow up the guy's family. The husband can't have that, no way, *José*. So he tells her they need to talk and they rendezvous at a secret location, the lake or the woods, and they argue, it gets out of control, and the husband ends up strangling her.

And on and on Nathan's mind went, playing out the various scenarios, knowing any one of them could be the way it all went down, except there was the small problem of the mask. None of the scenarios he imagined ended with the killer putting a mask over the girl's face, especially one as obscure as one fashioned in the form of the Unknown Girl of the Seine. What did it mean? What did it symbolize? It hadn't been Batman or Mickey Mouse or Winnie the Pooh. Any one of those masks could have been purchased at a Walmart or a Target or a K-Mart for less than five bucks. If it had been any of those, Nathan wouldn't have attached as much significance to it. But this was different and he made a mental note to do some research once they were back at the office, thinking maybe if he read up on the details of *L' Inconnue de la Seine* he would find some connection to the unknown dead girl that had been dragged out of Crater Lake.

They reached Alton at 8:45 A.M. and by 8:51 they had pulled up to the back entrance of the hospital and parked.

Nathan had called Mathers on his cell several minutes prior to them getting there, and when they exited the patrol car, the medical examiner was waiting at the back door, holding it open for them.

"Thanks for letting us slide around the formalities, Gene," Nathan said on his way in.

Once they were inside, Mathers led them down a long hallway, down a flight of stairs, to the morgue located in the bowels of the hospital. He showed them into a large room done up floor to ceiling in white tile, an analog clock on the wall, a stainless steel table standing in the center of the room, a scale suspended from the ceiling to the right of it.

The dead girl lay on the stainless steel table. The skin of her chest and stomach had been flayed back, her ribs sawed through and pulled back to reveal her internal organs.

A tall man dressed in scrubs, blue gown, cap, gumboots, thick gloves, and wearing a surgical mask stood over the girl. Mathers introduced him as Robert Grayling, the forensic pathologist.

They gathered around the steel table. Carl cupped a hand over his nose and mouth.

"Are you all right, Deputy?" Mathers asked.

Carl nodded without removing his hand from his mouth.

Nathan hadn't known what to expect. He hadn't been present during or after an autopsy before, and seeing the girl's body spread open, the internal organs exposed beneath the harsh white light for all the world to see, made his stomach do somersaults. His skin went cold. The smell, whatever it was, was the worst, and he did his best to breathe through his mouth and to keep his shaking hands hidden in his pockets.

He glanced up at Carl, but Carl was oblivious, gaze fastened on the dead body that lay on the table.

Mathers looked to the pathologist and said, "Go ahead, Robert."

Grayling proceeded to give them the facts in a clipped and no nonsense fashion. Nathan turned his ears on, told himself he didn't want to miss anything, but as hard as he tried, the body on the table was a distraction and he ended up catching only snippets of the conversation.

"...*bruising around the neck,*" Grayling was saying, "*fracturing of the hyoid...indications of petechiae and subconjunctival hemorrhaging.*"

Grayling pointed to the girl's open chest cavity. "*Lungs were devoid of water, indicating that she died on land.*"

Mathers said, "You mentioned the fishermen who found her said the body was floating in the water, right?"

Nathan nodded.

"Another sign that she died before going into the water. If she would have drowned, her lungs would have been filled with water and she would have sank to the bottom. The air in her lungs helped keep her afloat."

"*As to lividity...pooling evident in chest, abdomen and face...placed face down...*"

The girl's eyes were closed. Nathan was thankful for that. Her hair and been swept back and hung off the back of the steel table.

"…*maceration of the skin consistent with being submerged for between five to ten hours*"

Carl gagged, went into a coughing fit, excused himself as he fled from the room in a hurry.

"*Tearing of the vaginal walls…presence of seminal fluids… blood…*"

Nathan let that last sink in. The girl had been sexually assaulted before she had been killed.

Grayling paused briefly and then continued on. Nathan hoped to God the man hurried because before long he would be fleeing the room in a similar fashion.

"*…evidence indicates manual strangulation resulting in death.*"

"Like I said," Mathers said. "Death by strangulation. Have you identified her yet?"

Nathan shook his head.

"That's a pity. She must have been a beautiful girl in life. I can't see how she wouldn't be missed. Come on, I'll walk you out."

He followed Mathers out of the room, up the stairs, through the hallway again, until they reached the rear exit door. Again, Mathers held it open.

Once he was outside, Nathan paused, searching for the right words but coming up empty. He settled for, "I appreciate it, Gene."

Mathers nodded, lips tight, a sympathetic look in his eyes. "Forget what I said before. Just find the man who did it. Crater Lake wasn't made to handle something like this, but I guess the outside world was bound to creep in sooner or later. If you need me, you know where to find me."

Nathan thanked him again, started toward his car.

"One more thing," Mathers called after him. "If you get another one, make sure it isn't on a Sunday. Sundays I go golfing. I'm not good, perhaps not even average on my best days, but what it is is an excuse to get out of the house and leave the wife home. So no dead bodies on Sundays. Is that doable?"

Nathan smiled, nodded, said, "I'll see what I can do," as he got into his patrol car.

5

the hunt

HE WAITS IN the woods, hunkered down behind the thick trunk of a tall tree, enjoying the silence. He has done this for a long time, is an old hand at it, used to waiting. It has taken many years, but he has succeeded in learning patience. It is a skill possessed by a sacred few.

He isn't a hunter by trade, but has become proficient at it, hunting and stalking his prey. There is a line from a book or a movie claiming that Man is the most dangerous game of all. But he doesn't agree with this, because it isn't true. There are things out there that are far more dangerous than Man, things that have walked the Earth for much longer.

The moon shines down from overhead, light streaming between the trees. He knows the darkness as well, has spent more than his fair share of time in it. From somewhere nearby, he hears a twig snap, a sharp crack amplified by the silence. His heart starts to race. He takes a deep breath, calm and steady, and, most important of all – *patient*.

This is a dangerous hunt. There's no fooling himself, no getting around it. He knows this, keeps it at the forefront of his brain, never allows himself to become complacent. This isn't his first rodeo. And his prey might be dangerous, but *he* is dangerous too. He takes comfort in this fact.

It hasn't always been like this.

A long time ago, longer than he can remember, he had been innocent like the rest of them. He had been naïve and soft and weak, another sheep, until circumstance had shown him that there were wolves in the world. They were predators and they were hungry, and they came for the sheep when they least expected it. After he had seen them, after he had become aware of their existence, he had decided he wanted to be like the wolves. Not *a* wolf, but *like them*. The wolves had great power, but they had no souls. He wanted to be a wolf, but didn't want to give up his soul. So he had done the next best thing. He had read and read, trained and trained, until he was no longer a sheep. He became something else. A predator like the wolf, but different because he had taken an oath to protect the sheep, and the secret to protecting the sheep was to kill the wolves. Only the wolves were secrets themselves, and he knew he must keep that secret because to not keep it would only serve to panic the sheep.

He had made the mistake once of trying to tell the sheep, and the sheep had been too dumb to believe him, had laughed at him, had not taken him seriously. Worse yet, they hadn't wanted his protection. In fact, they had treated him like *he* was a wolf, a wolf that meant to do them harm. They had tried to put him away, lock him up, cage him, never realizing that his purpose was to protect them.

After that, he had learned to steer clear of the sheep. He knew how to walk among them because blending in with them was a necessity sometimes, but mostly he kept to himself, and he had never tried sharing his secret with them again. They might not believe him, they might call him hurtful things, but he would go on protecting them anyway because he had made that promise to himself. A man, according to his father, was good for nothing if he couldn't keep a promise.

This is all in the past, he tells himself. He tries not to think about it because it makes him sad and angry. Maybe one of these days he will make a kill and keep it, something to take back to the sheep and show them, give them proof that he isn't crazy, that they have been wrong all along. He doesn't understand how they can spend their lives in the dark the way they do. But try as he might, they refuse to open their eyes.

He is alone now.

He has always hunted alone.

It's better this way. Almost peaceful.

Another twig snaps, and his prey is closer now.

He fishes into his pocket, pulls out a small square mirror, takes a deep breath, holds the mirror up in front of his face, exhales when he sees his reflection staring back at him. He isn't one of them. If he was and if the folklore is to be believed, then he wouldn't be able to see himself in the mirror. He gets confused sometimes, always chasing, always thinking like them, always afraid that maybe one day he will look into the mirror and his reflection won't be there. The bright blue eyes, the rugged face, the scraggly beard…

He tells himself not to worry. His reflection stares at him from the wedge of mirror. He isn't one of them, isn't a wolf. He will perform the ritual again tomorrow and the day after and the day after that. If the day should ever come that he looks into the mirror and doesn't see himself, he will deal with it. The Bible tells him that it is a sin to take his own life, but he has come to find that the Bible doesn't always get it right, there are mistakes from time to time, and…

Deal with it if and when the time comes.

He pockets the mirror, digs quietly into his rucksack, pulls on a pair of worn leather gloves, searches some more until his fingers wrap around the long cylinder of wood that tapers to a sharp point at one end. The stake is fashioned out of ash. He knows this because he made it himself, spent hours carving it with a sharp knife until the tip could puncture flesh with ease and the weight of it felt right in his hand. The tip is stained black from much use.

He leaves the rest of his tools of the trade in his rucksack for later. There is a ritual to the hunt, and as long as he sticks to the rules things will be fine.

His prey runs through the woods noisily, alone, scared. He knows the feeling. It runs by the tree without noticing him. A woman. Lost. She doesn't know that she is a wolf, that she is part of the darkness now. He almost feels sorry for her. It's always like this, the confusion, the terror, the feeling of being lost and alone and of being chased. But he knows what she is, what she will become, and it's better this way.

He springs from his hiding spot by the tree, and he is on her, tackling her to the ground. She screams, but not for long. He pins her there, in the dirt and the dead leaves, straddling her, feeling himself grow hard as she struggles against his weight. She is wearing only underwear and a t-shirt that is too big for her. Her bare legs are milky white in the moonlight.

He leans over her, grabs a handful of her hair, lifts it up, examines the back of her neck quickly, sees the tell-tale mark. He removes the wedge of mirror from his coat pocket, twists her head to the side, holds the mirror up to her face, close enough that her breath fogs the glass. Her reflection doesn't appear in the mirror.

She squirms and struggles as he rolls her over until she's on her back, staring up at him. He straddles her again as she screams, and tries to tell himself that he doesn't enjoy the terror in her wide eyes, or the fear that contorts her face as he raises the wooden stake, brings it down, lets the tip hover over her chest, pressing into her t-shirt, then through it, until the first stains of blood seep through to paint the white fabric.

He's throbbing now, can't lie to himself anymore because he enjoys it, making her suffer like this. She continues to struggle for a while, but eventually the fight goes out of her.

He smiles and says, "I'm sorry."

But he isn't sorry.

Not even close.

She becomes calm. He doesn't like it, exerts pressure on the wooden stake, watches as it slides deeper into her chest. The terror returns and he smiles.

"Please," the girl says. "Please don't."

The words are music to his ears.

"Please."

He presses down against the wooden stake. The crimson stain on her shirt grows larger as though it is a living thing.

"*Please.*"

A whisper, without conviction.

She tries to form the word again, but instead there is only the hiss of air, blood trickling down her lower lip.

"I give you peace," he whispers and drives the wooden stake home.

6

second victim

NATHAN'S PHONE WOKE him at 6:20 on Tuesday morning. Carl was on the line.

"You up?"

"Getting there."

"We got another one." Subdued panic in his voice, just below the surface.

"Say that again."

"Another dead body. Jesus, Nate, they're starting to stack up."

Nathan sat up in bed, tried to get his mind to focus, ignored the powerful ache in his testicle, got moving, already throwing on his uniform while he still had Carl on the phone.

"It's the Struthers girl," Carl said. "*Becca*. Rick and Cheryl's daughter. It's bad. *Real* bad. A massacre. I know Rick pretty good, went to school with him, played football with the guy. How am I supposed to break this to him?"

"Where are you?"

"Coldfall. I'm in way over my head here."

"Give me ten."

"I'll have Iverson posted on the path," Carl said. "He can bring you to us."

Nathan hung up the phone, buttoned his shirt, fastened his badge to it, wrapped his duty belt around his waist, secured it to the inner belt with two keepers. He grabbed his Glock from the nightstand drawer, holstered it, repeated the process with his ASP baton and OC spray.

Jess mumbled something from her spot on the bed, lifted her head, brushed hair out of her face, stared at him with sleep-filled eyes. "What time is it?"

"Little after six. How'd you sleep?"

"I was up and down all night. *Your* child was busy throwing a party."

Nathan moved into the bathroom, stared at his face in the mirror. He opened the medicine cabinet, took out the bottle of ibuprofen, jiggled several of the rounded pills into his hand, tossed them into his mouth and chased them down with water from the faucet. The pain in his testicle was worse this morning, but he didn't waste time thinking about it, didn't have time to worry about things like life's little problems, problems like cancer, because there was a much bigger problem waiting for him in Coldfall Woods.

"You're in an awful hurry."

"Duty calls."

"Nate, what is it?"

He stopped what he was doing, stood in the bathroom doorway, stared at her.

"Oh my God. Another one?"

Nathan nodded his head.

He expected more questions, but to her credit, she didn't ask any. She said, "You better go," which was as close to a blessing as he was going to get, so he went to her, gave her a peck on the lips, rested a hand on her stomach, and then he was out the door and going.

He had prepared himself for the worst and that was exactly what he got. It was 6:35 when he pulled up to the dirt path that circled Coldfall Woods.

Deputy Chad Iverson was waiting for him on the path. Normally, Iverson was the optimistic type. He had been with the Chickasaw County Sheriff's Department for just over a year, still a little wet behind the ears, and if this had been high school, Nathan would have pegged him as the class clown. He was the guy that always had a joke handy, knew a million of them, but today he looked pale and stiff and somber.

"It's about a quarter mile in," Iverson said as he led Nathan into the woods. The sky was overcast. The weatherman had promised rain and it looked like they might just get it.

"How bad is it?" Nathan asked.

Iverson didn't look around, kept walking, trudging through the underbrush, ducking here and there to avoid the occasional low-hanging branch. "It's probably better if you see it for yourself."

Those were the only words spoken between them as they made the quarter mile hike into the woods.

Up ahead, he saw the bright yellow caution tape stretched across several trees, Carl standing beyond it, watching them as they approached the crime scene.

Despite the pills, the throbbing pain in Nathan's crotch hadn't subsided. It was still going strong, a dull stabbing sensation that increased with each step he took. The ibuprofen hadn't touched it, and the deadline Jess had imposed for making an appointment with Kobayashi was fast approaching.

Iverson stopped, lifted the caution tape, allowed Nathan to pass under it before following after him.

Carl had left everything exactly as he had found it.

Nathan saw the body now. A young girl with dark auburn hair, wearing only underwear and an over-sized t-shirt, green eyes open and staring up at the sky. None of those details were what stood out to him.

Two things caught his attention:

The first was the wooden stake stuck in her chest, an amorphous circle of dried blood decorating the white cotton of the t-shirt surrounding the puncture wound.

The second was that her head had been severed from the rest of her body.

Carl waved his hand at the body. "What kind of a psycho… c-cut her fucking head off, Nate…what the hell are we dealing with here? This isn't like the first one. This is w-way worse, man."

Nathan waited, gave Carl time to get it all out of his system before he started asking questions of his own. Iverson hung back, facing in the opposite direction, staring off toward the lake.

"It's Becca Struthers, man. Becca-fucking-Struthers. Last time I saw Rick he told me that she had been accepted to Wayne State. But you know what? She's not going. Because somebody sawed off her head and put a fucking stake through her heart."

Carl paced back and forth, kicking up dead leaves, forgetting about this being a crime scene. Nathan let it happen. He had known the man for a while now, ever since they had attended the Academy in Johnston together, and he knew that Carl was the type that could usually keep his shit together, but this thing they were dealing with now was stretching it, stretching it thin.

"What the fuck are we supposed to tell them?"

Nathan was anything but calm, but he didn't let it show. He kept his voice smooth and even when he said, "We'll deal with it. Are you finished?"

Carl ceased his frenetic pacing, stared at Nathan. Several seconds passed. He swallowed hard and nodded.

"Paramedics on their way?"

"Yeah, not that that means jack shit to her."

"Mathers?"

"Yeah. Iverson called him."

"Okay. Good. All of that's squared away. Now, who discovered the body?"

"Couple of hunters. Brad White and Mike Brody. Neither of them have got much sense, but they're decent guys overall, when they aren't busy getting tanked."

"What time was this?"

"I wrote it down." Carl consulted his notepad. "Dispatch logged the call at five forty-five. I was here by six. I wish to God I would have called off sick. Just look at her for God's sake."

Nathan looked. Her too-large t-shirt was pulled up, revealing a taut stomach, her arms down at her sides.

The stake protruded from her chest, five or six inches of wood poking out of a black hole of dried blood and cold white flesh.

Right where her heart would be, Nathan thought, eyes working their way up to the small gap of dead space between her head and her neck. Nathan had never been a hunter, had never skinned or butchered an animal, but it looked like a clean cut, performed with an instrument that had been very sharp.

"Different M.O.," he said dispassionately.

"You think it's the same guy?"

Nathan nodded.

"This isn't like the last one," Carl said, steadier now, but his hands were still shaking. "He butchered her. No mask this time."

"Victimology is the same. Young, female, attractive. Lake's within half a mile of here, so location's about the same."

"Except I know this girl. She's from town. And what about the mask? Or the fact that he cut her damn head off?"

"Could be that he's getting better. Or maybe his fantasy is evolving. Maybe the other vic was his first, and he's improving on what he didn't get right the first time around."

"Damn, Nate. I didn't realize you were such an expert."

"I read a few books when I was in college. I think we're dealing with the same guy. Mainly because I don't want to think about what it would mean if we aren't."

Iverson joined them. He was still pale. "You know what it looks like, don't you? Like the guy who did it thought he was killing a vampire."

"A vampire?"

"Sure, yeah, haven't you seen all the old Dracula movies? They were hokey, but way better than that *Twilight* crap they put out now. Remember how the only way to kill them was to jab a stake through their heart and then they'd cut the head off. Sometimes they'd burn the body after that, just to be sure."

"So what are you saying?"

Iverson shrugged, gaze moving off in the direction of the lake again, acting like the dead girl's body wasn't even there. "Maybe nothing. Or just maybe the guy believes in vampires and thinks he's some big vampire killer."

"That fits," Carl said.

"Of course," Iverson said, "everybody knows that vampires aren't real. Right?"

They finished taking photographs and searching the crime scene by close to eight. Mathers had arrived, looking tired and grim, and declared Becca Struthers dead with a simple glance. Her mutilated body was hauled away to the morgue, Mathers saying he would make sure the pathologist got to it that same day. Like Carl, he knew Rick and Cheryl Struthers personally. Maybe that was the worst part of it: that this time they knew the victim, there was a name to go with the face.

Nathan and Carl skipped breakfast, neither man believing that his stomach could handle solid food after seeing what they had, and so they swung through one of the local gas stations for coffee before heading back to the office.

Nathan felt like he should be doing something, doing *more*, but there was a strange stillness to the day, and it seemed like the only decisions to be made were hard ones. Carl asked if he should call the Struthers family and have them come down to the Sheriff's Office. More often than not, in the event of a death (which came few and far between in Crater Lake, and none of those had been cases of homicide) they would have someone from the family come down to positively ID the body. Given the condition of Becca Struthers, Nathan decided that might not be the best way to handle things this time, so he told Carl he would handle it.

He phoned Cheryl at her place of employment around ten o'clock that morning, asking if he could meet her and Rick at their home. Of course, she was curious, who wouldn't be, but Nathan had told her that it was best if they spoke about it in person.

He met them at their modest ranch style home, pulling into the driveway at 10:45, taking a minute before he exited the patrol car.

His testicle was on fire. It was painful to walk. Not unbearable, but getting there. He reached into the glove compartment for the bottle of ibuprofen, shook out four pills this time, swallowed them with a sip of what remained of his coffee.

It was hard finding the words. Nathan climbed the wooden stairs to the front door, stood there without knocking, trying to plan what he was going to say, but the words wouldn't come, at least not the way he wanted them to. Finally, he gave up, knocked, waited.

Cheryl Struthers answered the door almost immediately, flustered and worried. Nathan couldn't say he blamed her, it wasn't everyday you received an early morning phone call from the Sheriff of Chickasaw County, and most people, even the ones prone to optimism, couldn't help but view that in a negative light.

Rick Struthers appeared behind his wife, staring over her shoulder, lips pursed below his mustache, looking at Nathan like the bad news had already been delivered.

Nathan wasn't surprised. They were intelligent enough, could do the math, knew that the both of them were present and accounted for, so through an elementary process of elimination, they had already guessed that it was about their daughter, that it was about Becca. From what Nathan had gathered, the girl had still been living at home for the summer, wouldn't move into a dorm at Wayne State until late August. The first thing Cheryl would have done would have been to try Becca on her cell phone, and when Becca didn't pick up, she would have made a mad dash home, checked her daughter's room, would have found it empty and then commenced searching the rest of the house.

Cheryl's mouth bobbed open and closed, no words coming out. She looked to be on the verge of tears, her eyes pleading, begging him for good news, and from behind her, Rick said, "It's Becca, isn't it?"

Nathan nodded.

"Just tell us."

Nathan thought it was funny how people always prepared themselves for the worst. There had never been a murder in Crater Lake since he had lived there, and Carl had lived in the small town all his life and couldn't recall there ever being one. Traffic fatalities weren't unheard of, but they were few and far between. Standing there on the porch, Nathan knew the looks on their faces would be stamped in his memory for the rest of his life, just like the body of Becca Struthers would be, and the girl in the mask. All of them dark stains that would later come back to haunt him.

He took a photo from his pocket. It was one they had taken with a digital camera at the crime scene earlier that morning and then printed out at the office. Given the condition of the body, they had cropped the image so that it was a close-up of Becca's face, revealing nothing below the chin. Nathan thought it best to deny them the gory parts. The details would come later, but for now he focused on dealing as little damage as possible.

"I'm going to need you take a look at this," Nathan said.

"Just show us, *Sheriff*," Rick Struthers said, and there was acid in his voice. The way he stressed the word "Sheriff" told Nathan in no uncertain terms that the man hadn't voted for him in the last election.

He handed the photo to Cheryl. She took it, stared at it, her face changing, flitting from one emotion to the next until the tears finally came. The photo slipped from her hand and fluttered to the ground. Nathan bent down, picked it up, held it in his hands, addressed them both. "Mr. and Mrs. Struthers, can you tell me, is it Becca?"

Cheryl turned to her husband, sagged, melted. Through the sobs, she wailed her answer, giving the one that Nathan had expected. Yes, the girl in the photograph was their daughter.

Rick Struthers wrapped his arms around his wife, held onto her, supported her weight. His face was stoic, his eyes filled with a sorrow unlike anything Nathan had seen before.

Nathan stood there, silent, feeling incredibly small at that moment.

Don't shoot the messenger, he thought, which was what he thought every time he was the bearer of bad news. He felt the familiar sense of guilt crawl over him. Of course they blamed him, because there was no one else, and he was the one standing there, something tangible they could aim their fury at. That was how it always worked. First the sorrow, then the rage.

"I'm sorry," he said, already knowing it wouldn't make a difference.

Cheryl broke free from her husband's arms, taking deep hitching breaths that racked her entire body. "It can't be her," she said, and stared at him in disbelief. "There has to be some mistake. It can't be Becca. I just talked to her yesterday, before she left for work. I remember her saying that she was going to Jimmy's house after – that's the boy she's been seeing – and they were going to watch movies or something like that, and I didn't hear her come home, but that's happened before, where she's stayed out too late and ends up falling asleep over there. So, you see, it can't be Becca. She can't be dead. I can call Jimmy right now. The first time it happened where she didn't come home, after that, well, I made her give me his number since they're glued at the hip, and I knew if I couldn't reach her, then maybe I could get a hold of him. See, it's all just a mistake, Sheriff. That girl in the picture can't be our Becca."

She looked at him for a long time, defiantly, as though daring him to contradict her beliefs.

Nathan stared at her, then at the photograph. He folded it carefully and slid it into his back pocket.

"I know this isn't easy," he said, "but if I could ask you a few questions…it might help give us something we can use…or if you'd rather come down to the station after you've…processed for a bit…"

Rick took his wife in his arms again, glowered at Nathan until Nathan thought he might crumble under the other man's gaze.

"You've already done enough, Sheriff."

And then the door slammed closed in Nathan's face.

7

blood loss

ON THE DRIVE over to Chickasaw County Memorial, Nathan recounted the story of his visit with Rick and Cheryl Struthers. When he finished, Carl only nodded.

"Better you than me," he said.

"What did I ever do to them?"

"Well, let's see. First, you aren't a native of Crater Lake. Meaning you weren't born here, didn't grow up here, didn't spend every waking moment of your life here."

"I grew up in Des Moines. That's barely an hour away."

"Yeah, but it's what folks in these parts consider 'The Big City.' And city people can't understand small town life. At least that's how most people around here think."

"I've lived in Crater Lake for over six years."

"Doesn't matter. Unless you were born and baptized here, it just doesn't matter. You'll always be an outsider. Somehow, by the grace of God maybe, you ran in the election, against a man that had been Sheriff for the past twelve years, and then, maybe also by the grace of God, you won. That right there rubbed a lot of folks the wrong way. It's intolerance at its finest."

"Is that how you think of it?"

"Of course not. Give me some credit. We went through the Academy together, we've played for the same team for a while. You're practically blood now. Besides, I'm the progressive type. Most people that are born here grow up with one thing on their mind: getting the fuck out."

Nathan shook his head.

"But I haven't even gotten to the worst part," Carl said. "And I think you already know what it is."

"I broke the news to them about Becca."

"Right on the money. That was like the third strike against you. A wiser man might have let a lifer deliver the bad news. Like me, for instance."

"I thought I was doing you a favor."

"You did. A big one. No way did I want to be the one that gave them that kind of news. They probably would have hated me for it, but it wouldn't have been as bad because I wouldn't have been going into it with two strikes against me already."

They were silent for a while before Carl said, "Don't let it eat at you. They'll get over it."

"I don't even care if they do."

"Yeah, you do. I know you, man. You care what other people think, at least up to a point. But I'm telling you, you can't be friends with all of them. Because, in the end, they'll turn on you. Small town folk are fickle. They can be the best at greeting you with open arms or they can be as stubborn as a mule. It really doesn't matter. You're here. You won. It isn't about making friends anymore." Carl smiled. "Unless, of course, you're planning on running for another term."

Of course, that last was a bit of an inside joke. The whole idea of running for Sheriff had only come up because of a simple, childish dare. Nathan and Carl had been assigned to the third shift, and in a town like Crater Lake, when you worked the graveyard, the toughest part of the job was staying awake. There wasn't a lot of action. Period. Weekends and holidays were usually the busiest. Mostly, they got called out on noise complaints, kids playing their music too loud. There was also speeding, careless driving, reckless driving, underage drinking, DUI, possession, B&E, trespassing, and a lot of other nonsense that usually wasn't enough to whittle away the time until the sun decided to open its bright orange eye on the world.

So they spent a lot of time drinking coffee and talking. Nathan did most of the coffee drinking; Carl did most of the talking. They had a system. They would go hard and heavy up until around midnight, at which time they would meet up at the only place in Crater Lake that stayed open 24/7.

Wayside Junction was one of two gas stations in town. It stayed open all night, and its reputation was built on the fact that it served some of the worst coffee available between Des Moines and Omaha (some rumors purported that its reputation extended even farther than that).

Carl wasn't a big fan of coffee, so usually he settled for Red Bull or Rockstar, averaging three or four cans a night, as he and Nathan sat in their patrol cars with the windows rolled down, the tunes on low, chatting about any number of things to get through those quiet witching hours. Usually, Carl would tell stories about growing up, about what it had been like to serve a life sentence in Crater Lake. Nathan had grown up in West Des Moines, and although he had grown up in the city, their lives weren't all that different.

It was on one of these nights, going on three or four in the morning if Nathan remembered it right, that Carl had gotten started on a long-winded tirade about Abraham Talley, then Sheriff of Crater Lake. Turned out, Carl had a laundry list of things he despised about his boss, and had a lot of his own ideas about how the Department should be run. Nathan had listened, letting Carl go on and on, which was how it was most nights, until, after he was reasonably certain that Carl was finished, he had said, "Maybe you should put your money where your mouth is."

Carl had first laughed and then scoffed at the idea. "Me? No way. I don't have the stomach to play the game. But...you're the smarty pants, you've got the degree, maybe *you* should."

Nathan had scoffed at the idea as well, but as Carl went on, the idea had slowly started to take shape in his mind. It didn't happen overnight, but over the course of weeks and months, it gained weight, and pretty soon it was all he could think about. (This had been back before they had known that Jess was going to become pregnant. If he had known that, he might not have gone through with it, but at the time, the pros had seemed to outweigh the cons).

Abe Tally had been the Sheriff of Chickasaw County for twelve years, had won the last three elections, had gone unopposed for two of them. He was in his sixties, but had held onto his physical prowess and mental shrewdness. Nathan's laundry list wasn't anywhere near as long as Carl's, but he did have his fair share of qualms.

Talley was notorious for being a micro-manager. He questioned everything. Arguably, for some that could have been viewed as a favorable quality, but Talley took it to the next level. Nathan had gotten his Bachelor's in Sociology. He was smart, well-educated, and respectful of the established hierarchy, but he didn't tolerate being made to feel like a fool. Talley treated all his employees as if they were fools; as if they wouldn't be capable of tying their own shoes without his hawk-like supervision.

But perhaps the thing that irked him most was that Abe Talley didn't know how to accept criticism. You couldn't just waltz into his office with feedback or an idea and expect to be heard. Doing something like that was akin to mutiny, and Talley seemed to view it as an all out declaration of war.

Nathan hadn't been so naïve to think that the Department would be a total democracy, but he hadn't expected a dictatorship either. He had raised what he considered to be several fine points during his career with the Chickasaw County Sheriff's Department, points that had been born of the intention of making the world a better place, but all of these had been summarily dismissed by the good Sheriff Talley.

Over the years, Nathan's resentment had grown, little by little, without him even realizing it. He had bitched to Jess about it on several occasions, but he hadn't really given it much thought until that serendipitous night when he had jokingly offered up the idea that Carl run in the next election. He had never expected to have it all backfire on him, for Carl to turn the table on him, or that his mind would latch onto the concept and run with it.

At some point, after discussing it with Jess, he had made up his mind, knowing full well that Talley wasn't the kind of man that would accept one of his deputies running against him. No. Talley wouldn't like that, wouldn't like it at all, and Nathan knew that if he didn't pull off the win, that he would find himself standing in the nearest unemployment line.

It had meant a lot of risk, but Nathan was determined. Jess thought it was a grand idea. (Again, this was before they had known she would be getting pregnant shortly thereafter, and Nathan often wondered if she would have been as supportive had she been privy to this information ahead of time). Carl was in love with the idea (the idea, in a roundabout way, had been his after all), and had gone full-steam ahead with it, spreading the word, helping have the signs made up, posting it all over Facebook, telling anybody that would listen.

Nathan had broken the news to Talley himself. Word got around, got around fast in a small town, and rather than have Talley hear it from someone else, Nathan had gone into Talley's office, informed his boss that he would be running against him, and had marched back out with his heart racing and a smile on his face. He had been both giddy and mortified, a sensation that had stuck with him for the duration of the campaign.

Long story short, he had won.

In Crater Lake, it was considered to be a minor miracle. No one had expected it, let alone Nathan, who, when he wasn't actively campaigning, had been sending out resumes to other departments, figuring it would behoove him to hedge his bets.

After winning the election, they held a public after party. Talley showed up, shook Nathan's hand, bowed out gracefully, wished him luck. But there was something in the handshake that had suggested to Nathan that the man wasn't being entirely sincere.

Those last months with Talley had been hell. Nathan had survived because he had had the foresight to know it was coming, had given himself pep talk after pep talk, counting down the days until he took office and Abraham Talley became a thing of the past.

He hadn't been prepared for it, hadn't given it a lot of thought, what it would be like, now that he was occupying the throne Talley had abdicated. The last several months had come with a steep learning curve, but he *was* learning, and after a while he thought things might level out, that there was a chance he would get the hang of it. Until now. Now the body count was sitting at two, in a town where murder was unheard of.

They sat in silence for the remainder of the trip. Mathers met them at the rear entrance again.

"Didn't interrupt your golf game, did I?" Nathan asked.

Mathers shook his head, showed them in, led them down the hall, down the stairs, through the door and into the morgue.

The smell was appalling, worse than he remembered it. Was it possible to *taste* a smell? He thought it was and was experiencing it now. He would have asked for a mint if his eyes hadn't immediately been drawn to the lifeless body of Becca Struthers laid out on the polished steel table, nude and impossibly pale.

Grayling was there, decked out in his cap, gloves, boots and gown, his mouth and nose hidden behind a surgical mask.

Mathers said, "Are you thinking these are related?"

Nathan nodded.

"I assumed as much. If it wasn't for coincidence, however, I don't think I would have lumped them together."

Grayling turned to a metal tray, picked up a plastic bag containing the wooden stake he had dislodged from the girl's chest. The last few inches of the wood were stained black. "The weapon pierced her heart, causing death. The decapitation was performed afterward. Judging from the pattern of the wound, the blade would be between eight and twelve inches in length." He grabbed the sides of the girl's head in his gloved hands, lifted, held it upside down, used a finger to point at the jagged seam of flesh and tissue. "Notice how it isn't a clean cut? The blade was probably serrated."

Nathan listened. He glanced at Carl. Carl was pale, but determined to stay for the duration.

"There are also indications of significant blood loss occurring *prior* to sustaining her injuries."

"Hold up. *Prior to*?"

Grayling nodded. "Yes. Help me turn her over."

Mathers was already wearing gloves. He assisted Grayling in turning the body over so that it laid stomach-down on the cold metal.

Grayling motioned for them to come closer, and as they did, he pointed at a small mark on the back of her neck.

Nathan leaned in close, studying the injury. It appeared to form the shape of an inverted 'Y' surrounded by a circle around two inches in diameter.

"See this upside down Y shape? It appears that three minute incisions were made. The circle seems to be some type of suction device. I believe this is how the blood was evacuated from the body."

"You're saying that the killer used some kind of device to drain most of the blood from her body *before* he killed her?"

Grayling nodded, pulled down his mask, stripped off his gloves. "That's exactly what I'm saying. If that hadn't been the case, we would have seen quite a lot more blood from her other injuries."

"You said the first girl was sexually assaulted."

Nathan nodded toward Becca Struther's body.

Grayling said, "It looks as though she had intercourse sometime within the last forty-eight hours, but there are no indications of sexual assault with this one. I also collected samples of the drainage coming from the wound in her neck. I sent it to the lab for analysis."

"Thank you, Robert," Mathers said.

"You can take this with you," Grayling said, handing them the plastic bag that contained the wooden stake.

"Are we finished here, gentlemen?"

Nathan said that they were and let Mathers lead them back the way they had come.

"Have you ever seen anything like this?" Nathan asked.

Mathers raised his eyebrows. "Not even close, Sheriff. I've been doing this for twenty-five years and I haven't seen anything that comes close. You speak with the parents?"

Nathan said that he had.

"How'd they take it?"

"You have to ask?"

"No. I suppose not. After my daughter – she's in her thirties now – graduated from high school, she was dead set on moving away. She needed to find herself, she said. Needed to live life. I pleaded with her to stay away from the big cities. I told her that she wasn't prepared for what was out there. Of course, she didn't listen. She lives in Chicago now. For a long time, I laid awake at night worrying about her, alone out there in the world. But after seeing this, I'm starting to think that maybe she had the right idea. I don't envy you. I don't envy you one bit. You need to find the responsible party, and you need to make sure he can't do something like this again. I guess what I'm saying is, maybe there's more than one kind of justice. The kind that relies on the courts, and the kind that doesn't. If I were you, I'd lean toward the latter."

"You're talking about vigilante justice," Nathan said.

"I didn't' say that, and you didn't hear me say it," Mathers said. "What I'm saying is that you're one of us now, and sometimes that means doing things a different way."

"I'll be sure to keep that in mind, Gene," Nathan said.

After Mathers had gone back inside, Carl said, "What he was saying, I think, is that if we catch this guy, maybe we shouldn't bring him in alive."

"I know what he was saying."

"I hate to say it, but that idea doesn't sound half bad."

Nathan stared at him.

Carl shrugged, said, "Just sayin.'"

On the ride back, Carl kept shaking his head. Nathan had worked with the man long enough to know that it meant Carl was twisting an idea over in his brain. Nathan didn't want to hear it. Not right now. But Carl kept doing it, shaking his head back and forth, starting to make little noises in his throat to get Nathan's attention, trying to get him to take the bait.

Finally, Nathan asked.

"What is it?"

"What?"

"Don't play dumb. You've got something to say, so say it."

"I was just thinking back to what Iverson said. About vampires. It sort've fits, you know."

"If you're saying that you think a vampire did this, you might as well leave your badge and your gun on my desk before you leave the office tonight."

"That's not what I'm saying. Not exactly, anyway. But that stuff the pathologist was saying, about the Struther's girl having her blood drained *before* she was killed. That's what a vampire would do. Drain a person's blood."

"It sounds like you're saying you think it was a vampire that did it."

"No. But what if the guy *thinks* he's a vampire?"

"I'm not sold on the blood thing," Nathan said. "At least not yet. And you're forgetting our suspect staked her through the heart and then cut off her head."

"Yeah, and that fits, too. If you thought somebody was a vampire, that's exactly how you would do it. Stake it through the heart, sever the head."

"Just a second ago you were making it sound like the guy thinks he's a vampire. Now you're saying he thinks he's a vampire killer. You can't have it both ways. Which is it?"

"Well, who says it can't be both? If the guy thinks his job is to go around killing vampires, he wouldn't get very far if there weren't any vampires around."

"I'm not following."

"Maybe he goes out creating vampires so that he can kill them. So he kidnaps somebody, drains most of their blood, waits for them to regain consciousness. Then he kills them."

"That's pretty far out there."

"It's *way* out there, but *what if*? It's not like we have a lot leads."

After that, they made the rest of the trip back to Crater Lake in silence.

8

killers

RICK AND CHERYL Struthers made the trip down to the
Sheriff's Department around three-thirty. Both appeared gaunt
and somehow thinner. The death of their daughter was already
taking its toll. As Carl led them into the interview room, their
grief was almost palpable, a physical manifestation, thick in the
air, and when they passed by Nathan's office, neither looked in
his direction, content to pretend that he didn't exist. They hadn't
thought highly of him in the past, and after he had brought them
the news of Becca's murder, they thought even less of him. Carl
said he thought it would pass, that they were in mourning, and
somewhere down the road when they managed to pull themselves from the depths of sorrow, they would come to appreciate
the fact that Nathan had delivered the news in person. Nathan
wasn't so sure, but he let the subject drop.

Because Carl had had his hands full with the Struthers, Nathan had run another missing persons check himself. There was nothing new. An amber alert had been issued for a four-year-old boy, last seen leaving in a dark green Toyota sedan with his father, who had been a no-show for his meeting with his parole officer. A black woman, 37, had been reported missing by her husband. She worked the graveyard at the Walmart in Alton, and hadn't come home the next morning. There were maybe a dozen or so others, all having occurred within the past twenty-four hours, but they were all out of Des Moines or Omaha, and none of them matched the description of the girl in the mask.

The Struthers departed the station shortly after five, Carl showing them out, extending his condolences, looking more than a little like a rat trapped in a maze. After they were gone, Carl entered Nathan's office, let out a deep sigh, pulled out a chair, sat down across from Nathan.

"How'd it go?"

"How do you think? Cheryl can barely walk on her own. She's practically a tear factory. Rick kept it together, but I'm pretty sure he's ready to murder somebody. They were cooperative. I asked if they'd noticed anything out of the ordinary lately, did Becca have any enemies, had she been acting strange. No, nothing like that, they said. She'd been happy-go-lucky, high spirits, excited to go off to college after the summer. Just in case, I asked did they know if Becca kept a diary or a journal. Isn't that what teenage girls do? Write down their feelings? Anyway, Cheryl wasn't sure, but she said she'd check, and if anything turns up, she'll let us know."

"What about the boyfriend?"

"Jimmy Bennett. I know his parents. He's eighteen. Graduated with Becca's class. Unemployed. I ran a background check. Came back clean."

"Make contact," Nathan said. "See if he'll come in voluntarily."

"You think he had something to do with it?"

"No, not really, but let's talk to him anyway. Maybe he can help establish a timeline, tell us if anything was going on with Becca."

"She was a smart girl, Nate. Really bright, from what I've heard. Honor Roll and all that. Wasn't much of a partier, didn't touch drugs as far as I know. If this guy tried to pick her up, offered her a ride or something, I can't see her going willingly."

"No, probably she wouldn't have. He would have had to take her by force."

"You heard what the pathologist said. She wasn't raped. That's contradictory to what happened to the unidentified girl. Why do you suppose that is? Why would he sexually assault one and not the other?"

"I don't know. Maybe he didn't have time. He didn't cut off the other girl's head, either. Took the time to cover her face with a mask. Trying to make it impersonal, or maybe it *was* personal and he covered her face because he felt guilty about what he'd done. Like I said before, it's possible the girl in the mask was his first and he's getting more proficient, more elaborate with his work, trying to make it match his fantasy. Maybe the second time around he didn't feel bad, didn't need to hide her face anymore. Guy's deranged, so who knows."

"What about the public? You planning on saying something anytime soon? Word gets around fast, you know that, and it's probably better you give an official statement before the rumor mill starts churning out bad product."

Nathan leaned back, sank down in his chair.

"Yeah, I know. I was hoping to have a solid lead before we made a statement, but it doesn't look like it's going to work out. We'll put it out there tomorrow."

"It's going to cause a panic."

"No way around it. Who knows? Maybe it'll help. Maybe we can run a photo in the paper of the unidentified vic. Get some more eyeballs on it. Someone might know her."

"Rick and Cheryl are having Becca's funeral on Friday. Closed casket, of course. You've gotta be there."

"Why?"

"People will expect it."

"I'm the last guy they want showing up at their daughter's funeral."

"You're going," Carl said. "You can ride with me and Carol if you want."

Nathan stared at him, opened his mouth to say something, closed it again, nodded solemnly.

"Good. I'm glad you can still see reason. What else?"

Nathan threw up his hands. "For now, that's it. We'll talk to the Bennett kid tomorrow. Put out the press release, see if we get any bites on the unidentified girl. We're still waiting on lab results on the semen, and the stuff Grayling took from that mark on the back of Becca's neck."

"Some kind of weapon, you think?"

"Some kind of siphon is what I think," Nathan said. "Grayling said whoever did it drained some of her blood before killing her."

"Medical device?"

"Grayling didn't act like he recognized the markings."

"Weird shit."

"Only kind of shit there is lately."

"I'm beat, man."

"Go home. We'll pick it up tomorrow."

"What're you gonna do?"

"I'm heading out too. My head's killing me."

Which wasn't true. Something was killing him all right, but the pain wasn't in his head. His testicle was on fire, aching worse than ever, and the ibuprofen he had taken earlier hadn't helped, so he thought it was time to up the ante. In the back of his mind, there was a little voice whispering to him, clinically detached, telling him it was cancer with a capital C, better come to grips with it, prepare himself for the battle of his life. But there was another voice, a louder one that demanded that he suck it up, he didn't have time deal with cancer or anything else at the moment. He had two dead girls rotting down at the meat locker and their killer was still on the loose.

Carl stood, moved the chair back to where he had found it. "You know, you guys should come over for dinner sometime soon. Carol's a decent cook, and she's been dying to meet Jess. I think the two of them would hit it off."

"Have you seen Jess lately?" Nathan asked. "She'd probably eat you guys out of house and home."

"Sounds fine to me. Pregnancy'll do that to a woman. Or so I hear. Truth is, I think Carol's feeling lonely. Moved here a year ago, but she hasn't met that many people on account she does medical transcription at home. Doesn't get out much."

"She's got you."

"Sure, she's got me, and I listen well, but I don't always fit the bill."

"How long have you guys been dating now?"

"Seven months come July."

"And you moved in with her when?"

"March."

"How's that working out?"

"Not bad. For a little while, there was a learning curve. She doesn't like it when I leave wet towels on the floor, or when I clutter up the dining room, but otherwise it's good. Anyway, think about it, would you? She could use some female companionship."

"I'll do that."

"Night, boss."

"Night."

It was 7 P.M. by the time Nathan left the office. There was still plenty of light, but the sky was a dreary gray and the first drops of rain began to spatter against the patrol car's windshield by the time he pulled into his driveway.

When he went inside, Jess was in the kitchen, cooking a late dinner consisting of oven-baked porkloin and instant garlic mashed potatoes. Lately, they had been having porkloin at least once a week. Jess stretched it out so they usually had leftovers for a few days. She wasn't a natural in the kitchen, but the pregnancy had given her weird cravings. Porkloin seemed to be her go-to of choice, that, and in the middle of the night she liked to get up and fix herself a bowl of Fruit Loops, carrying them back to bed, using her stomach as a shelf to rest the bowl on as she ate and watched reruns of *Law & Order: Special Victims Unit*.

Nathan asked her how much time he had, asked if it would be all right to jump in the shower. Jess said it was, and Nathan stripped out of his uniform, showered quickly, put on jogging pants and a t-shirt. Before going back to the kitchen, he opened the medicine cabinet, snatched out the ibuprofen, shook a few into his hand, swallowed them. The pain was fierce, but he couldn't let Jess catch onto that. She would only push him to see the good doctor again. For now, she seemed to have forgotten about his ailment, and he was determined to keep it that way.

Jess pulled the porkloin out of the oven and whipped up the instant potatoes. Nathan grabbed the plates and silverware, helped Jess plate their dinner, and they both sat down at the kitchen table.

Nathan hadn't expected to have an appetite, but it was there in full force, and he practically inhaled it as they watched through the French doors to the back patio as the daylight faded away.

He knew Jess was going to ask about the murder, that it was only a matter of when, and she did, finally, as he was scraping the few scraps of food that remained of his dinner into the trash.

He weighed his words before he spoke them, telling Jess about Becca Struthers, leaving out the finer details, the gruesome parts. He didn't mention that she had been staked through the heart or that her head had been removed from her body; didn't mention that her blood had been drained; didn't mention Carl's theory about how maybe they were dealing with a psychopath with a vampire fetish.

Jess had known the Struther's girl. She had a checking account at the bank where Jess worked. She knew the parents as well, and she paled noticeably as Nathan told her about his visit with Rick and Cheryl, leaving out the part about the door being slammed shut in his face. Like Carl, Jess had spent her entire life in Crater Lake. She couldn't fathom the idea of the good people of Crater Lake treating someone differently, or that such a form of bias existed at all. It was a form of denial that Nathan had become accustomed to.

"It's terrible," she said, pushing around uneaten mashed potatoes with her fork. "And he's still out there. You don't have any leads?"

Nathan said, "We're working on a few things. Too soon to know whether any of them will pan out or not. We'll probably issue a statement tomorrow, see if anyone comes forward with information."

"I just can't believe it. A killer in town. It's like something that happens in a movie, not in real life. Not here."

Her hand went to her protruding stomach as she said it, as if willing their unborn child to cover its ears.

Nathan squirmed in his chair. The ibuprofen hadn't kicked in yet and he was beginning to wonder if it ever would. The pain was intense.

"What's wrong?" Jess asked.

"Nothing's wrong."

"Don't lie. You can't sit still."

"Just antsy. This stuff at work, I can't decide if I'm coming or going."

She stared at him for a minute, her eyes drilling into him, searching, but finally she seemed to accept his answer and said, "It's terrible," again.

She stood, picked up her plate, but Nathan grabbed it from her, carried it to the sink, said, "You cooked. I'll handle clean up duty. Just relax."

She did so without protest, adjourning to the living room, sinking into the recliner, putting her feet up.

When Nathan finished with the dishes, he joined her and they watched several episodes of *Criminal Minds* until Jess started to fall asleep in the chair. Nathan patted her on the shoulder gently, helped her up, escorted her to the bedroom. "I've got to go pee," she said, and Nathan waited while she did, helped her take her shoes off afterward, and once she was in bed, he laid down next to her.

Within minutes, she was fast asleep. Nathan closed his eyes, but couldn't shut out the thoughts running through his brain. He thought they might pass eventually and that exhaustion might finally overtake him. But neither of those things happened. He lay awake for a long time, staring up into the darkness, and soon it was after midnight. His left testicle burned, ached, throbbed, stabbed.

He freed himself from the covers, quietly got out of the bed, trekked down the hallway and into the bathroom. He slid his pants down, then his boxer briefs, cupped his hands over his balls and began feeling and squishing around. He winced as his fingers closed over the left one, could tell it was swollen, nearly twice the size of its neighbor.

There was something out of the ordinary, he wasn't sure if it was a lump exactly, but his mind ran with the idea, hammering another nail into the coffin of self-diagnosis. Hadn't he read about that online? How one of the symptoms of testicular cancer started as a noticeable lump on one of the testicles? And here he was, standing in the bathroom at twelve-thirty in the morning, his pants down as he fondled himself, looking at himself in the mirror above the sink, seeing the fear in his own eyes as his pregnant wife lay sleeping in their bed.

Nathan tried to ignore it, but the pain wouldn't let him. Maybe Jess was right; maybe it was time to bite the bullet and make that appointment with Dr. Kobayashi. If the pain kept going the way it was, he wouldn't have a choice.

But not yet. He told himself he could wait a few days, watch it, reevaluate. No use jumping the gun. His mind screamed cancer, but this wasn't a truth he wanted to face, at least not right now.

He pulled his pants up, ran the faucet, palmed cold water onto his face.

He crept down the hallway, past the open door to the bedroom that would soon be the baby's room, and took the stairs down to the basement.

He and Jess shared a home office they had set up in the basement's unused den area. There was a small L-shaped desk they had purchased at Walmart positioned in one corner. Next to it, a metal two-drawer filing cabinet where they stored receipts, past tax returns, and other important documents. The remainder of the room was empty space. The plan had always been to set up another living area down there. Get one of those fancy couches with the fold-out footrests and the console in the center with a storage compartment and cupholders, maybe a big 60" TV, a nice surround sound system, convert the area into a place of entertainment, a place they could go and watch movies without waking the baby. They just hadn't gotten around to doing any of that yet.

Nathan sat down in the swivel-chair, scooted up to the desk, opened the laptop. Blue light flooded the otherwise darkened room.

Are you really entertaining this idea?

Carl's theory. The one that had the killer believing he was a vampire or a vampire killer or maybe both.

He brought up Google, typed in *vampire serial killers*, waited. There weren't as many results as he had expected, but two popped up at the top of the list.

The first was a man named Richard Trenton Chase. Nathan clicked into one of the sites, was looking at a grainy black and white mugshot of Chase. Thin face, shaggy dark hair, mustache. He appeared rather ordinary. Maybe not an upstanding member of society, but when Nathan stared at the photo, he didn't see any trace of the monster that had killed six people in the span of a month in Villa Park, California.

Nathan scanned the article.

Robert Chase had been born in San Jose, California. Abusive mother. By age 10, he was exhibiting signs of something called the MacDonald triad: bed-wetting, arson, cruelty to animals. Chase was an alcoholic, drug user, and a hypochondriac. He was committed to a mental institution in 1975 after he tried to inject rabbit's blood into his veins. He fantasized about killing rabbits, had been caught with blood smeared around his mouth, and hospital staff discovered he had been capturing birds and drinking their blood.

It was at the mental institution that Chase was diagnosed as a paranoid schizophrenic. After receiving treatments involving psychotropic drugs, he was released in 1976, after being deemed to no longer be a danger to society.

A year later, Chase murdered a man in a drive-by shooting with a .22 caliber rifle. Several weeks after, this was followed by attempted breaking and entering into a woman's home. The article went on to say that Chase took locked doors as a sign he wasn't welcome, and then he would move onto the next, until he found one unlocked, which he believed to be an invitation for him to come inside.

His next victim was a woman named Teresa Wallin. She was three months pregnant. Chase attacked her in her home, shot her three times, raped her corpse while stabbing her with a butcher knife. He then went on to remove her organs, cut off her nipples, and, this was the kicker – drank her blood.

He committed his final murders several days later, killing four people, including a 6-year-old and a 1-year-old. Again, he engaged in necrophilia and cannibalism of the victims' bodies.

Nathan continued on, reading about how Chase had been startled when a neighbor knocked on the door to the house of the family he had just slaughtered. When police arrived, they found that Chase had left bloody handprints in one of the victim's blood. He was apprehended, went to trial, found guilty of six counts of first degree murder, and was sentenced to die in the gas chamber. But he never made it there. Prison guards found Chase dead in his cell, a case of apparent suicide.

Before Chase's death, an FBI Agent, Robert Ressler, conducted a series of interviews with the killer. During the interviews, Chase elaborated on his fears of Nazis and UFOs, claiming he had only killed all those people in order to keep himself alive.

Nathan stared at the photo again, studied it. He wanted badly to see something there, something in the eyes that would betray the fact that the man was a cold-blooded killer. Some sign or curiosity that differentiated him from other human beings.

Next on the list was Peter Kürten.

There was a mugshot of Kürten from the 1930s. He was German, a gaunt figure, short hair combed over to the side, dressed in a suit, white collared shirt, striped tie. Nathan studied the photo the same way he had studied the photo of Robert Chase. Again, he couldn't see a monster. What he saw was an accountant, or maybe a math teacher, or a mid-level executive.

But Kürten was none of those things. What he was was a man that committed a series of murders and sexual assaults that later earned him the nickname *The Vampire of Düsseldorf* or, alternately, the *Düsseldorf Monster*. He was considered a vampire because he repeatedly tried to drink the blood of his victims.

Like Robert Trenton Chase, Kürten was born into an abusive family. As a child, he regularly witnessed his alcoholic father sexually assaulting both his mother and his sisters. Allegedly, Kürten committed his first murders at the tender age of 9, when he drowned two young boys he was swimming with. He served time for various crimes, including theft and arson, and moved on from torturing animals to attacking people. His weapon of choice was a hammer.

He was arrested in 1930, tried, convicted, sentenced to death, and was later executed by guillotine.

A doctor who interviewed Kürten prior to his death said that Kürten stated that his primary motive was in receiving sexual pleasure. Nathan thought about the first murder, the girl in the mask, how Grayling had said there were signs of sexual assault.

It wasn't a surprise to him that the man they were hunting got his kicks by making people suffer, that the act of killing gave him pleasure. That was par for the course. Another point in the article that stood out to him was that Robert Chase had been diagnosed as a paranoid schizophrenic. He had a hunch their killer suffered from a similar mental disorder. If Carl was correct in his theory, then the killer believed in vampires, thought he was hunting them. But his delusion had progressed, and, Nathan thought, this could be due to any number of reasons. Maybe killing an innocent wasn't doing it for him anymore; maybe he had to believe that the person he was stalking actually *was* a vampire, and the only way to accomplish that was to convince his mind that they really *were* vampires. Becca Struthers had been partially drained of blood.

The article about Chase mentioned that after he had been released from the mental institution, his mother had weaned him off of the medications they had been giving him.

Bad idea, Nathan thought.

And maybe they were dealing with a similar case now. What if their killer had been on medication prior to the killings, and the drugs had done their job by keeping him in line. Only at some point he had decided to stop taking them for whatever reason, and, with his illness left unchecked, his delusions had spiraled out of control.

Nathan took the yellow legal pad from the top desk drawer, grabbed a pen, scribbled a quick note: *check with neighboring hospitals/mental institutions – recent releases/escapes.*

He didn't know if anything would come of it, but it couldn't hurt. They weren't exactly drowning in leads.

It was one-thirty. He had been staring at the laptop screen for the last hour. He rubbed his eyes, closed the lid, sat in the darkness for a minute.

He went back upstairs, poured himself a glass of milk, drank it, stopped in the bathroom for another round of pain-killers, exceeded the recommended dose, prayed he wasn't causing any long-term damage to himself. He walked back to the bedroom, quietly slid into bed. Jess shifted and mumbled something incoherent, but didn't wake up.

Gradually, the pain in his testicle dulled. Enough so that just after two o'clock, his eyes grew heavy and he was able to fall asleep.

9

jimmy bennett

Jimmy Bennett was 6'1", with dark, wavy hair, brown eyes, and a build like the actor Jay Baruchel. Carl had contacted him the previous evening and asked if he would mind making a trip down to the station for questioning. Before answering Carl's question, Bennett had had a few questions for him first. *Did they think he did it? Did they think he killed Becca? Did he need to get a lawyer?*

Carl had done his best to assuage the kid's fears, telling Bennett that they just wanted to ask him a couple of routine questions, basic stuff.

Bennett had agreed. He arrived at the station at five past ten (the interview had been scheduled for ten o'clock sharp) on Wednesday morning. Carl escorted him into a cramped interview room. Nathan joined them a minute or two later.

The kid looked nervous. Fidgety, eyes darting around, shifting in his chair a lot. These weren't tell-tale signs of guilt. This wasn't the movies. Nathan didn't think for a minute that the kid had done it, but that didn't stop him from sizing the kid up, staring at him, studying him the way he had studied the photos of Robert Trenton Chase and Peter Kürten, searching for some inner monster.

Bennett was eighteen, unemployed, had attended Crater Lake High, had graduated with the same class as Becca Struthers, didn't have the slightest idea about what he wanted to do with his future. He hadn't applied to any colleges, but had been entertaining the possibility of moving to Nebraska when Becca headed off for Wayne State. He said the plan had been to get a job, rent an apartment, and see if Becca would ditch the dorms after her freshman year and move in with him.

From everything Nathan knew about Becca Struthers, she had been hard-working, ambitious, goal-oriented, gotten good grades, and had had a concrete plan for her future. Unlike Bennett, she had known what she wanted to do with her life, or at least had a tentative idea about it. Nathan thought it was a case of opposites attracting. Yin and yang. He could vaguely recall his own state of mind during his high school days, and thought his mindset had been similar to Jimmy Bennett's. He had never been one of those people that had a plan, that had mapped out their life ahead of time. So he couldn't fault the kid for lacking in the motivation department.

They offered Bennett water or coffee. Bennett said he would appreciate a water, and Carl exited the room, fetched the water, returned, handed it to Bennett, who unscrewed the cap and took a long swallow.

They exchanged the usual pleasantries, Nathan thanking the kid for coming down, saying it was a terrible thing that had happened. Then he said let's start from the beginning, where was Bennett on Monday night.

"I was home."

"Was Becca with you?"

Bennett nodded. "Yeah, she came over after she got off work. I rented a movie."

"When was this?"

"Around five-thirty, I think. Maybe a little after. She ate dinner with us."

"Who's 'us'?" Carl asked.

"My mom and I."

"So you ate dinner around five-thirty. Then what?"

"After dinner, Becca and I went down to the basement – that's where my room is – and we put on the movie."

"Did you notice anything different about her? Acting strange? Anything out of the ordinary?"

"No. She seemed like her normal self. She was always so happy. I know she wasn't happy all of the time – who is? – but she almost always acted like it. Like nothing could get her down. Always cheerful. Sometimes it got to be annoying."

"Annoying?"

Bennett shrugged. "I don't know. You know, like sometimes it could be exhausting, her acting happy all the time, even though I knew she wasn't. She was always so mature. Even when we would argue, she acted like it was no big deal. She never raised her voice."

"Did you argue often?"

"Not really. I think that's why Becca liked me. I'm pretty laid back most of the time. Her last boyfriend, Dylan, those two were always fighting. They went out for most of our junior year and broke up right after we were seniors. She couldn't handle it. She didn't come out and say that, but Dylan's a really negative guy, and Becca had a hard time being around negative people like that."

"What's Dylan's last name?"

"Mulroney."

Carl said, "You mean Dylan Mulroney, the starting quarterback for the Crater Lake Pythons?"

"Yeah, that's him. He's got a real temper."

"Did he have a problem with you and Becca dating?"

"Not that he came right out and said, but he'd give me dirty looks a lot. People would say stuff about how he didn't like it. Like how he wanted to meet me in a dark alley."

"But he didn't ever do anything?"

"He still called Becca sometimes. Just out of the blue. Wanted her to give him another chance, talking about how he'd *changed* and if she would give him another shot, he'd get it right this time."

"She would tell you that he would call her?"

"Yeah," Bennett said. "We didn't keep secrets from each other."

"And how did you react when she would tell you?"

"I didn't like it. Me and Dylan never got along, were never in the same circles. I thought he was a dumb jock. I don't know what she ever saw in the guy."

"The two of you would fight about it?"

"No. Not really. Like I said, Becca didn't like to fight. So whenever I'd bring it up, she'd just kind of humor me, tell me there wasn't anything to worry about. Of course, I *was* worried. I mean, he was the star quarterback. This big athlete, popular, good-looking. I guess I could be a little insecure about it."

"Okay, what about Monday night. The two of you had dinner with your mother, then you went to your room to watch a movie. Did you guys have a fight?"

"No. I mean, it wasn't really a fight. I would never hurt her."

"I don't think you would," Nathan said. "But we're trying to be thorough here. Any small detail could help. You did fight on Monday night then?"

"Like I said, it wasn't really a fight."

"All right. What was it about?"

"The same thing it's always about. Her going off to school. Leaving me behind."

"You didn't want her to go."

"It wasn't like that. I wanted her to go, I just didn't want her to go so *far*. I thought she could go somewhere closer. They've got the community college in Alton. But she had her heart set on Wayne State, and I took it as she was willing to leave me in the dust for that."

"You were upset about it," Nathan said. "Did your arguments ever turn physical?"

"What? No. Of course not. I'd never hurt her. I just felt like she was ditching me. I know college is important, and I wanted her to be happy, but, and maybe it's selfish, but I didn't want to lose her. I knew if she went off to Wayne State, well, the long distance thing, it doesn't work. Maybe it would be okay at first, but it doesn't last, she'd be meeting all these guys at school."

"Like Dylan Mulroney," Carl suggested.

"Guys *like* him, sure." Bennett was going red in the face now, passionate, spilling his guts in front of the whole world, which was really only Nathan and Carl, but might as well have been the entire planet. "I don't stack up. I'm not talented in sports or anything else. I was afraid if she went...that I'd lose her."

Nathan and Carl waited for the kid to get it all out of his system.

"You guys probably think I killed her now."

Nathan and Carl exchanged a quick glance, Nathan shaking his head.

"I know this is hard, Jimmy. Believe me" Nathan said, "I really do. And nobody here thinks you would have hurt Becca. But the more we know, the better we can flesh out a timeline, try to put it all together. That way maybe we *can* find the person that did it."

Bennett sniffled a few times, palmed his eyes to dry the tears, started the process of putting himself back in order. He nodded a few times, said, "I get it. I'm sorry. I usually…I…I still can't believe she's gone."

"I know. Take your time. Think. It's Monday night, you guys are downstairs watching a movie, you get into an argument about Becca going off to school. What happened after that?"

"Nothing. I kept pushing it. Not outright doing it, but I'd make these little jabs here and there, and she took it in stride like she always did, not getting mad at me or anything, but I could tell she was getting impatient. When the movie got over, I went to start another one, but she said she should be getting home. That wasn't like her, that's how I knew she was upset. She didn't storm out. She didn't work that way. Just made it sound like she wanted to go home and sleep in her own bed. A lot of times when we stayed up late watching movies, she'd just fall asleep at my house, we'd both sleep on the couch and she'd go home the next morning to get ready for work. I told her I was sorry. I was being selfish. I thought maybe if I apologized I could get her to stay, but she had her mind made up."

"What time did she leave?"

"It must've been ten-thirty. She loved *Titanic*. You know, with Leonard DiCaprio and Kate Winslet. She could watch it over and over again. We usually watched movies I like, but that night we ended up watching one of hers, and it's like three hours long…so, yeah, it must've been at least ten-thirty when she said she was going."

"So she left between ten-thirty and eleven, you think?"

"That's about right."

"Did she have her car?"

"She walked over. My house is only a few blocks from the store. She usually left her car at the store and would walk over to my house when it was nice out."

"Did you talk to her after that?"

"I tried calling her a little after, but she didn't answer. She tended to ignore me when she was angry. She'd just pretend it wasn't happening. Drove me nuts."

"You didn't hear from her after that?"

"I texted her later that night, probably around one in the morning, I'd have to check my phone. When I still hadn't heard from her the next morning, I texted her some more, apologized some more. I thought about going by her work, but I thought that might make me seem like a stalker, so I didn't. Usually, if I gave her some space, she'd start talking to me again."

Nathan said, "Okay, Jimmy, I think we've got everything we need. We appreciate you coming down. Why don't you go on home."

"Do *they* think I did it?"

"Who?"

"Becca's parents."

"I don't know," Carl said.

"They probably do. I tried calling them, you know, to offer my condolences, but they haven't returned my calls."

"They're grieving. I doubt they're returning anyone's calls. Give it some time."

"Her funeral's on Friday," Bennett said. "I want to go, but..."

Carl stood. "Then you should go," he said, guiding Bennett out of the interview room, through the lobby, holding the door for the kid on his way out.

Bennett turned to him before he left. "I loved her you know. If I ever saw the guy that did it, I'd kill him. With my bare hands if I had to. I *want* to kill him. I think I could if I ever saw him. Does that make me bad?"

Carl was silent for a moment, before he said, "If it's bad, then I'd say we're all bad right about now, Jimmy."

"Think he did it?"

"Not even a little bit."

"Me either. Puts us back at the drawing board."

"She was on foot," Nathan said.

"Not unheard of."

"Run down to the store later. See if the kid's story checks out, that Becca's car is there. When you find it, go over it with a fine-toothed comb."

"Jimmy said she left on foot, so I doubt there's any evidence in the car."

"Probably not, but let's cover all our bases. And put in a call to see if any results have come back from the lab."

"What about missing persons?"

"Check that too."

"What are you going to do?"

"I'm on my way to make a statement to the Press."

"By now, the news has already made its way around town."

"We'll run a photo of the girl. Maybe somebody will call in, maybe offer a reward."

"Word on the street is that Rick and Cheryl are starting their own crusade. Five thousand cash to anybody that comes forward with information that leads to the arrest of Becca's killer. And so it begins."

"The more eyeballs the better, I guess."

"Did you have a chance to talk to Jess?"

Nathan stared at him, saying *What was I supposed to talk to Jess about?* with his eyes.

"Dinner, with Carol and me?"

"I spaced it."

"Uh huh, sure."

"I'll ask tonight."

"And I'll hold my breath."

10

fractured

HE STARES AT himself in the mirror for a long time, study-ing his face, not liking what he sees, but grateful that his reflec-tion is still there.

This is how it always goes. Always.

When he's in the thick of it like this, deep into the hunt, things start to get fuzzy after a while. He takes more and more time to remember who he is, what he looks like, going through the steps, the rituals, making sure he isn't one of them. It's a fine line sometimes.

Reality has always been weird for him; has always been stretched thin, like the skin of a balloon. If he stretches it far enough and gets up close, he can almost see through it, imag-ines he can see the shapes of things, but the details are unclear.

The motel is a dump. He's used to it by now. He's stayed in far worse places. The shower is going, steam fills the tiny bathroom, and the mirror above the sink starts to fog up every couple of minutes, so he wipes it clean, staring at his reflection again.

Still there…

That's all that matters.

How long has he been at this game, this crusade? More years than he can count. When he first started, he would go for long periods without shaving, and his beard would come in dark brown. These days, when he let it get out of hand, there was white mixed in with the brown, lots of it, so he shaved it every two days now.

He has been trailing the Elusive One for what seems like forever, always close, but never close enough. His prey always leaves a trail of bodies in its wake, a string of innocents, leaving them like scattered breadcrumbs.

For a long time, the man has fooled himself into believing that the Elusive One isn't aware of his presence, doesn't realize it is being pursued. But those days are over. He sees all the signs now, all the clues, and understands that it has become a game. Maybe the Elusive One has always known.

He isn't afraid of death. He's afraid of what comes after. If the Elusive One catches him, there won't be death at all, but something far worse, and he will no longer be in control of himself.

He thinks this, chuckles at his reflection in the mirror. Has he *ever* truly been in control of himself? Don't ask any of the people that know him, or any of the hospital doctors from the old days that acted like it was their mission in life to keep him locked up, make sure he never saw the bright light of day. If only they had realized the things that walked in the dark, they might have understood.

Mirrors are the only thing he can trust these days. He fishes into his pocket, takes the fragment of mirror from it, looks at his reflection, switching back and forth between the one above the sink and the one in his hand.

The feeling comes over him. Soon now, he thinks. It has been almost two days. The Elusive One operates on a schedule, and he knows there will be another any day now, maybe tomorrow, maybe the day after, he isn't sure, but what he knows for certain is that there will be another.

Finally, satisfied, he puts the mirror into his pocket, leaves the bathroom, enters the living area with the single queen-sized bed, the bureau, the ancient 25" console TV, the wall lamps, the telephone, the window with a majestic view of a concrete sea crowded with cars, trucks, vans, and motorcycles.

Nothing but sheep. All of them. Sheep. He is the reason they can sleep easy at night. He hates them. Time has taught him to. But he protects them anyway.

His own car isn't parked in the lot. He's smart. Knows all the tricks. He uses stolen plates, so they wouldn't be able to identify him by his vehicle, but he doesn't want them to get that far, and so parks his car several blocks away. He uses a fake ID to book the motel room, pays in cash, wears a disguise, tries to look nondescript, intensely average, easily forgotten. It is like being invisible. They never remember him. He is a ghost that operates in a land of make-believe.

Moving over to the table by the window, he sits down in one of the hard plastic chairs, begins unpacking a plastic sack of supplies. He brings out a dozen bulbs of garlic, breaks them apart, separates the cloves, peels away the skin, uses a long needle he takes from his backpack to pierce each of them, deftly threading the cloves together. He leaves several inches of slack at each end, ties the ends together, forming a necklace of garlic, which he pulls over his head and wears around his neck. For protection. He fashions a new one every few days, wants to keep the garlic potent.

The heavy curtains are parted slightly. He goes about his work in the semi-darkness, glancing out the window every so often, can see his reflection in the glass.

Where was the Elusive One now? Close, no doubt. Things had only just begun. It would get much worse before it was over.

He travels often, following the trail, criss-crossing the country. There never seems to be any rhyme or reason to it. There is a map of the United States folded neatly in his backpack. On it, he has detailed all the places he has been, number of victims, locations of their bodies.

Ten months ago, he was in Southern California; San Diego, near the Mexican border. After that, came Pueblo, Colorado, followed by New Mexico. He spent three weeks in Carlsbad, cleaning up the mess, preventing another outbreak.

Before it came to Iowa, it spent a month in some rinky-dink town not far from Grand Forks, North Dakota. This was late January, the middle of winter. The Elusive One didn't mind the cold.

He didn't like killing in the snow. It always left stains, crimson flowers that seemed to blossom on a blanket of virgin whiteness.

Everywhere he goes the sheep always chase him, unaware they are chasing the wrong thing, searching in the wrong places. Two years ago, they almost caught him, but he managed to slip away. He had gotten a new identity after that, switched cars, changed plates every day or two.

He still hasn't figured out where the Elusive One is going. For a while, it has been vaguely west to east, toward the East Coast, and he wonders what will happen once his prey reaches the Atlantic. Will it turn back and head west again, or will it cross the ocean to wreak havoc on a new continent?

He doesn't know, perhaps never will, but he will follow it. He has never been as close to catching his prey as he was in

Colorado, but he has a good feeling about this one. It is only a matter of time.

And he has to be prepared, has to have his tools sharp and ready.

He digs into the sack, hauls out a bundle of wooden dowels, inspects each of them, then unsheathes his knife, begins carving the ends, making sure they are razor sharp.

11

the funeral

The funeral service for Becca Struthers was held at Our Lady of the Lake Parish. Nathan had never understood the difference between "funeral service" and "memorial service," but, apparently, a funeral service meant that the service was held with the deceased's body present. With a memorial service, the body was absent. In the case of Becca Struther's funeral, it was something of a mystery. Becca's casket was positioned in front of the carpeted stairs leading up to the altar, but it was closed, and Nathan had no idea if Becca's body rested within it.

Attendance was high that Friday morning. The pews packed with people. Nathan spotted Rick & Cheryl Struthers, seated at the front, Rick looking blank and forlorn, Cheryl dabbing at the tears pouring from her eyes with a silk handkerchief.

Nathan had let Jess dress him that morning. He owned two suits, a black one and a gray one. She chose the gray one for him, pairing it with a white button-down shirt and a light blue tie with angled horizontal stripes streaking across it at regular intervals.

He hadn't slept much the night before. At eleven-thirty, Jess had started to stir, tossing and turning, unable to find a comfortable sleeping position. Finally, after midnight, she had given up, sighing loudly as she threw off the covers and traipsed into the kitchen. She returned several minutes later, carrying a bowl of Fruit Loops. She slid back into bed, lay on her back, switched on the television, put on an episode of *Criminal Minds* and perched the full bowl of cereal on her stomach, spooning Fruit Loops into her mouth as she watched TV.

Despite this distraction, Nathan had been serious about getting to sleep, so he turned onto his side, faced away from her, closed his eyes, tried to ignore the noise coming from the TV and the thoughts that spun themselves round and round in his head. Around one, he gave up, turned onto his back, two pillows behind his head, and lay watching the TV. He had stayed awake through two episodes of *Criminal Minds*, when he finally fell asleep a little before three. Jess had roused him a mere three and a half hours later, at six-thirty, nudging him awake, telling him it was time to get up and get ready.

As he dressed that morning, he had tried to find reasons to skip the funeral. He could think of a million of them, but Jess only shook her head, told him he was going and that was that.

He sat now, in a pew toward the back of the church, Jess next to him, Carl and Carol sitting to her left.

The priest said a few words, took a seat to the left of the altar as a young woman ascended the steps to the lectern, paused to take an inordinate amount of time to adjust the microphone, and then began a long and drawn out eulogy about Becca Struthers.

Nathan found himself zoning out, trying to pretend that people weren't staring at him, silently blaming him for what had happened.

When it was over, they watched as the pallbearers took hold of the casket's handles, carrying it out of the church, down the steps, to the hearse that was parked out front.

Nathan waited, watched Rick & Cheryl pass down the aisle. He looked at them, willed them to look back, but neither of them did. In their minds, he had been wiped from their existence the moment he had delivered the news of Becca's death and had the door slammed the shut in his face.

As they exited the church, Nathan saw Rick and Cheryl at the bottom of the stairs, talking to Abraham Talley.

From behind Nathan, Carl said, "Oh boy, here we go. Probably already campaigning for the next election. Think we can make it past without being seen?"

Nathan wasn't sure, but he moved over to the side, closer to the handrail, grabbing Jess's hand as they tried to make a quick getaway.

But Talley spotted them when they were halfway down, turned back to the Struthers, smiled, shook their hands, helped load them into their vehicle, and then turned toward Nathan just as he reached the sidewalk.

Jess leaned in close to Nathan's ear, whispered, "Behave."

"Sheriff," Tally said, all smiles, extending his hand.

Nathan shook it vigorously, smiled back, cursed fate under his breath. "Hi Abe."

Tally proceeded to shake Jess's hand, then Carol's, and finally Carl's, saying, "How's your new boss working out for you?"

Carl grinned, said "just fine," and then snatched Carol's hand, dragging her toward the car.

Tally looked sharp and well-rested, already deeply tanned from having spent long hours out on Crater Lake, fishing.

They moved out of the way of the stairs, Talley saying, "You heading out to the cemetery?"

Nathan nodded.

"It's a real shame." Talley lowered his head, shook it back and forth a few times. "Sounds like you've got a serious shit-storm on your hands. Making any progress?"

As if you give a flying fuck, Nathan thought. Jess was staring at him, probably reading his thoughts, probably trying to tell him to behave telepathically.

"We've got a few leads," Nathan said, knowing it was bull-shit, but determined to not let Talley catch onto that fact.

"Saw the other girl's picture in the paper yesterday. If you ever get an itch to put a fresh eye on things..."

"I think we've got it covered."

"Sure, absolutely, I wasn't implying that I had anything but complete faith in your abilities, Sheriff. Just sayin', I don't harbor any hard feelings about the way things turned out. The people spoke, for better or worse, and that, as they say, is that. But I'm still available, the old mind is still sharp, and I'm more than willing to take a peek at what you've got."

Nathan stared into the man's eyes, saw the resentment there, plain as day.

"I'll keep that in mind."

"Do that. I'm always one of two places these days. At home or out fishing. So you know where to find me."

They shook hands again. Talley left them, moved onto the next, making the rounds.

"Asshole," Nathan said under his breath.

Jess touched his shoulder. "You handled that very well."

"If only I had been armed..."

"Oh, calm down. He even offered to help."

"Yeah, because he's busy campaigning, making sure everyone sees how he isn't a sore loser. I'm sure he's telling everyone how incompetent I am in his own delightful way."

"You don't know that."

"I *do* know that," Nathan said and started for the car.

"Well, still, you handled it well. Very professional. And maybe he was just putting on his campaign face so everyone will think he's wonderful, but everyone also saw you being polite back. People aren't dumb. They elected *you*, didn't they?"

When they reached the car, Nathan held the door open for Jess, closed it after she was in the passenger seat. He pulled out, followed the procession through town, and once they reached the cemetery, he parked on the shoulder of the gravel path that formed a large circle within the confines of the tall wrought-iron fence.

Carl and Carol were exiting their car when Nathan arrived. Carl waited for them to catch up, started to apologize profusely about ditching them so abruptly outside the church.

"I couldn't do it," Carl said. "I thought I could, but if I would have waited around, I would've ended up smacking the guy in the face."

"Nathan wanted to shoot him," Jess said.

"Should've brought your Glock," Carl said, smiling at Nathan.

"If I was a wiser man."

"So anyway," Carl said, "I got a call on our way over. From Mathers. Test results came back from the lab."

"Carl, we're at a funeral for God's sake," Carol said. "Can't it wait?"

Carl stared at her, shrugged. Jess grabbed Carol's arm, said, "Let them talk about their work stuff," guiding her toward the crowd that had gathered around the open grave thirty yards away.

"Okay, so what did he say?" Nathan asked.

"It's the weirdest thing," Carl said. "I guess I'll cover the easy stuff first. The fluids they swabbed from the first girl's…privates…tested positive for semen. But we already knew that would be the case. All the blood samples they took from Becca's clothes were her own. But here's the strange thing. You know that funny mark she had on the back of her neck? The one the pathologist thought was how the guy drained off her blood? Well, they were able to get a DNA sample. Of course, some of it tested as Becca's, but there was also something else."

Nathan stared off toward the slightly upward-sloping hill to where the crowd had gathered around the open grave. A three-sided shelter had been erected around the site to protect the visitors from potential rain, but it proved unnecessary because the sky was blue and cloudless, the sun beating down from above.

"Listen closely," Carl said, pulling a small notepad from his shirt pocket, flipping it open, reading over his scribbled notes. "Mathers said the foreign DNA, they identified it as coming from the *Hirudinea*. Carl struggled with the pronunciation. *He-ro-do-nee-ah.*

"Am I supposed to know what that is?"

"*Leeches.*"

"Leeches?"

"Yeah, they pulled leech DNA from around that mark."

Nathan shook his head.

"Mathers didn't believe it either, so he did a little research. Those markings, that upside down 'Y' on the back of her neck, he said that makes sense now because that matches up with the way a leech's mouth is. It has these three blades and a sucker, and when they latch onto somebody, that's the mark their mouth leaves, the circle around the Y is from their lips. It's basically how they make the incision into the flesh so they can suck out blood. They're" – Carl glanced down at his notepad – "*hemato-phagous*. Meaning they feed on blood. From what Mathers said, they produce this anticoagulant enzyme so the blood doesn't clot. There's something in their saliva that acts like an anesthetic, so when it sucks your blood, you don't really feel it. They aren't supposed to be particularly dangerous, but Mathers said that sometimes they carry parasites in their digestive tract, and they can transfer the parasites into the host, maybe get them sick that way."

"That mark on the back of Becca's neck was at least two inches across," Nathan said. "It would have had to have been one big leech."

"Mathers said that, too. He made sure to mention that he wasn't an expert on the subject, but the size of the mark would have made whatever did it unusually large."

"Who carries a giant leech around with them?"

Carl shrugged.

"Did he say how long it would have taken a leech to drain that much blood out of her?"

"I didn't think to ask. My guess is that it would take a while, but if it's that big, maybe it would have been faster."

"It doesn't make sense. If you wanted to get the blood out of a person, there are faster ways, not to mention easier ones."

"Kind've makes sense though, doesn't it?"

"How do you figure?"

"This sicko killed Becca like he thought she was a vampire. We're operating under the theory that he needs to *believe* his victims are vampires before he kills them –"

"*You're* operating under that theory."

"Right. Anyway, it's kind've ironic…he used a bloodsucker to drain her blood."

"Wouldn't it make more sense to use a bat? Aren't vampires associated with bats?"

"Have you ever heard of a trained bat before? I haven't. I don't think he has a bat that he can tell to go suck blood on command, so a leech would have been easier to manage."

"That's stretching it thin."

"I'll admit, it's a little far out, but do you have a better explanation? As unbelievable as it is, the pieces fit, Nate."

"A *leech*?"

"A big one."

"Jesus."

"I think we can say beyond the shadow of a doubt that this guy is a real whacko."

"Did Mathers say anything else?"

"Just that he hadn't seen anything like it before, and hoped he never would again."

"Nothing on the unidentified girl?"

"Nobody has called the hotline if that's what you mean."

They started walking toward the graveside service.

"Something just doesn't add up," Nathan said. "The first girl wasn't mutilated. There weren't any marks on the back of her neck, which doesn't do anything to reinforce your vampire theory."

"I didn't say it was perfect. You said yourself that maybe he had changed his style or whatever."

"*Signature.*"

"Yeah, he's evolving. Or if he's off his meds, maybe his delusions are getting worse."

"That reminds me, I was meaning to check on that. See if there have been any patients released recently out of any of the mental hospitals."

"Or escaped, maybe."

"We would have heard something if there was an escape."

They fell silent as they reached the gravesite, joining Jess and Carol as Father Morrison droned on, reciting prayers. Rick and Cheryl were on the other side of the casket, standing close to the priest, Cheryl leaning into Rick for support, their lives shattered by the brutal death of their child.

Nathan thought about his own child, the boy or girl still cooking inside of Jess, ready to burst out of the oven any day now. He tried to imagine what it must be like to be Rick and Cheryl, to have your child there one minute and gone the next. He couldn't fathom it. When he tried, his mind clamped down on itself, refused to play. There were certain things too terrible to comprehend, and the cold spike he felt stab at his heart just pretending to know what it might feel like made him frightened of the real thing.

He slid his arm around Jess's waist, pulled her close, and held her tightly.

12

false hope

THE CALL CAME in at around nine-thirty on Saturday morning. Jess was busy tidying up the house. Nathan was outside, mowing the lawn, when she came down the front steps, carrying his cell phone, holding it out to him. She shouted at him over the high whine of the lawnmower. "It's Steph from Dispatch."

Nathan released the lever that kept the mower going, waited for it to die down, took the phone, said, "This is Nathan," and listened as Stephanie Phippin frantically tried to explain how they had just received a phone call from a concerned citizen who thought she maybe knew the identity of the girl from the photograph in the newspaper. Nathan listened patiently, waited for Stephanie to finish, and then had her recite the phone number the caller had given. He had her repeat it twice, saying it over and over in his head as he went into the house, found a pen, scribbled the number down. "Got it. Thanks for the good work, Steph."

Nathan debated finishing the lawn, but decided this new development wasn't something he wanted to sit on.

When he was off the phone, Jess asked, "What was that about?"

"Someone called the hotline saying they think they know who the girl is."

He wiped sweat from his forehead, took a glass from the cupboard, filled it with tap water, gulped it down.

"Are you leaving?"

"I think I better."

He grabbed the keys to the patrol car from the hook above the trashcan, clipped his off-duty holster to the waistband of his jeans, holstered his Glock, headed for the door.

"Are you going out like that?"

Nathan glanced down, took inventory of himself, shrugged his shoulders. "You're right."

He went to the bedroom, grabbed his badge from the nightstand and clipped it next to his holster. "Better?"

"That's not what I meant," Jess said.

He stopped long enough to touch her belly and gave her a quick kiss and was out the door, in the patrol car, backing out of the driveway, already dialing the number that Stephanie had given him into his cell phone.

It rang three times and Nathan was sure it was going to go to voicemail, but then a female voice answered. Nathan told her who he was, asked if she had a few minutes to talk, and he listened to her as he drove, not sure where he was driving to.

The call lasted for five minutes. The woman's name was Gwen Harms, and she thought she had gone to school with the girl in the photograph, she couldn't be one hundred percent sure, but she was pretty sure, like seventy-five percent sure, that they had been friends, both of them on the cheerleading squad their senior year. She hadn't spoken to the girl in a while, so God knew where she was, but last she knew the girl was living at her parent's house in Alton. Gwen said the girl's name was Katie Elm, last name spelled the same way as the tree. Gwen gave him the address to Katie's parent's house in Alton.

Nathan thanked her, hung up, turned onto the highway and headed for Alton. He didn't know why he was in a hurry, but he was, he was excited, and he didn't want to let this lead slip away. It was the first lucky break they had received.

He dialed Carl on his way to Alton, briefed him, Carl saying, "Want me to tag along?"

"I'm already on the road."

"Sure you want to solo this one? The only thing Carol has planned is trying to get me to fix up the backyard, so I'm dying for a reason to skip out."

"I'm halfway there."

"You sound hot to trot."

"I am."

"Well, call me after."

Nathan promised he would, hung up, punched his foot down on the accelerator. Traffic was light for a Saturday. He reached the Alton city limits in ten minutes flat, checked the scrap of paper he had scribbled the address on.

A few minutes later he pulled up in front of the house, got out, walked up to the front door and rang the doorbell.

An elderly woman wielding a walker answered the door.

"Ma'am, I'm looking for a girl named Katie Elm?"

"That's my granddaughter," the elderly woman said, and then she turned her head and shouted over her shoulder. "Debra!" She turned to face Nathan again. "Debra's my daughter. Katie's mother."

Another woman appeared in the doorway, crowded out the elderly woman. "Yes? Can I help you?"

"Debra Elm?"

"Debra *Stayer*. Elm was my ex-husband's last name. I changed it when I remarried. What's this about?"

"But you have a daughter? Katie?"

"Yes."

Her eyes went down to the badge and the gun, taking them in, widening, panic starting to set in.

"Has something happened? Is she all right?"

"I was hoping you could tell me," Nathan said. "Have you spoken to her lately?"

She paused to think about it, calculating it in her head. Nathan could see she was flustered, worried now, and wanted to tell her to calm down, take a deep breath, think, but his own mind was racing, and he gave her the time she needed.

"Yes. Well…I guess it's been about a week ago or maybe a week and a half. Last Friday night, I think."

"You haven't spoken to her since last Friday?"

She thought some more. "Friday, yes. She goes to Iowa Western in Sioux City. I tried to talk her into coming home for the summer, but she got an internship at one of the clinics up there, so decided to stay."

Nathan was thinking this was it, he had the right place, the woman hadn't spoken to her daughter in over a week, and they had pulled the girl's body out of the lake on Sunday meaning it was probably put there on Saturday night. He went over the timeline in his head. It was cutting it a little close, Friday to Saturday, especially if the girl lived in Sioux City. The question in his mind was how the girl had ended up in Crater Lake. Sioux City was an hour and twenty minutes to the north.

"Your daughter didn't mention anything about coming down to visit when you talked to her last Friday?"

Debra shook her head. "No. She would have been working. She works the graveyard shift on the weekends. She looked up then, saying, "Please tell me what this is about now. Has something happened to Katie?"

"Do you think you could try calling her?"

Hope flashed in her eyes. "Let me get my phone." She disappeared, leaving the elderly woman in the door, leaning over her walker, staring at Nathan through the screen.

"She doesn't call as much as she used to," the elderly woman said.

"Pardon?"

"Katie. Since she went off to college, we rarely see her. You know how kids are these days. Can't wait to fly the coop. Only call when they *want* something."

Nathan nodded, wasn't in the mood to disagree.

Debra reappeared in the doorway, holding her phone, swiping at the screen, scrolling through her contacts. She was on the verge of hysterics. Nathan couldn't blame her.

She found the number, dialed it. Nathan waited, already knowing that no one would be home on the other end, that no one was going to answer because they had pulled Katie Elm's body from the lake almost a week ago now and that, presently, her pale corpse was laying on a rolling metal slab in a refrigerated locker at the Chickasaw Memorial morgue.

Debra kept the phone pressed tightly to her ear. "It's ringing," she said.

Nathan realized then that he was going to be the bearer of bad news once again, that in a moment he would have to tell Debra Stayer that her daughter had been murdered. He kept a copy of the photo from the newspaper in his patrol car. It was resting on the passenger seat even now, and he knew that here any second he would have to go to the car and get it and show it to Katie's mother, asking her if the girl in the photo was Katie, knowing that she would say it was as she broke into tears the same way Cheryl Struthers had when he had delivered the news about Becca.

But someone picked up on the other end because Debra suddenly shouted, "Katie!" into the phone. "Are you all right, honey…where are you …is everything okay?"

Nathan couldn't believe it. There had to be some mistake.

"It's her," Debra Stayer said, holding out the phone to him.

Nathan took it. "Katie?"

"This is Katie."

"This is Sheriff Murphy from the Chickasaw County Sheriff's Department. Are you all right?"

"Um, yeah, I think so. Is something wrong?"

"You're all right?"

"I was sleeping. What is happening? Is my mom okay?"

"She's fine. It's just…my mistake."

Nathan handed the phone back to Debra. Debra *was* crying now – tears of joy. She spoke to her daughter for a minute, hung up. When she looked up, she was glaring at him.

"Satisfied?"

"I apologize, ma'am. A caller phoned the hotline this morning and said they thought your daughter might be in danger. It's all just a big mistake. I'm sorry."

"Next time you should check your facts first, before you show up on someone's doorstep and almost give them a heart attack."

Before he left, he apologized again, walked to his car with his head hung low.

The drive back to Crater Lake was a miserable one. His testicle was on fire again, raging, and when he checked the glove compartment and found the bottle of ibuprofen, it was empty.

He fought down the pain, pounded the steering wheel with the palm of his hand. He had convinced himself that the lead about the dead girl was a solid one, mostly because he had wanted it to be. He had played this game before, knew that of all things *disappointment* was a constant in any case, but he had had a good feeling about this one. Now they were back at the beginning – dead in the water.

Nathan didn't feel like talking to anyone, but he phoned Carl because he had said he would. Carl answered right away, sounding optimistic. Nathan broke the news, told him that it was all a dead end, and Carl was silent on the other end of the line for a while before he said something would come along, but he didn't sound convinced.

After he hung up with Carl, Nathan pulled into a gas station, paid the exorbitant fee for a travel-size bottle of Aleve and a bottle of Ice Mountain, carried them back to the car, peeled away the safety foil from the bottle of pills, shook several out, took them with a swallow of water.

By the time he got home, Jess had finished cleaning the house. She could read his face, but she read it wrong, or only half-right at least. He was dejected about the false lead, but his testicle was still throbbing dully.

"It didn't go well?"

"I basically convinced a mother that her daughter was dead, when in reality it turned out she was alive and kicking."

"You were doing your job."

"I don't think she saw it that way."

"She should have been relieved that her daughter was alive."

"Don't get me wrong, she was, but she wasn't thrilled about the false alarm."

"But she has to understand…"

She let it hang there. Nathan nodded.

"It's lunch time. Want me to fix you something?"

"I think I'll finish the lawn."

"The lawn can wait."

"It's supposed to rain later. Besides, the neighbors will think less of me if I don't keep the lawn neatly manicured."

"Well, we wouldn't want that."

He left his badge and gun in the kitchen, started for the door.

"Oh, and by the way," Jess called after him.

"Yeah?"

"We've been invited to dinner."

"Carl?"

"Yep."

"What did you tell them?"

"According to Carol, Carl has been asking you about it for quite a while now. Apparently, it just plain slipped your mind."

"Naturally. You said we'd be there, didn't you?"

"Of course I did. Six o'clock sharp."

Nathan rolled his eyes. "I'm not dressing up."

"You're dressing up."

He looked at her, aware that the battle was already lost.

"No tie," he said.

Jess appeared to weigh this for a moment.

"One condition."

"Anything."

"I told Carol we'd bring the wine. You'll need to run to the store and pick something up."

"Red or white?"

"Hmm…" Jess cocked her head, contemplating, hands sliding down to her stomach and resting there. "Let's ask your unborn child, see if she has a preference."

"Funny. And, once again, you're wrong – you should have said if *he* has a preference."

"Wishful thinking, Daddy-O."

13

the urge

HE KNOWS THAT if it had gone on for much longer that he wouldn't have been able to resist. The urges come and go, but they never leave for long. They always come back. Completing his work satisfies him for a little while, but the time in between has gradually grown less and less, and then the urges are back again.

The Elusive One knows him, or at least he imagines it does. Knows about these urges, these cravings, and maybe they are alike in some way, maybe it can understand, but these days it makes him wait, makes him suffer, as if taunting him.

The urges are bad. He can't remember when they started, but it was a long, long time ago, since he was a child, since his alcoholic father would do bad things to his mother and his sister, and, sometimes, if his father was in a particular mood, to *him*. He has blocked many of these memories out. He doesn't like to remember them anymore. He has explained all this to the doctors back when they had imprisoned him in a tiny room, feeding him pills – *medicine* they called it – and he always took them, but they made him feel funny, like a ghost of himself. The medicine made the urges go away, but he was never himself when he was on the medicine. It always made him stupid in the head.

After he decided he wanted to be done with doctors and the other men whose job it was to mess around in his head, he had sworn off the medicine. It was nice the urges disappeared, but the cost was high, he could never think straight. When he stopped taking the pills, his head became clear again, he could think, reason, could remember what his duty was.

He waits on the corner in his car, his backpack on the passenger seat next to him. He rolls down the window. The garlic around his neck is cloying, almost overpowering, and he is thankful for the fresh air. He isn't happy about lingering in one place for too long, but the urge is on him and he is helpless. His saving grace comes in the form of a lost girl wandering the sidewalk in frayed blue jeans and a halter-top. Up ahead, the girl stumbles, catches her balance.

His hand finds the door handle as he debates the best way to capture his prey. Does he drive up to her, charm her, offer her a ride. This is something he is capable of, turning on the charm, but it's dangerous…someone could spot the car, take down the plate. The plate is stolen, so he isn't overly concerned, but if they remember the make and model, the color, it could mean trouble.

Or should he come in on foot, sneak up on her, go for the blitz attack? She will never know what happened, she'll be incapacitated, unable to fight back. But there's a chance he could be spotted, and if he is, it will be more difficult to escape on foot.

He hates urban settings. The woods are better. More isolated. Fewer people. Less likelihood of there being witnesses.

He believes the Elusive One has done this on purpose, has become bolder, to mess with him. It knows he will have a tougher time in a populated area. The chance of being caught is greater.

Put it out of your mind, he thinks. *Focus on the task at hand.*

When the urge is on him, it clouds his judgment. He has to compensate, remember to be patient.

The girl staggers, falls, picks herself up.

A neon sign flickers nearby, advertising a local bar. The sheep will mistake her for being drunk because they don't understand how to read the signs, and because they are oblivious.

He starts the car's engine, lets it idle. He shifts into drive, lifts his foot off the brake…

…but then slams it down again, waits, watches as a group of young men exit the bar, stumbling and hollering. He knows they will spot the girl – and they do. They approach her, huddle around her. She is fresh meat, easy prey, and he knows these young men are drunk and horny and looking to take the girl home.

He waits in the car. He can't intervene, can't risk them seeing his face or his car.

With the car's driver's side window rolled down, their voices carry, he can hear them, talking loudly, joking, making an attempt at drunken charm.

Leave, he thinks. *Go away. You have no idea what you're getting involved in.*

"*Hey sweetheart, you okay?*"

"*What's your name?*"

"*You high or somethin'?*"

"*She's wasted as fuck.*"

"*Need a ride?*"

Laughter comes next. Real comedians. None of them are in any condition to drive, and even if they had considered attempting it, they're all probably too wasted to find their cars.

"Come on, you can't talk or something?"

"Let us walk you home. Streets can be dangerous at night, especially for a girl all alone, in the kind of shape you're in."

The girl stumbles into them, tries to break past the huddle, but they maintain their formation, more aggressive now.

He knows he could kill them all. Part of him wants to. But it would be sloppy, would draw a lot of attention. His work isn't done yet. He reminds himself why he is here, of his mission, of the Elusive One.

"Maybe we should call her a cab?"

"Fuck her."

"You see that? Is that fucking blood?"

"Are you hurt?

"Maybe she needs to go to the hospital."

"Maybe she's one of the crazies from the institution."

"Last chance, baby. Sure you don't want us to walk you home?"

He pulls his backpack into his lap, unzips it, rummages inside of it until his hand finds one of the wooden stakes, closes around it, holds it against his leg. He won't allow them to take the girl. She can't go to the hospital, can't go home with any of these men. They don't understand that she is infected, that she can spread the virus to them, and if that happens things could get out of control.

Finally, the men disperse, leaving the girl alone.

He watches her move on stilted legs. She might not look it, but she's standing on death's doorstep. She can transmit the virus now.

He can't waste any more time. He pulls away from the curb, sliding the car forward, trailing her slowly. When he's close enough, he parks, jumps out of the car, clubs her from behind, catches her as she goes limp and sinks into his arms.

The trunk is already open. He drags her over to it, crams her in, slams the trunk closed and drives away.

He glances in the rearview mirror. The street behind him remains deserted, empty.

The urge grows in him, a crawling sensation over his skin. It tells him to take her back to his motel room, to do things to her. His penis hardens.

No.

He must maintain discipline. He reminds himself how easy it would be to become infected himself, and that is a fate worse than death. It is something he has thought about for a long time, but he has always resisted it.

He drives until the lights are behind him, turns off onto a gravel road, drives a little farther, parks, exits the car, stares up at the clear sky, all the stars, hears a thumping noise coming from the trunk.

The thought of what he is about to do excites him. It's a difficult thing to control.

He digs into his pocket, pulls out the fragment of mirror, holds it up to his face, gazes at his own reflection. It's still there, thank God. His heart is racing, beating fast, and he goes over what he's about to do in his mind, play by play, visualizing it, continues this until his hard on subsides.

He opens the trunk, stares down at the frightened girl. She is conscious, just barely, and her eyes are partially open, gazing up at him. He bends over her, gently wraps his arm around the back of her head and lifts upward, using his free hand to bring the mirror close to her face.

"See? Nothing. So I'm sorry, but I don't have a choice."

He pockets the mirror, clumsily turns her over, inspects the back of her neck. The tell-tale mark is there, the inverted Y-shape within a faint circle. The Elusive One has branded her, has infected her with its seed.

He tears the girl's shirt open, exposing her breasts. He stares at them for a long time, and then his gaze goes to her eyes, open and staring, and he covers them with a gloved hand as he pulls the wooden stake from the waistband of his jeans, locates the sweet spot, plunges it downward, feels his heart race faster as the stake pierces her heart. Her eyes widen for a moment, mouth drops open and closed, open and closed, and within seconds she goes completely still.

The night is quiet. He leans against the side of the car until his heartbeat slows, and then drags the girl's body out of the trunk, over to the side of the road. He goes back to the car, to his backpack, brings out the knife with the serrated blade, kneels down beside the girl, tilts her head back and finishes his work.

14

dinner date

THEY PULLED UP in front of Carol's house at 5:55 P.M. Nathan got out first, went around the front of the car, helped Jess out of the passenger seat. She was holding a Pyrex container full of green bean casserole she had whipped together earlier that afternoon. Nathan leaned into the car, grabbed the brown paper bag containing the bottle of wine he had purchased at the store after finishing with the lawn. He had gone with a white wine, a Moscato. He was lousy at wine, and the Moscato had seemed like a safe choice.

Carol greeted them at the door. Jess handed her the container of green bean casserole, said, "Whatever you're cooking, it smells wonderful."

Which, lately, could be considered high praise coming from Jess. For the last few months, it had been hit or miss as to what Jess found appealing when it came to food. Fruit Loops had become her staple, but there were other foods, foods she had always enjoyed, that she just couldn't stomach anymore. This was normal, she explained, a side effect of the pregnancy. A pregnant woman's sense of smell could become hyper-sensitive. Nathan was no stranger to making late-night food runs, catering to Jess's sudden cravings.

Carl appeared behind Carol, nodded to him, and Nathan stepped around the ladies, made his way over, handed over the bottle of wine.

"Wine? Jesus, you've gotten fancy on me."

"Fancy doesn't apply if the bottle costs under ten dollars."

"Come on, I've got beer in the fridge."

Nathan followed Carl into the kitchen. Carl took out two cans of Bud Light, handed one to Nathan.

"Come on, let's take this outside," Carl said.

Nathan glanced over his shoulder. Jess and Carol were still chatting in the entry.

"Don't worry about them, they'll be fine. Carol'll take care of her."

They went out to the back porch, climbed the wooden stairs to the second-story deck. Carl plopped down in one of the folding lawn chairs, motioned for Nathan to take the other one. This was Nathan's first time at the new house. Prior to moving in with Carol, Carl had rented an upstairs unit in a restored Victorian that had been divided into four apartments. A real pit. Whenever it rained hard the ceiling would leak; the new furnace the landlord had installed hadn't had the strength to heat the entire house comfortably, so the two upstairs apartments were always cold. During the winter months, Carl had taken to wearing winter hats and thick sweaters before crawling into bed for the night. There had been no central air, so in the summers, the apartment became a giant oven, cooking Carl like a Thanksgiving turkey. Despite all this, Carl had loved the place. Yes, it was a dump, but it was *his* dump.

"This is an improvement over your last place," Nathan said, popping the tab of his beer.

"I know it sounds funny, but I sort've miss the old place."

"It had character, I'll give you that. Comparatively, this is a mansion."

"The seller fucked Carol on the selling price. She was so desperate to find a place, she didn't bother to haggle, and the inspector didn't catch some of the plumbing issues. Every couple of months, the tree roots get out of control and clog shit up, so she has to call in a plumber to have them snake the pipes out. Hundred bucks a pop. She's in way over her head on this place."

"Then she's lucky she has you."

"Yeah, I'm a real handyman. Anyway, enough with the small talk. What the hell happened with the lead on the unidentified girl?"

Nathan took a drink of his beer. "There's nothing else to tell. It was bogus."

"Another nutcase trying to help, you think?"

"I don't think so. The girl that called it in, she sounded sincere on the phone. She was mistaken is all."

"Why is it that Good Samaritans always wind up being a big pain in the ass?"

"Tell me about it. This girl's mother, the one I basically implied her daughter was dead – she didn't laugh when it got to the punchline."

"No, I don't suppose she did," Carl said. "Just another satisfied customer."

"Another tale of incompetence Talley can spin when he's busy tossing a few back with all the mummies down at the Moosehead."

"You still worried about that old fart?"

Nathan shook his head, drank his beer.

"You are, aren't you? Give it up, Nate. You aren't a good liar, and maybe that's part of your problem. Talley's an old hand at pulling the wool over peoples' eyes. Thing of it is, he can't do shit about it for the next three and a half years. There's a chance he might keel over by then."

"I'm not that lucky. I'm pretty sure he's going to live forever."

"I wouldn't put it past him. But if push comes to shove, we can arrange for a little boating accident or something."

Carl mentioning the hypothetical boating accident made Nathan think about Crater Lake, which in turn made him think about the dead girl in the mask they had pulled out of the water. Then he thought about Becca Struthers. How she had been staked through the heart, and how before that someone had taken the time to drain most of the blood from her body. He thought about Carl's vampire theory, and it wasn't long before his mind was calculating again, sifting through the details, trying to fit the puzzle pieces together in different ways, hoping they would eventually form something recognizable.

"Can't get it out of your head either?"

"Nope."

"I can't even remember what she looked like. All I can see is that damn mask. What a twisted fuck. Which reminds me, I heard back from the hospital *and* the loony bin in Des Moines. There's only been one recent release, a female, and supposedly they put her on a plane for some place in North Carolina because she has a sister there."

"No escapes?"

"No escapes. Nothing new with missing persons. The hotline has been silent, other than that woman that called in with the bad lead. I've been thinking about it, and the more I do, the more I think I'm right. About the vampire angle."

They talked a while longer. Carol called to them from downstairs to say that dinner was almost done. Nathan finished his beer, said he had to take a leak. He followed Carl down the stairs, back into the house, and Carl said, "Bathroom's down the hallway."

Nathan wandered down the hallway, opened the door to the first room he came to.

It wasn't the bathroom. It was a bedroom, bathed in black-light, the walls decorated with posters of monsters and metal bands. There was a dresser next to the bed, the top of it cluttered with dozens of esoteric objects.

He let curiosity get the better of him. Walked in, took a quick look around. There was a desk in the corner, a sketch-pad resting on top of it. He opened it, leafed through the pages. It was filled with drawings of pentagrams, nightmare visages with rows of teeth dripping blood, strange symbols that Nathan hadn't seen before. The skull of a small animal, probably a cat, hung from a nail in the wall, gazing at him with hollow eyes.

Nathan figured it had to be the kid's room. Carol had a son, Nathan remembered Carl telling him that, but he couldn't' recall the kid's name.

He exited the room, closed the door behind him, continued down the hallway until he located the bathroom. His testicle ached again. It wasn't bad yet, but it was getting there. He searched the cabinet and the linen closet, feeling slightly guilty about rummaging through Carol's things, but soon the pain would become unbearable, and it would be tricky business getting through dinner if he didn't medicate first. Finally, he found a wicker basket hidden in the vanity under the sink that was piled high with bottles of pills, first aid supplies, extra tooth-brushes, deodorant, nail clippers, and an open box of tampons.

Nathan rooted around in the basket until he discovered a bottle of generic Tylenol, shook a few into his hand, washed them down with a drink from the faucet. He slid the basket back under the sink exactly as he had found it, glanced at himself in the mirror, and then headed back to the kitchen.

Dinner was already on the table. The main course was brown-sugar glazed ham. Carol had also prepared buttered carrots, mashed potatoes, fresh rolls, and Jess's casserole. The bottle of white wine was also present and accounted for, already open, Carol's glass full of it. Carl had placed a new can of Bud Light next to Nathan's plate.

They made small talk as they ate, steered clear of the nasty business about the two dead girls, but Nathan could sense it wasn't far from any of their minds.

"The ham is excellent," Jess said as she chewed down a piece, followed it with a drink of water.

Nathan thought it was a little dry but didn't say so.

"It came out a little on the dry side," Carol said. "I've never been a great cook."

"It's perfect."

Jess nudged him under the table, and Nathan nodded, said, "Tastes good to me."

His beer was disappearing fast. He forced himself to slow down, pace himself, because he could already feel it starting to go to his head. He wasn't a heavy drinker, especially since Jess had gotten pregnant.

"I think I accidentally went into your son's room," Nathan said.

Carl and Carol exchanged a glance.

"It's a trip, isn't it?" Carl said.

"Unique."

"He worships Satan, we think."

"Speak for yourself," Carol said. She glanced up at Nathan. "Peter's just going through a phase."

"Yeah, it's a phase. Where he makes animal sacrifices to the Devil."

"He does not."

"Did you see the skulls?"

Nathan shook his head. He had told them he had stumbled into Peter's room, not that he had taken the tour.

Carl said, "He's big into all that kind of stuff. The occult. Paganism. *Vampires.*"

"Like I said, it's just a phase."

"My ass."

This time, Carol spoke directly to Jess, as though she might be the only one left that could see reason. "You know how kids are. Their beliefs are always changing. He's just taken an interest in those kinds of things now. Because of all the movies is what I think."

"He dresses like every day is Halloween. You should see it, Nate. Dyed his hair black, all his clothes are black. Paints his face white and wears black lipstick. I woke up the other night and found him in the kitchen. Scared the hell out of me. Thought it was a ghost. I almost shot him."

Carol was looking at Jess again. "He's exaggerating."

Carl shook his head. "Like hell."

Carol shot him a look that was very clearly meant to let him know that he was treading on thin ice. Carl shut up then, pushed his plate away, sulked as he worked on his beer.

The conversation shifted to sunnier topics. The weather, gossip around town, mostly the women gabbing. When dinner was finished, Nathan helped clear the table, thanked Carol for the amazing meal, and then Carl invited him back outside, carrying an ice-cold six-pack of Bud Light. When they were out of earshot, Carl said, "She thinks that kid can walk on water."

"She's his mother. Of course she feels that way."

"What he is is creepy. Wearing that makeup and shit. I really did almost shoot him once."

"Carol wouldn't have been too happy with you."

"She coddles the kid. Carol thinks it's a phase. Me, I don't think it's normal at all. When I was a kid, we wanted to grow up to be major league baseball players or astronauts. We didn't decorate our rooms with dead animals and pictures of demons. If I'd tried doing that, my dad would have kicked the shit out of me. Granted, I don't think the kid's really into worshipping Satan or anything like that. It's probably harmless. He's actually pretty smart, but you'd never know it from looking at him. When all this first started, at least after we found Becca Struthers the way we did, I almost started to think maybe Peter did it on account of the weird shit he's into. He's all about vampires, has stacks of books about them in his room. He's an awkward kid, not very social. I don't know if he was a nerd or anything, but I don't think he's got a lot of friends, kind of a loner. Plus, he's the same age as Becca was, graduated from the same class, so he knew her. I got to thinking maybe he had a crush on her, maybe she blew him off, seeing as how she was popular and on the Honor Roll and all, and that might've pissed him off."

"You think your girlfriend's kid is a serial killer?"

Carl swallowed some of his beer, smiled, shrugged. "Yeah, insane, I know. But it did cross my mind, and once it did, things started to kind've add up against him."

"Have you told Carol?"

Carl laughed, swallowed more beer. "Now *you're* the one sounding insane. If I went to Carol with something like that I'd be out on my ass lickety-split. You know how it is, no parent believes there kid is capable of something like that. I'm just sayin', it crossed my mind. I chalked it up to coincidence. Peter's an oddball, but I don't think he's a killer."

"Any history?"

"Possession. Marijuana. Got busted when he was sixteen, put him on probation for six months. Made him take piss tests and all that. It was expunged a few months ago when he turned eighteen. But he still smokes. I know it. He burns this nasty-smelling incense shit in his room all the time, thinking he's masking the scent, but I know weed when I smell it."

"Ever call him out on it?"

"Shit no. What would be the point? Carol would never believe it, and it *is* only weed after all. Hell, didn't you toke up once and a while when you were younger?"

"Twice, when I was in college."

"See, no big deal, right? See no evil, hear no evil."

"Think he's dealing?"

"I doubt it. Probably recreational. Like I said, he's smart, but he's still just a punk kid. If he was dealing, people would be knocking on the door at all hours, or at least his phone would be ringing off the hook. What I do know is that he's got a nickname, I've heard it come up now and again around town. *Hashbrown*. Like hashish, on account of he likes to smoke the stuff so much."

"Yeah, I get it."

"Fuckin' pothead."

"Leave no stone unturned," Nathan said.

"Wouldn't that have been a hoot? If it turned out I was dating the killer's mother. I'd never live it down and neither would you."

"Christ, if Talley caught wind of a rumor like that, he'd take it and run with it."

"Old fart would just love that."

Nathan's cell started to ring. He took it out, checked the caller ID, whispered, "It's Iverson," answered it, listened. His left testicle started to ache again; an intermittent stabbing sensation that kept time with his heartbeat.

The call was brief. When it was over, Nathan held the phone in his hand, stared at it numbly.

"I don't like the look on your face, Nate. What did Iverson want?"

Nathan shook his head and went on shaking it. "They found another one," he said.

part

II

closing in

15

playing with fire

THEY DIDN'T RECOGNIZE the girl. Not because her face was unfamiliar, but because she hardly had a face left.

Her body still smoldered on the side of the road, blackened and charred, and the only reason they knew it was a girl was because one of her shoes had come off during the struggle and hadn't been destroyed in the fire. It was a purple running shoe, white tread, the familiar Nike Swoosh in hot pink running up the side.

"Jesus Christ," Carl said, the words muffled because his hand was cupped over his nose and mouth. The stink was awful.

Iverson leaned against the rear panel of his patrol car, looking sickly and pale. Before Nathan and Carl had arrived, Iverson had vomited, but had at least had the good sense to do it far away from the crime scene.

Nathan gazed at the body for a while, stood up, walked over to Iverson. Iverson managed to pull himself together long enough to tell Nathan that a farmer had called in to report a fire. Iverson had responded to the call, and when he had arrived the flames had still been raging, and that was when he had noticed what was beneath the flames. He had phoned Nathan and then lost the contents of his dinner immediately after hanging up the phone.

Despite the condition of the body, it was apparent that this hadn't been a tragic accident. A charred cylinder of wood protruded from the body's chest, and the head lay several inches away. It was mostly bones that were left, the blackened skull tilted slightly to the side, teeth exposed, seeming to grin up at them.

Nathan glanced at Carl. "Burnt the body. Fits with your theory."

"I hate being right," Carl said.

It was the middle of nowhere; one of many gravel roads on the outskirts of town, separated by large swaths of farmland. The night was mostly silent, a cool breeze running through the air. Nathan felt like he was on another planet, far away and alone on this isolated road.

"I already called the ME," Iverson said. He tried taking a step, stopped, hunched over, dry heaved. He used his forearm to wipe the spittle from his chin. "Damn, sorry."

"Don't be," Nathan said. "You did fine."

"I haven't seen anything like this before. First the Struthers girl, now this. Whacko burnt her to a crisp."

Nathan made his way over to the body, knelt down, ignored the stench of burnt meat that wafted up from the corpse. "Seal it off," he said. "Let's search the area quick while we're waiting for Mathers to show."

Iverson worked on taping off the crime scene while Nathan and Carl switched on their flashlights, began searching the area.

Once the caution tape was up, Iverson grabbed the digital camera from his car, proceeded to take photos of the body, captured it from different angles, photographed the Nike shoe after that.

"Go ahead and bag it."

They searched for half an hour, the beams of their flashlights crisscrossing in the darkness, working their way into the low ditches on either side of the road, wading through the tall weeds, searching for something – *anything* – that might give them something to work with.

"Had to have abducted her," Carl said. "No way she just happened to be walking around out here this time of night."

"Could have been jogging," Iverson said.

"Way out here?"

"It's possible. Some people like to be alone when they do it."

"Maybe. But I doubt it. Probably grabbed her in town, tossed her in the trunk, drove her out here where there wouldn't be any one to see."

"What's with this guy? He changes it up every time."

"I don't know."

"Hey, guys, come take a look at this."

Iverson was crouched down next to the shoulder on the opposite side of the road. His flashlight was pointed at the ground, illuminating a small patch of gravel a few inches from where the gravel turned to grass and sloped down toward the ditch.

"What is it?"

Nathan knelt down, spotted the object, had Iverson take a picture of it before he slipped on a latex glove and picked it up. It was off-white, crescent-shaped, like a shrunken sliver of moon. He twisted it over between his fingers, brought it close to his face, sniffed it. He wrinkled his nose and said, "Garlic."

"Wild, you think?" Iverson asked.

Carl said, "I'm not a fucking gardener, but have you ever seen garlic just growing out in the middle of nowhere?"

Iverson produced a small baggie, opened it. Nathan dropped the clove into the baggie, watched Iverson seal it shut.

"You know what hates garlic, right?" Iverson asked.

Nathan let the question hang.

It was ten-thirty by the time Mathers had made an appearance.

Loading the remains into a body bag had been gruesome work. They arrived back at the station close to midnight, and Carl started the coffeemaker going, knowing that sleep was a distant thing.

Iverson was still looking sickly, and Nathan sent him home, told him to get some sleep, Iverson asking how the fuck he was supposed to do that after seeing what they'd seen. Nathan hadn't had an answer for him.

There was a modest conference room in the back of the station where they occasionally held briefings for incoming and outgoing shifts if there was anything noteworthy to pass along. Nathan and Carl sat on opposite sides of the long oval table, drinking coffee.

Nathan was smoking a cigarette, tapping ashes into an empty coffee mug. He had broken down and stopped at the gas station on their way back to town and bought a pack. He hadn't smoked going on almost twenty years now, not since high school, and the cravings were few and far between, but if there was ever a reason to start again...

"I didn't know you smoked."

"I don't. Not since before I graduated high school."

"Guess this is a good time to start."

"What I figured."

"Bet Jess'll throw a fit."

"Jess doesn't have to know."

"Carol's mom was a smoker. Something like sixty years. Died a few years back."

"Cancer?"

"Emphysema. I was telling you how she thinks Peter is a saint, can't do any wrong. Well, that's mostly true, but she was cleaning up a month or so ago, happens to come across a pack of Camels in his room. That was it. She lost her fucking mind, man. I knew she could get angry, had a little bit of a temper if you pushed her far enough, but when she found out Peter was smoking cigarettes…she went nuclear. I thought she was gonna kill him, and when she confronts him, she waves the pack of smokes in his face, asks him what the hell he thought he was doing, telling him how cigarettes killed his grandmother, and did he want to end up like her, how could he pollute his lungs, and then she crumples up the pack in her fist, says no son of hers is going to smoke, and that she'll kill him herself if it happens again."

"What did he say?"

"I told you, he's a smart kid when he wants to be. He didn't say shit. I'm pretty sure keeping his mouth shut saved his life. God only knows how she reacted when he got busted for smoking pot." Carl pointed to the pack of Marlboros on the table. "Give me one of those."

Nathan picked up the pack, slid it across the table, pushed the lighter after it. "Just so long as you don't rat me out to Carol when she busts your ass."

Carl selected a cigarette from the pack, lit it, inhaled, went into a coughing fit.

"It's a bad habit," Nathan said, sliding the mug across the table.

Carl crushed his cigarette out in it, slid the mug back to Nathan.

They had procured three pieces of evidence from the crime scene. All three of them sat at the center of the conference table, neatly bagged and labeled: the Nike running shoe, the remains of the wooden stake, and the clove of garlic.

"Maybe it's like you said. He's *evolving* or whatever."

"Could be. Perfecting the fantasy. I hate admitting it, but your theory might just hold water."

"This is one time I don't like being right," Carl said. "Thinks he's killing vampires." He reached across the table, picked up the baggie with the garlic clove in it. "Even down to using garlic for protection. That's some old school shit." Carl's eyes went to the shoe on the table. "You know, right now there's a mother out there that's worried sick because her daughter hasn't come home."

"Assuming the girl still lived with her parents."

"How are we gonna catch this guy? He doesn't seem to make any mistakes."

"He's methodical. Mostly organized, but not entirely."

"Not entirely?"

"The shoe. If he was really trying to cover his tracks, why didn't he make sure he got rid of it?"

"Maybe he was in a hurry?"

"Guys like this don't make stupid mistakes. He made two. The shoe and that thing you're holding in your hand."

"Yeah, but it doesn't get us any closer to figuring out who this guy is. Maybe he knows that and didn't bother. Thinks we're a bunch of idiots."

"Or he's getting sloppy. These guys, they fantasize a lot first. Maybe for a few days, maybe a lot longer than that. They go over it in their minds, plan all the little details. When the time comes and they actually act on their fantasies, the murder has already happened in their heads a long time ago. If he's making mistakes, I think it's because he's starting to unravel."

"Why Crater Lake? There are a hundred small towns around here. Why did he pick this one? Do you think there's a reason? Like he knows someone around here or is familiar with the area?"

Nathan crushed out his cigarette, lit another. His head swam and he realized the tobacco was actually getting him the slightest bit high. The pain in his testicle had subsided after taking the pills back at Carl's house, but now it was staring to creep up again.

"I don't think he's local. We would have seen the signs before this. And he doesn't hide the bodies. Becca Struthers was left in the woods. The one tonight was on the side of the road. Sure, they're both isolated areas, but he had to know someone would probably find them. If he was really worried, he would have taken the time to bury them or dump them somewhere they wouldn't be found."

"You're forgetting about the first girl. The girl in the mask. They pulled her out of the lake. Seems like he was hiding it to me."

"Yeah, and she was different from the rest, too. She wasn't killed the same way, wasn't mutilated like the others, but he took the time to hide the body. Maybe that means something."

"Think we'll figure out who the new girl is?"

"If she's local, yeah, I think we will."

"They'll have to identify her by her shoe," Carl said. It wasn't a joke, but he uttered a nervous laugh. "Iverson doesn't look so hot."

"He'll bounce back."

"I'm not so sure. He's just a kid really. Seeing something like that…"

"He'll be okay."

"What about you? Are *you* okay?"

"Not even close, but I'll live. I could use a full night's sleep."

"What's bothering you?" Carl asked, laughed because it was a silly question.

"Other than three dead bodies and a killer on the loose? For starters, Jess stays up all night watching bad TV, can't sleep, just tosses and turns and finally ends up having a midnight snack in bed. Fruit Loops. Couldn't stand them before, but now they're like speed to a junkie. And all I hear in the middle of the night is her crunching away – crunch, crunch, crunch – as she watches *Criminal Minds*, which is crap by the way."

"Carol's really into all the *CSI* shows. Doesn't matter if they're about as authentic as a three dollar bill. It's entertainment, she says. Says maybe I should pay attention, maybe I'll *learn* something."

"Then there's this thing with my nut," Nathan said.

"Okay, now you've peaked my curiosity, boss. Don't stop there. I wanna hear all about this problem going on with your balls."

"*Ball.* Singular. I don't know, it's been killing me the last couple of weeks. It started out like a dull ache, like when somebody hits you there and you get past the part where you feel like you're going to shit your pants. But lately it's been getting worse."

"Taking anything for it?"

"Just over the counter stuff."

"I'm just spitballin' here, but a lot of folks, what they do when they're having problems like that, they go and see someone that knows about that sort of thing. They call them *doctors*."

"Yeah, yeah, I've heard that *spiel* before."

"Jess?"

"Ordered me to see Kobayashi."

"And you didn't?"

"She forgot all about it."

"So now you're hiding it," Carl said. "What the hell's the big deal about going in to have it looked at?"

"What if it's bad?"

"What if it's nothing?"

"What if it's something?"

"That's right, I forgot, you've got this thing about cancer. So what if it is? They'll cut out your nut and after you're well, we can all make fun of you."

"That easy, huh?"

"That's right."

"What if I caught it too late and its spread. Once they tell you, it's as good as a death sentence."

"Man, the shit you get worked up about."

"Like you wouldn't be shitting your pants."

"Maybe. But I'd have the balls – pardon the pun – to have it checked out. What's it gonna look like if you could have caught it early, but you sat on it and then it's too late? You gonna tell your kid that daddy could have been around to see you grow up, play catch and go to baseball games, but instead he decided to be a giant pussy?"

It sounded silly when Carl put it like that.

"Giant pussy?"

"Just sayin."

"How did we get hung up on talking about my nuts?"

"You started it. Had to start sharing your feelings."

Nathan put his cigarette out, debated another, rubbed his eyes, told himself one more wouldn't hurt before he packed it in. He lit one, watched the smoke hover in the air.

"What are we gonna do about all this? If we don't figure it out, heads are gonna roll."

"Another pun?"

"You know what I mean. It'll be *our* heads. Talley's probably sleeping like a baby."

"I don't give a fuck about Talley."

"Sure you do. He's a prick, and he's gunnin' for you. That would piss me off."

"I don't have time to be pissed."

"I'm trying to be motivational here. I know how your brain works. You're good at this kind of stuff. So figure it out already. What are we missing? Maybe you should sleep on it. Or think about it while you're laying awake at night listening to Jess pig out on her Cheerios."

"Fruit Loops," Nathan corrected, but his mind was already a million miles away.

Was Carl right? Were they missing something?

"Whatever. I'm beat. I think I'm going to mosey on home, have nightmares about that woman being roasted alive."

"Maybe you're right. Tomorrow's another day."

"You mean *today* is another day. By the way, you smell like shit. You've got the smoke on you. I keep some spray-on deodorant in my locker. Mouthwash, too. If I were you, I'd take advantage of that before you go home to Jess. If Carol finds out I so much as *looked* at a cigarette, she'll ream my ass. She'll have me bunking up with Peter, and I'm tellin' you, that kid's room scares me."

Nathan told Carl he would see him the morning, waited until he had left, and then lit another cigarette. It tasted bad, but not as bad as the first one had. How quickly the old habits came back, how they became second nature and stayed that way for the long haul.

He sat there by himself for a while thinking about what Carl had said, thinking about the girl they had found tonight, about Becca Struthers, about the girl in the mask, trying to add it all up, searching for some minute detail they had overlooked the first time around.

There wasn't much use to it. His mind was tired, his thoughts scattershot.

He tried playing an association game in his head:

Lake.

Girl.

Female.

Young.

Mask.

Stake.

Woods.

Blood loss.

Stake through heart.

Head severed.

Blood drained.

Gravel road.

Isolated.

Incinerated.

Running shoe.

Mistake?

Sloppy?

Garlic.

Leeches.

Vampires.

How did you kill a vampire?

Stake through the heart.

Beheading.

Destroy with fire.

Sometimes the game worked. But not tonight. It seemed too difficult a task to put everything in order, to complete the puzzle using the individual pieces.

What were they missing?

Nathan stubbed out his cigarette, thought about pitching the rest of the pack, thought better of it, walked to the locker room, opened Carl's locker. Both the deodorant and travel-size bottle of mouthwash were on the top shelf, above Carl's winter jacket, a change of clothes, and a pair of sneakers.

He sprayed a mist of deodorant on his shirt and neck, removed the mouthwash from the shelf, carried it over to the sink, gargled for thirty seconds, stared at himself in the mirror. There were dark circles under his eyes, he looked thinner, had a kind of crazed appearance. He studied his reflection the same way he had studied the faces of Robert Trenton Chase and Peter Kürten, wondered what separated him from the killers of the world, hoping he wouldn't be driven mad before this thing was through.

He placed the deodorant and mouthwash back on the shelf where he had found them, at the last minute placing the pack of Marlboros next to the clutter of other items, smiling to himself, knowing it would get a rise out of Carl later.

Then he headed home.

16

false alarm

IT WAS TWO-THIRTY by the time he got home. Jess was in the living room, leaned back in the recliner, body cocooned beneath a thin fleece blanket.

There was an empty bowl on the end table next to the recliner.

The room was mostly dark, dimly lit by the glow of the TV.

Nathan approached her. She hadn't spoken, hadn't moved, so he thought she was asleep, but then when he was closer, she said, "You're home."

"I'm home," he said, sitting down on the edge of the couch, which, because the living room wasn't really big enough for the both of them, almost touched the recliner's armrest.

"You were gone a long time."

"Why are you sleeping in the chair?"

"I was waiting up for you. I failed. Have you been smoking?"

He didn't hesitate before shaking his head and saying, "If I smell like smoke, it's probably because I was near a fire."

She shifted, sat up, winced, touched her stomach. "A fire? The way you and Carl rushed out, I knew it had to be something bad."

"It was."

He told her about the girl, but, again, spared her the details. She winced again.

"What's wrong? And don't tell me it's nothing this time."

"I've been having some bad cramping."

"How bad?"

"I thought maybe if I sat in the chair for a while, it would go away."

"Are you going into labor? It's close enough, isn't it?"

"I don't know. I've never gone through it before."

"I'm taking you in."

"No. I'll be fine."

He almost accepted her answer. He was exhausted, and crawling into bed was about the only thing he thought he could muster the energy for, but he had an idea that Jess was minimizing, fibbing about the severity of the pain.

Oh what a hypocrite you are, he thought, thinking about the fire raging in his left testicle.

"Come on, let's go."

"You have to be tired."

"I am."

"Really, it's not that bad. Maybe we should just ride it out for a little bit."

But Nathan wouldn't take no for an answer. He helped her out of the chair, escorted her down the hallway and into the bedroom, picked out clothes for her, and after she had dressed, she sat down on the bed and allowed him to help her get her shoes on because she wasn't as flexible these days.

Ten minutes later, they were in the car, headed for Chicka-saw Memorial, Nathan speeding because there was no traffic on the roads at this hour of the morning.

"Slow down," Jess said.

The posted speed limit on Highway 6 was fifty-five miles per hour. Nathan glanced at the speedometer, saw that he was doing in excess of eighty, brought it down to seventy.

"Better?"

Jess nodded, winced again.

When they reached the hospital, Nathan pulled up around the side in front of the ER entrance. It was the first time he had been to the hospital lately that he wasn't there about a dead body.

Nathan had expected the ER to be hopping at this hour on a weekend, but, thankfully, the waiting room was mostly empty. They were seen by the triage nurse almost right away, and then another nurse came in pushing a wheelchair, had Jess sit in it, and they wheeled her through the maze of rooms.

They waited for twenty minutes. Jess sat on the examina-tion table. Nathan pulled one of the chairs up next to it, held her hand, Jess squeezing hard on his whenever another cramp took her.

During the wait, he started thinking about his own pain, the fire in his testicle, thinking that Jess would probably remem-ber him complaining about it a week or so ago, and might men-tion it to the doctor, wouldn't put it past her, and the last thing he wanted was to be dropping his drawers in front of his wife while some PA fondled his nuts with cold hands like they were Chinese stress balls.

The doctor finally arrived, greeted them, had Jess de-scribe the pain. He used the fetal Doppler, checking for the ba-by's heartbeat, found it, and they listened to the weird pulsing sound. Next, he checked her cervix, estimating she was roughly a centimeter dilated, nothing abnormal about that. Just to play it safe, he ordered an ultrasound, and Nathan followed the nurse pushing Jess in the wheelchair to another room where the sonographer was already waiting.

Jess gasped as the cold gel touched her belly. The sonographer moved the probe around, located the baby.

"Do you already know the sex of the baby?"

"No," Nathan answered.

"Do you want to?"

"No," Jess said before he could respond.

Everything looked normal. By the time they were released, the cramps had started to subside and Jess was feeling like herself again. She complained about being hungry, and now that it was after 4 A.M., Nathan swung through McDonald's, let her order breakfast before they left Alton.

"Told you it was nothing."

"Better safe than sorry."

"You take such good care of me."

She worked on her sausage and egg McMuffin and hashbrown patty while he drove. She made it halfway through, decided McDonald's wasn't what she wanted, and tossed the remains into the paper bag, curled up the top, put the bag on the floor.

Back at the house, he helped her into bed, and she mentioned again that he smelled like smoke. Once she was tucked in, he handed her the remote in case she wanted to watch TV, and then stripped out of his clothes, showered, took some ibuprofen, and got into bed.

Jess was already snoring, the remote still perched on her stomach. He knew that before long she would be grinding her teeth.

It was 5 A.M. Outside, twilight had arrived.

Nathan set his alarm for seven-thirty, rolled onto his side, closed his eyes.

Sleep didn't come right away. He lay there for a while, thoughts running through his mind, replaying the events of last night. It didn't help his cause. Neither did knowing that his alarm clock would go off in a little over two hours.

He listened to Jess snore, caught the rhythm, and before long his mind cleared and he slipped away.

17

reflection

HE WATCHES THE sun rise from the window of his motel room. The world yawns, wakes up, but this is when he starts to feel drowsy, because he works at night, because the night is when the sheep need protecting.

He sits at the table. A bottle of Wild Turkey stands at the center of the table, along with a glass half-full of ice cubes. He's gone on this way for a long time, many years, but has never gotten used to it. Humans weren't meant to live at night, he knows this, but the Wild Turkey helps. Lulls him closer to sleep. This is always when the thoughts start to come. And he lets them. Maybe this isn't much of a life, no one is there to reward him, no one is there to pat him on the back. But it beats being locked away, beats being drugged and living under a veil of fog so thick his brain won't work right.

Now, at least, there is clarity. *Purpose.*

He pours Wild Turkey into the glass, drinks it, enjoys the burn as it works its way down his throat, the warmth it brings to his stomach.

The sliver of mirror is in his pocket. The impulse is strong to look into it, to see his reflection, but he doesn't need it this morning. Today, he knows who and what he is, believes in the nobility of his calling. The daylight always makes him feel better. The daylight is safe. The monsters only come out at night. Or at least...

...the *real* monsters, the ones that people don't believe in anymore. He has been called a monster before, a long time ago. This still makes him laugh. *Him?* A monster?

No no no no no no.

If they only knew. Because they were sheep, they had no idea about real monsters. He supposed he should forgive them their ignorance.

As he works on his bottle of Wild Turkey, staring out the window into the sun, the sound of traffic getting louder, he thinks about the girl from last night. It was a close call, picking her up in town like that. The real monster, the Elusive One, had left her as a trap. How long had it known about him? How long had it known it was being chased?

Did it matter?

It wasn't afraid of him. Wasn't worried that someone knew its secret. No, it had made a game of it, leaving the innocents to be found.

It isn't afraid of me, he thinks. *It has been around for too long to fear anything, especially Man.*

Where would the game go next? Did the Elusive One want him to be caught?

Maybe it knew about him.

He knows it has powers, can read peoples' minds, at least to some extent. Perhaps it wants him to be caught, locked away, knowing that the secret was safe because no one was going to believe a lunatic that ranted and raved about monsters. He thought of them as sheep, but even sheep were capable of bad things, acting out of fear, and this time they would lock him away for good and throw away the key and the Elusive One would laugh.

The question that lingers on his mind this morning is this: why had he made a mistake? He had gotten sloppy with the girl. The shoe. He knew that it had escaped the fire. Why hadn't he corrected this oversight? Was the Elusive One getting to him, controlling him?

Did he want to get caught?

No.

It wouldn't do any good to start doubting his abilities now. The shoe was a minor mistake. Nothing, really. It wouldn't help them identify the girl (which he didn't care if they did), and it wouldn't lead them to him.

So why are you worried?

He doesn't want to be caught. He is certain of that.

But maybe, just maybe, he wants them to know. Some part of him wants others to know of his work, the good he is doing, to understand it. It isn't guilt. He has never felt guilty afterward. Recognition? Is that what it is?

He shakes his head, uses his hand to scoop a handful of ice from the bucket, drops it in the glass, pours more Wild Turkey.

His head is swimming a little now. He is drinking too much. It loosens his tension, but it is also dangerous. If he doesn't watch himself, he could lose control, and losing control is the last thing he needs.

No, not recognition. He isn't asking for a medal.

He wants them to know. *Period.* Doesn't want to be alone in his knowledge. He wants the sheep to *see*, goddammit, to see the truth, but they insist on living with their eyes closed. He can't make them see anymore than he can make a blind man see.

He gulps down the Wild Turkey, refills the glass, does it again, shoves the glass away, drinks straight from the bottle.

His vision blurs, clears, blurs again.

He puts his hand in his pocket, wraps it around the mirror.

You don't need to look…

…you know who you are…

…don't…

…don't look…

…the sun…look at the sun…it's shining…

…see…

…you know who you are…

…I don't…

…you do…

….I need to…

…don't!

But he does.

He brings out the hand holding the mirror, draws it close to his face. His reflection is there. He stares at it, at the blood-shot eyes, the day's growth of stubble.

He thinks about the girl again. He had been too quick, hadn't taken the time to enjoy his work. The potential of being caught had gotten to him, and he had rushed it, and now he felt empty. The thrill wasn't as strong as it should have been. He should have felt more as he drove the stake through her heart, but the elation had been missing.

It meant the urge would return sooner than usual. It demanded perfection, and would go on demanding until he got it right.

When he gets it right, it is like heaven. There isn't a better feeling in the whole wide world. He wants it to feel right again.

Not just good. It needed to be great, like the girl he left in the lake. He gave it to that girl, gave it to her good, and it had been sweet, *she* had been sweet, had made him feel like he was worth a million bucks.

He carries the bottle of Wild Turkey over to the bed, lies down, clutches the bottle to his chest. He closes his eyes, thinks about the girl in the lake. Thinking about her makes him feel better. He considers masturbating as he thinks of the girl, but decides against it. It wouldn't be the same, wouldn't feel as good. He wishes he could feel her again, his hands on her throat. His eyes grow heavy. He falls asleep thinking about her.

18

remains

THEY FOUND OUT who the dead girl that had been incinerated was on Monday morning.

Her name was Kathleen Black. She was twenty-one, a junior at the University of Iowa, and had just returned home to Crater Lake to spend summer vacation with her family. She had been home for less than a week when she was murdered.

Kathleen Black hadn't come home Saturday night. Her parents, Jack and Audra, said that Kathleen had left the house around five on Saturday evening to meet friends for drinks at the Hawkeye Bar. Audra Black had explained that Kathleen didn't typically frequent the bars, but she hadn't seen her girlfriends in a while what with being off at college and all, and they had wanted to make the Hawkeye's happy hour, which ran from four-thirty to six, spend a nice evening catching up.

Kathleen hadn't come home on Saturday night or on Sunday morning. Audra had been worried but not overly concerned. Her daughter was twenty-one after all, and her initial thought was that she had spent the night at a friend's house.

Later on Sunday, she had tried texting Kathleen on her cell to no avail. Then came the phone calls. Still nothing. She wasn't panicking yet, but close to it, and next she started calling around, talking to Kathleen's friends, and then she really did start to panic when all of their stories were the same: they had met Kathleen at the Hawkeye at the predetermined time, had chatted, had a few drinks, maybe gotten a little tipsy, and then a man had approached the table and struck up a conversation, singling out Kathleen, and after a little while the two of them had went off somewhere to talk in private.

About an hour later, they saw Kathleen leaving with the handsome stranger. One of Kathleen's friends (her name was Jordyn, and Nathan had scribbled it on his notepad as J-O-R-D-A-N, crossing it out and rewriting it after Mrs. Black corrected him) had stopped them before they left, pulled Kathleen aside, asked her what she was doing, if she was sure about leaving with a man she had met only an hour prior. According to Jordyn, Kathleen hadn't seemed drunk – a little *tipsy*, but not drunk – and appeared to have her wits about her. And, hey, the guy really was quite handsome, a real catch, they all agreed on that.

That was the last they saw of Kathleen.

Audra Black had reported her daughter missing at 4:45 P.M. on Sunday. She received the usual law enforcement response: had she been missing for over twenty-four hours? Did she have reason to believe her daughter might be in danger? Was it possible she had run away? Was it unusual that her daughter failed to check in?

Nathan had received the news on Monday morning and had immediately phoned the Blacks and asked them to come down to the station. He asked them to bring a recent photograph of Kathleen with them.

Of course, seeing the photograph of Kathleen Black didn't help all that much given the condition of her remains. Nathan didn't want to show them the body. He showed them the shoe. The purple running shoe with the pink swoosh, and when Audra Black saw it the tears started to come then, grinding her palm against her mouth, and all Nathan could do was watch the train wreck unfold in front of him in slow motion.

Yes, she thought it looked like the same kind of shoe that Kathleen wore, the same size even, and she knew this because she had purchased them only a few weeks ago. Only she left room for doubt, saying they *looked* like Kathleen's shoes, but couldn't they have been anyone's? Surely, Kathleen hadn't been the only one to own shoes of that make and model, probably hundreds, maybe thousands of people owned shoes identical to the one Nathan removed from the evidence baggie.

Still, she wailed, nearly fainted, sunk down into one of the chairs in the conference room with her husband's help, buried her face in her hands and sobbed some more because as much as she wanted to believe that this was simple coincidence, the truth was there in bright purples and pinks, shiny and new and unmarred.

Nathan didn't offer her much hope. He believed in coincidence, mostly because he encountered it on a daily basis, but he didn't believe that was what they were dealing with now.

The Blacks asked to see the body. He advised against it, provided them the details, but they were undeterred. Reluctantly, they were allowed to see the remains, and, as he had expected, Audra Black screamed, wailed some more, fainted for real this time. Jack was stoic, but Nathan could tell that he was holding on by a thread, barely keeping it together.

Of course, they couldn't identify the body. So Jack and Audra Black left the station with a kind of fragile hope. Nathan said he would be in touch, and now that he had something to go on, they left it in the hands of an expert. Two days later, on a Wednesday, the body was positively identified through dental records as being that of Kathleen Black.

He made sure both husband and wife were home that same day, made the drive over. He stopped a block from the Black residence, stepped out of his patrol car, smoked a cigarette before completing his journey. He hadn't let the habit come back fully, was still working on the pack he had bought in the wee hours of the morning the previous weekend.

He delivered the news. It went as badly as he had assumed it would, and he stopped again on his way back to the station and smoked another. He had already polished off the small bottle of mouthwash Carl kept in his locker, and had replaced it with a new one. It was still a secret from Jess, but the guilt was building, and he would probably tell her soon if he didn't kick the habit within the next few days. She wouldn't be happy, but maybe she would understand, would maybe even grant him a temporary reprieve seeing as how he was up to his elbows in dead bodies lately.

Nathan stood next to his patrol car, and in the four minutes it took him to smoke the cigarette, he realized two things. First, he was in over his head. Way, way over. And, second, was this: they needed help. Desperately. As much as he hated to admit it, room for denial was shrinking by the minute.

By the time he arrived back at the station, he had formulated a plan, and the plan was to do what Carl had recommended in the first place and seek the assistance of the FBI's Behavioral Analysis Unit.

"Took you long enough," Carl said.

"You want to run with it or not?"

"Damn straight I wanna run with it. I thought you'd never ask."

And Carl *did* run with it. With unusual diligence and attention to detail, Carl put together everything they had in a neat little package and composed a request for assistance letter to the BAU. He called ahead, and then overnighted it via FedEx the next day.

"Now what?"

"Wait, I guess."

"We can't just sit on our hands, Nate."

"I'm listening."

19

the handsome stranger

THEY STARTED BY interviewing Kathleen Black's girlfriends, the ones that had been with her at the Hawkeye Bar last Saturday night. There were four of them in all. Nathan interviewed Jordyn Fine and Darcy Gallas; Carl handled Alex Boseman and Tina Steinmeyer.

All their stories matched up, the timeline and the appearance of the handsome stranger, Kathleen going off with him to talk in private, leaving the bar with him a little while later.

About the handsome stranger: that's where things became vague.

They all agreed that he was tall and thin. Nice eyes, hypnotic almost. Deep voice. What had they talked about? None of them could quite remember. Frivolous stuff, nothing important. He was handsome, but none of them could pinpoint exactly why. Jordyn Fine mentioned that her initial impression was that there was something dangerous about him, but couldn't give any specifics as to why she felt that way. She had been the one to stop Kathleen on her way out, ask her if she was aware of what she was doing.

Did Kathleen seem to be in control of herself?

Yes.

Was she drunk?

No, I wouldn't say that. Buzzed, a little tipsy maybe.

Did she use drugs?

Never.

When you spoke to her, she seemed coherent?

You mean, like, was she slurring her words?

Sure. Anything like that.

No. She seemed lucid. I don't think she was drugged, if that's what you mean. At least not while she was sitting with us. You can't be too careful about that these days. Guys trying to slip something into your drink when you aren't looking. I pay close attention to that kind of stuff.

Did Kathleen have a habit of doing that? Meeting men in bars and going home with them?

She wasn't promiscuous. That was one of the reasons I stopped her before she left. We always stuck together. She'd never left with a man she just met before.

Tell me about the guy she left with.

He was tall, good-looking.

You didn't recognize him?

No way. He wasn't local, I'm positive about that. He seemed easy to talk to. His eyes…

What about his eyes?

I don't know how to explain it. He had these great eyes, like I had a hard time looking into them, but once I did, it was like they pulled you in, and I couldn't look away from them.

Do you recall what he was wearing?

I remember thinking he was overdressed. Too fancy for a small town bar.

Like a suit?

No. Not that fancy. Button down shirt maybe, black slacks I think.

Did he talk about himself? Say where he was from or what he was doing in town?

I don't think so. Mostly he asked questions, let us do most of the talking.

Did they leave on foot? Or did they get into a vehicle?

I stopped them before they got to the door, so I don't know.

Anything else?

I can't believe that Kathleen's dead. I mean...I shouldn't have let her leave. I should have stopped her. I don't know what I was thinking...she didn't even know the guy...but I'm not her mother, ya know...she was an adult, I couldn't really prevent her from leaving...but I could have tried harder...maybe if I had she would have stayed. He was just so...handsome. If it had been me, I would have left with him.

After the girlfriends, they interviewed the employees that had been working at the Hawkeye that night, flashed the picture of Kathleen the Blacks had left with them.

Another dead end. No one remembered Kathleen Black or the handsome stranger, which didn't surprise Nathan, since the Hawkeye would have been hopping on a Saturday night, and they weren't trained to remember faces.

"The handsome stranger," Carl said.

"I got the same thing."

"The prettiest eyes."

"Yeah, hypnotic almost. A real ladies' man."

"Only nobody can hardly remember shit about the guy."

"Other than he was tall. And his eyes. Great eyes."

"So we put out an APB on a male model with fuck-me eyes. What a fucking waste."

"Maybe not."

It was late on Thursday night by now. The station was empty except for Nathan and Carl. They were seated on a bench in the locker room, Nathan smoking a cigarette, the next to last from the pack he had bought over the weekend.

"Pray tell," Carl said, swatting at the smoke wafting toward his face. "God damn, you quitting that shit anytime soon?"

"None of the friends seemed to think he was local."

"So he isn't from town. So what?"

"We know he's sticking around. In town, or somewhere close by."

"Yeah?"

"So where's he staying?"

Carl's eyes widened, the lightbulb going off. "You think he's staying at a motel."

"I think it's possible." He inhaled deeply on his cigarette. "Unless we go with your theory. Then maybe he's sleeping in a coffin."

"I'll get the shovel," Carl said, chuckling but not finding it particularly funny. "We get a list of everyone staying at motels or hotels in the area."

"Local ones first."

"Only two of them."

"Think they'll cooperate?"

"If I ask nicely, yeah. Both of them are locally owned. I know the girl that works the desk overnights at the Owl Night

Inn. Went to school together. Shouldn't be a problem getting her to cough it up. Cory Iverson owns the Candlelight."

"Any relation to our Iverson?"

"Yeah, it's Chad's uncle."

"They get along?"

"Far as I know. Cory's gettin' to be a mean bastard in his old age, but I doubt he'd give us much guff about it considering what's been going on lately. Chad's on tonight. I'll see if he minds playing quarterback on that."

"Okay, once we've got the lists, we can narrow it down by how many they've got staying in their rooms. We can rule out anyone that listed kids or more than one adult. This guy is a loner."

"Most of the people that stay at those dumps are loners, Nate. There's a few people that live there long term. Motel gives them discounts if they book by the week. Maybe we can weed some of them out, but even if we find somebody that looks good, what are you gonna do? We'd need a warrant to bust in on them, and the judge isn't gonna give us a warrant on suspicion alone."

"We'll cross that bridge when we come to it. For now, let's just keep it manageable and get the client lists. I've also been giving some thought to your theory. About this guy thinking he's a vampire hunter. Maybe that's the key."

"How so?"

"It means he's following a rulebook."

"I'm still not following."

"He thinks his victims are vampires. Goes so far as to convince himself they are vampires by draining their blood first. In his mind, he probably thinks he's performing a public service. He's staking them, cutting of their heads, now he's burning them. We found garlic at the last crime scene. That's all stuff that's mentioned in the folklore, isn't it? Maybe if we focused on the lore, we could use it to our advantage. Use it to predict what he's going to do next, or find a way to lure him into a trap."

"Look, I like the theory. I'm the one that came up with it after all. But what if I'm wrong?"

"We aren't out anything by giving it a shot. It's not like we're drowning in leads."

"Okay. Where do we start? You happen to know any vampire experts?"

"What about Carol's kid?"

"Peter?"

"Yeah, Hashbrown or whatever they call him."

"Tell me you're kidding."

"You said he's obsessed with the stuff."

"First of all, he's usually high as a kite. And second, I'm pretty sure the kid hates my guts just on principle. Despises authority. Plus, if Carol found out I tried wrangling him into a murder investigation, it'd only be one step below her finding out I actually considered him a suspect at one point. She'd throw me out of the house for sure. Huh uh, no way. I'm not coming near that one with a ten foot pole. You wanna recruit him, you're better off doing that on your own."

"Okay, I'll handle it."

"Try not to get me crucified in the process."

"Eggshells," Nate said.

"And quit hiding your contraband in my locker," Carl said, taking the pack of cigarettes from the top shelf of his locker and tossing them on the bench next to Nathan. "Oh, and you bought the wrong kind of mouthwash, too."

20

hashbrown

NATHAN REMAINED GOOD to his word and didn't involve Carl in the attempt to recruit Peter Hornick as their outside consultant on vampires.

Well…*almost* kept his word.

The thing about Peter, as Carl had mentioned before, was that he was both socially awkward and unpopular, which meant he spent a good deal of time locked away in his room. He didn't leave the house much.

He had already worked it out with Carl to have a "run-in" with the kid, but Carl was adamant that it not take place at the house, and so agreed that the best way to go about it was to use what they referred to as a staged coincidence. A staged coincidence was exactly what it sounded like, which was basically this: one party prearranged an event in hopes of reaching an intended outcome, while making it appear to be a complete coincidence to the other party.

The problem with this form of subterfuge was that it didn't always work the first time around. Nathan wasted three hours of his life on the first attempt, parked down the street from Carol Hornick's house, chain-smoking cigarettes and ignoring the fierce ache in his left testicle as he waited for Peter to leave the house. The three hours was divided into three parts, one hour increments. Once just after breakfast on Friday morning, again around noon, and finally in the late evening, after Carl was already home for the day.

That first day, Nathan came up empty-handed. After the two failed attempts, he had phoned Carl, said he would be back that night, and could he maybe orchestrate a way to get Peter out of the house. Maybe send him on an errand or something. Carl had promised to give it his damnedest, but by the time nine o'clock rolled around and there was still no sign of Carol's son, Nathan had called it a day.

Nathan had phoned Carl afterward saying, "What happened?"

"He wouldn't leave. The little fucker didn't even come out of his room for dinner. Look, Nate, I'm sorry. I know I'm making this a real bitch, but Carol…"

"You don't have to say it. I get it. If the shoe was on the other foot, I'd do the same thing."

"Look, I'll figure something out for tomorrow. I'll kick his ass and drag him to the street if I have to."

Nathan could hear the desperation in Carl's voice. He went home, spent a quiet evening with Jess, telling himself that they were doing everything that could be done. Word was getting around, spreading, and they were taking more calls down at dispatch, alleged sightings, strange occurrences, but nothing had panned out. It was the way of things he supposed. Nobody liked the idea of a killer being out there on the loose. Peoples' imaginations started to run wild. Saw things that weren't there. A person's mind could lie convincingly, fabricate things, see what it wanted to see. It was hard to ignore the voice in his head that kept telling him that they were getting nowhere. One, two, three bodies now and what did they have to show for it?

He didn't sleep much that Friday night.

The next morning – Saturday – Carl phoned him early, told him to get over to the house, Peter was getting ready to leave. Probably, Carl said, to visit his pot dealer.

Nathan headed over in a hurry, speeding down the street, slowing as he reached Carol's house, saw Peter coming out.

Peter was dressed in baggy black jeans, black long-sleeved shirt, the sleeves covering his hands. Long black hair, heavy with gel, slicked back. Painted white face, black lipstick, messenger bag resting against his hip. He was tall, maybe 6'2" in tightly-laced combat boots, pant legs tucked in. If a clown and a pirate fucked, Nathan thought their offspring would look an awful lot like Peter Hornick.

Nathan hung back. Followed.

When the kid reached the intersection, he turned left, walked a few blocks, hung a right, then a few more blocks, until they were coming up on the nicer part of town. All the well-to-dos had houses on Seever Drive, and that's where Peter was headed. If he was about to witness a drug deal, Nathan had assumed it would be on the east end, anything several blocks east of Main Street, which was considered the poorer part of town, as though a definitive distinction could be made in a town the size of Crater Lake.

But Peter kept going, headed north on Seever, past the fancy houses and heavily landscaped yards. Nathan tailed him, kept well back, knowing that he stuck out like a sore thumb in the patrol car. They didn't have a budget for undercover work, but a few years ago, Russell Pearson, who owned one of the used car dealerships in town, had donated an aging Chevy Caprice to the Sheriff's Department. Said he couldn't even give it away, might as well let somebody get some use out of it. At the time, Abe Talley had still been Sheriff, and he had accepted it gratefully. The car, bright blue and riddled with rust, had been parked in the one of the department's storage sheds ever since. Nathan could have used the car now, thinking maybe it would have been less conspicuous than his black and white.

At the intersection of Seever and Parkwild, Peter cut across the street diagonally, made his way toward a gray two-story house with an attached two-car garage. He bypassed the house, stepped up to the garage door, knocked, the door opened, and he went inside.

Nathan took a left on Parkwild, circled around, parked close enough that he had a clear view of the gray two-story, the front grille of his car pointed toward the house. He wouldn't be invisible. When Peter came out of the house, if he was paying attention, he would spot the patrol car, but at that point Nathan didn't think it would matter.

He waited. Several minutes passed. The pain in his testicle flared again (he still hadn't made an appointment with Kobayashi), and he reached into the glove compartment, pulled out the bottle of painkillers he had bought a week ago. It was almost empty. *Like candy*, he thought, shaking four into his palm, swallowing, cranking down the window, lighting a cigarette, letting his arm dangle out the window so smoke didn't get in the car.

Ten minutes later, the garage door came up, Peter ducking under it, starting back on Seever the way he had come.

Peter didn't see the patrol car. Or, if he did, he pretended not to.

Nathan let him get two blocks before he accelerated, pulled up alongside the kid, let the siren squawk briefly, rolled down the window.

"Hey Peter, got a minute?"

The kid kept walking like he hadn't seen Nathan pull up, hadn't heard Nathan talking to him.

Nathan kept pace with him.

"We need to talk."

Again, oblivious.

"I know you can hear me, Peter. Now, this is the last time I'm going to say it. You can either come get in the car and we can have a friendly little chat, or I can get out of the car, cuff you, take the bag of weed I have reasonable suspicion to believe you are carrying, then haul you down to the station and we can talk there. So, what's it going to be?"

The kid took his time pondering it. For a moment, Nathan thought Peter was actually going to run, and then he'd have a chase on his hands, thinking he would have to tackle him, and then what?

But Peter didn't run. He said, "The front or the back?"

"The front."

Peter came around the front of the car, opened the passenger door, sat down next to Nathan.

"It's bullshit."

"What?"

"You didn't have probable cause to stop me."

"Let me explain something to you, Peter. Do you like Peter, or would you prefer that I call you Hashbrown? See, Peter, probable cause is whatever I say it is. Besides, what we're really talking about here isn't probable cause but reasonable suspicion."

"That's fucked up, man."

"Maybe. But it's the truth. I saw you come out of that house. A known *drug* house, which leads a reasonable officer such as myself to believe you were there to purchase illegal narcotics."

"Bullshit, it is. It's not a known drug house."

"It is if I say it is. I saw you leaving, and if I want to make extra sure, I can say when I approached you that you smelled strongly of marijuana. There's your probable cause."

"A lie."

Nathan cocked his head. "Is it? And now that I've established both reasonable suspicion and probable cause, let's say I decide to search you, locate the weed you stashed in your messenger bag. Boom. Done deal."

"You're just like all the rest," Peter said. "You have power because you wear a badge and a gun and you think that gives you the right to abuse it."

"Spare me. This isn't a debate. And, if you're willing to hear me out, this won't turn into a drug bust either."

"And if I refuse?"

"Then we can take a ride down to the station."

"You're bluffing," Peter said, unsure.

"Am I?"

The kid was going to crack, Nathan could read it in his eyes.

"What is it you wanted to talk about?"

Nathan said, "I want you to tell me everything you know about vampires."

21

expert witness

"You want me to be a confidential informant?"

"Not exactly. More of an expert witness."

"Did my mom's boyfriend put you up to this? He works for you."

"Carl doesn't have anything to do with it."

"Really?"

"I plead the fifth."

"I *knew* it."

"Coming to you was my idea. Carl was against it."

"He knows I smoke weed."

Nathan nodded. "That's right. And he hasn't told your mother, so maybe you should cut the guy some slack. I'm guessing you're not the type of kid that runs off and tells Mommy everything that happens during the day. This can be our little secret."

"Why should I help? You aren't really going to bust me. Because of who my mom's dating."

"Because I'm asking."

Now that Peter had called his bluff, Nathan searched for something that would convince him. He lit a cigarette, blew smoke out the window.

"You smoke?"

"Temporarily."

"Uh huh, that's what they all say. What kind of police work is this? Wanting to know about vampires?"

"You've heard, I'm sure, that we've got a killer going around murdering people."

"Yeah. I heard about Becca. She was in my class."

"Talk to her much?"

"Me?" Peter smiled. "Look at me? Do I look like a social butterfly to you? Let's just say we didn't run in the same circles. Did you talk to Becca's boyfriend? *Jimmy.*"

"What about him? You know him?"

"A little."

"You think he could have killed Becca?"

Peter shook his head. "Can I have one of those?" He pointed at Nathan's cigarette.

"Your mother would kill me and bury the corpse."

"What she doesn't know…anyway, I'm legal."

Nathan took out his pack of Marlboros, handed it to Peter. Peter rolled down the window, lit, inhaled.

"No, I don't think Jimmy is capable of something like that. You've seen him. He looks like somebody tied a few twigs together and dressed it up in clothes. He loved Becca. A person can tell. Totally different type of guy than Dylan."

"Becca's ex."

"Now that guy, I can say unequivocally, that he's a major assbag. Treated Becca like shit when they were together, then when she'd have the nerve to leave him, he'd come crawling on his hands and knees, saying he couldn't live without her, and then she'd feel sorry for him, they'd patch things up, and the whole thing would start over again. I was ecstatic when she finally dumped him for good."

"You have a thing for her?"

"Who *didn't* have a thing for Becca? She was pretty, had the brains too. Only she wasn't into dating superheroes."

"Superheroes?"

"Yeah, I've got special powers. Most of the time, I'm invisible."

Peter continued smoking his cigarette. They were only a few blocks from Carol's house, Nathan wondering what kind of hot water he would find himself in if either Carl or Carol happened by, saw Peter smoking in Nathan's patrol car.

"Maybe we're looking at the wrong guys," Nathan said. "Maybe you did it."

"Killed Becca?"

"Why not? Maybe you were pissed she wouldn't give you the time of day."

"I didn't kill Becca. You know that. Anyway, I've got an alibi. I was home all night."

"Could have snuck out."

"Come on, are you serious? Carl said something to you didn't he? He started looking at me differently after I found out about Becca. Watching me. I think he thought maybe I had something to do with it. Because of the stuff I'm into."

"Can you blame him?"

"Did he tell you I worship Satan?"

"I stumbled into your room the other night when we were over for dinner. It isn't a big leap, thinking something like that."

"So if I was interested in learning about World War Two, would that mean I want to grow up to be the next Hitler?"

"Possibly."

Peter rolled his eyes, took a final drag of his cigarette, flicked it out the window. "I'm interested in the occult. I took a class on mythology and folklore when I was a junior. I wanted to know more about it. That doesn't mean I drink blood or sacrifice virgins."

"You could see why someone could get the wrong idea."

"Why? Because the way I dress? I dress like this because I want to make a statement. I don't want to be popular or cool or whatever unless it's on my own terms."

"You make a shitty clown."

"Fuck you."

"You didn't kill Becca."

"I didn't kill Becca. But you already knew that. That still doesn't explain your sudden interest in vampires."

Nathan reached over, opened the glove compartment, pulled out a manila folder, handed it to Peter. "Take a look."

Peter opened the folder. It contained a small stack of photographs. He flipped through them, his face changing. He didn't make it through the pile before he put them back, closed it, said, "Why are you showing me this?"

"You asked me why I was interested in vampires. Now you know."

"Did he really do that to her?"

Nathan nodded.

Peter's eyes were glued to the manila folder. Nathan waited, gave him time to make up his mind.

"Okay," he said finally.

"See, I knew you were an upstanding citizen."

"Don't say shit like that. You're an asshole, you know that, Sheriff? Showing me those pictures."

"I'm desperate."

"What now?"

"Now you give me that bag of weed you're holding."

22

traveling man

NATHAN DROPPED PETER off a block from Carol's house. Mum was the word, and Nathan didn't think the kid would have a problem keeping his mouth shut. Not after seeing the photographs.

He had hit Peter below the belt, but it had been a necessary evil. The stakes were high (again, no pun intended), and he wanted the kid to know that up front.

Carl was already at the station when Nathan arrived. He looked nervous, twitchy.

"How'd it go?"

"I don't know what you were all worried about. He's going to help."

"That easy?"

"I made a compelling argument," Nathan said, dug into his pocket, brought out the bag of marijuana he had confiscated from Peter, tossed it on his desk.

"He was holding?"

"You were right. Went to see his dealer."

"What a dumbass."

"Seems to have his head on straight. Just a normal teenager. They're all fucked in the head."

"You call *that* normal?"

"So what's new?"

"I heard back from the BAU. They worked up a profile."

"That's good news. What did they say?"

"Nate, they're sending someone."

"Really?"

"She'll be here on Monday. This thing is big. Bigger than we thought. Crater Lake isn't the first time something like this has happened. Apparently, this guy's been busy leaving bodies all over the country. They ran a check through ViCAP. Details matched up with cases in over two dozen different places. Never big cities, but places close to them. Small towns in Washington, California, Utah, Colorado, New Mexico, North Dakota, and that's just for starters, just the ones they know about. They think this guy has been doing this for years. Always the same way. They sent over a file. Take a look."

Carl handed him a stack of faxed photos. They were low quality, grainy, but Nathan recognized what he was looking at.

"Look familiar?"

"Same mark that was on Becca Struthers's neck."

"Yep. They're on all of them, at least the ones he didn't burn beyond recognition. Keep looking."

Nathan shuffled through the photographs, stopped when he reached the *L 'Inconnue de la Seine*.

He glanced up at Carl.

Carl was nodding. "That's right. It's happened before. But it's always only with the first body that shows up. And most of the time, they pull the body from a river or a lake or some kind of water."

"I was wrong."

"About what?"

"About that girl in the mask being his first victim. He isn't evolving. He's been doing this for a very long time. There's a pattern to it."

"Hell if I can figure out what it is."

Nathan studied the black and white photos for a long time, shuffling through them again and again until they were an indelible part of his memory.

"Did you talk to Iverson?"

"Yeah, his uncle gave him a list of the Candlelight's occupants, no questions asked. I also got the list for the Owl Night Inn."

"You have plans for tonight?"

"Carol wanted to go to Alton tonight. Dinner and a movie. I can cancel though. Why? What were you thinking?"

"I'm thinking this is time sensitive. The lists would change daily. The sooner we start narrowing them down the better. But you go on, have a nice night with Carol."

"No way, buddy. You're not getting rid of me that easy. I'll call Carol. She'll understand. Maybe Peter will go with her."

Nathan didn't argue. "You ate anything yet?"

"Nope. No time."

"I was thinking of ordering Chinese."

"You know the way to a man's heart."

The conference room table was littered with Styrofoam containers, remnants of Chinese dinner. It had taken until late into the night to go through both lists.

In all, there were fifty-two occupants between the Owl Night Inn and the Candlelight. Carl recognized several of them as locals, mostly men, who through fate or circumstance had found it easier to take up permanent residence at one of the two motels. After weeding out the ones Carl recognized, they had narrowed the list down to thirty. Carl spoke with the girl he knew that worked at the Owl Night Inn, and she confirmed a handful of others as being regulars, and so thirty became twenty-four.

Out of the twenty-four remaining, only half of those were sole occupants, meaning twelve of the twenty-four were renting a room with at least one other person.

"Leaves a dozen," Carl said.

"Manageable."

Carl's friend at the Owl was more than cooperative. They had known each other for a long time, had had a brief fling when Carl was a junior in high school, and when Carl called to ask if she could fax them over copies of driver's licenses, she had agreed whole-heartedly. They had the copies within twenty minutes, and he and Nathan began sifting through the details, studying the faces, running background checks, until they had eliminated another five, leaving them with seven. Three of them were staying at the Owl, the remaining four at the Candlelight.

Of those seven, only two of them had checked in more than a few days ago, one male, the other female, and Nathan immediately discounted the female occupant. It turned out she was a twenty-seven year old that had skipped town several years before, leaving her husband and nine month old daughter behind. She had returned now to reunite with her daughter, who was now three. Apparently, the guilt had caught up with her and she had returned to Crater Lake to make amends.

It was midnight now.

Nathan leaned back in his chair, rubbed his eyes, lit a cigarette. He had checked in with Jess a few hours ago, telling her not to wait up, that he would be home late. She hadn't complained, though she mentioned that it was always difficult getting to sleep when he wasn't home, when she had to man the bed all by herself. He had promised to be home as soon as he could.

"This is our guy," Carl said, staring at the low-quality copy of the man's driver's license. "Seymour Benton Jones."

"*Might* be our guy."

"We've eliminated everyone else. Seymour Benton Jones. Even *sounds* like a serial killer name, doesn't it? Kinda looks like the type too."

Carl pushed the paper across the table toward Nathan. Nathan looked at it, studied the face. In the black and white copy, Jones was a man with a round, bearded countenance, shaggy hair that came down over his ears. He looked like a vagrant. Nathan knew from experience that a photograph wouldn't tell him anything. He had studied the faces of killers, and none of them had given him any indication that there was a monster hiding behind their eyes.

According to his driver license, Jones was 6'3", 225 lbs, thirty-seven years old. Last known address was listed as a rental home in Des Moines. He drove a white 2005 Chevy Malibu, and that information matched the information he had put down on the guest card when he had checked into the Owl Night Inn.

"He checked in almost three weeks ago," Carl said. "Tell me, what does a guy stay that long in Crater Lake for?"

"Maybe he has family here," Nathan said.

"Why a motel room then? He could just stay with them."

"Maybe he doesn't get along with them that well. Maybe there isn't enough room."

"He lives in Des Moines for Christ's sake. You don't rent a motel for three weeks when you live an hour away. And he has two DUIs on his record."

"What about the handsome stranger?"

"Maybe he shaved his beard, styled his hair since this photo was taken. This is our guy, Nate. I can feel it in my gut."

Nathan glanced at the piece of paper, stared at the driver's license photo again. "We can't get a warrant."

"Doesn't mean we can't put eyes on him. Feel him out."

"We're spread thin as it is. Hard to spare someone to stake out a motel full-time. I don't have the budget to approve overtime."

"What about the reserves?"

"Gibson and Daniels? I barely trust them to write a speeding ticket. I'm not going to put them on a surveillance detail."

"You don't have to. Me and Iverson can trade off babysitting this Jones guy. I'll fill Chad in on it. You can call in Gibson and Daniels, they can handle the basic stuff."

"I don't know."

"Come on, Nate. We have to do something. At least let's give it a few days. This guy won't get out of our sight. There hasn't been a murder in almost a week now. He's overdue. But this time we'll be ready."

"I don't like the idea of putting all of our eggs in one basket."

"We've only got the one egg."

Nathan thought about it, stubbed out his cigarette, nodded. "All right. I'll call up Gibson and Daniels and see if they're available for coverage. If they agree, then you, Iverson, and I can trade off keeping eyes on Jones.

"Hell yes. I knew there was a reason I voted for you besides just your good looks."

"I want you to talk to Peter. See when he can make time to come down and school us on vampires."

"If I'm right, and I *am* right, man, then we won't need the little shit."

"Eggs – remember?"

"Yeah, yeah, I got it. I'll talk to him."

They chatted for another fifteen minutes. Finally, Carl stood up, got ready to leave, said, "You comin'?"

"I'm going to hang back for a minute."

"That's right, smoke another cigarette and then make yourself pretty so you can pass muster. I don't get it, man. For someone with a cancer phobia as bad as yours, I don't see how you can keep smokin' those things."

"I'm going to quit."

"Sure."

"Any day now."

"Sure."

"Get out of here."

Carl left. Nathan sat at the table, took out his pack of Marlboros, looked at it, considered tossing it into the trashcan, but couldn't bring himself to do it. Instead, he lit one, pulled the copy of Jones's driver's license in front of him, stared at it, wondering if he was staring into the eyes of a monster.

Jess was asleep when he got home, dead to the world for once. The TV was on. The bedroom smelled like Fruit Loops.

Nathan stripped out of his clothes, showered, taking extra care not to let the shower stream get anywhere near his testicles. The pain was bad now.

He dried off, took several Aleve tablets, sat down on the toilet seat, waiting for the pain to become tolerable again.

He returned to the bedroom. Jess didn't so much as stir, something he was grateful for. He found the remote, switched off the TV, and lay on his back, staring up into the darkness.

He slid his hand under the covers, searching, fingertips finding Jess's hip, moving up and over, his hand coming to rest on her stomach. He left it there, thinking maybe he would feel the baby kick. According to Jess, the kid was a real night owl, always squirming around, always hungry, hence her middle of the night addiction to Fruit Loops drenched in whole milk.

Nathan left his hand on Jess's stomach for a long time, until he grew tired. He felt nothing. No kicking baby, no late night hunger pangs. Tonight, their child slept.

23

the profiler

Nathan didn't know what he had expected, but Special Agent Lindsay Trujillo was a far cry from the image he had created in his mind.

She was 5'6" in flats, short dark hair framed her face, athletic, dressed in black slacks and white blouse.

Maybe Nathan had been watching too many of Jess's TV shows, too much *Criminal Minds*, because the woman standing on the other side of the conference table didn't look like an FBI agent. She looked normal, average, sans make-up.

The case materials Carl had sent her were laid out, neatly organized, taking up most of her half of the conference table. A stack of folders stood next to them.

Carl had arrived earlier, had already set about making coffee, asking how Lindsay Trujillo liked it, disappeared for a minute or two, reappeared with two cups, one for him, one for her.

He had taken the liberty of picking up a dozen glazed donuts from the bakery on his way to the station. The box of donuts sat open at the center of the table, only a single one missing from the box. It rested, uneaten, on a folded paper towel next to Carl's cup of coffee.

When Nathan had arrived a little later, Carl had introduced him to Special Agent Trujillo. Her fingers were long and delicate, but her handshake was firm, dark circles under her eyes from a night spent traveling. As she sipped her coffee, she briefly explained to them how her flight had been delayed, how she hadn't gotten into Omaha until after ten, and then driven the rental car to Crater Lake, making it almost midnight by the time she checked into her room at the Owl Night Inn.

When she briefed them on her background she was eloquent, succinct, well-rehearsed, Nathan wondering how many times she had delivered this same speech, how many times she had swooped in like a superhero to assist local law enforcement with a difficult case.

She told them about how she was surprised when the materials Carl had sent reached her desk, but how she had known it was coming. The Bureau had been dealing with this for a long time. There was always a short lull, but then it would start all over again in some small town, they never knew where, and then she would head off to pick up the pieces again.

"Two years," Lindsay said, testing her coffee, adding sugar, testing it again, leaving the spoon sticking out of the cup, drinking around it. "That's how long we've been pursuing this. It's always the same. The dead girl, the mask, pulling them from the water. Then things escalate. Stakes through the hearts, decapitated, the weird marks on the back of their necks. California, New Mexico, Colorado, Utah, Nebraska, North Dakota, roughly west to east, but sometimes he deviates, no rhyme or reason to it. And because he's always moving, we're always too late. By the time the pattern becomes apparent, it's always too late. He's gone and moved onto the next."

"We came to the conclusion that he thinks he's hunting vampires," Carl said.

"Yes, we've made that connection."

"Think maybe he's a dual personality? The blood loss…he has to create vampires so he can destroy them."

"He's methodical," Nathan said. "Organized."

"Both organized and *disorganized*, actually," Lindsay said.

"I assumed it's because he loses control sometimes. Gets caught up in the thrill, in his fantasy, and doesn't always stick to a script."

"Initially, it can appear that way. But this guy has been doing this for a long time, always sticks to the same pattern. If he makes mistakes, we believe they're intentional. Or he doesn't care. He's meticulous when he has to be. If it was an isolated case, I would tend to agree with you, but it always happens the same way."

"How many?" Nathan asked.

Lindsay gestured at the materials on the table. "Counting your three?"

"Yeah."

"In excess of fifty."

Carl whistled through his teeth. "Jesus."

"That's how many we know about. In the States. We think there are probably more. We've traced it back quite a few years to similar cases that occurred in Central America in the 90s and, before that, Europe back in the 80s. We can't say for sure that it's the same guy, if he's a copycat, or if it's just coincidence, but he's been doing this for a while, and he's managed to evade law enforcement the entire time."

"You're saying it's possible he's been doing this for nearly thirty years?"

Lindsay nodded, sipped at her coffee. "*If* it's the same man, yes. We're working with several of the international agencies to see if we can obtain files, but there's a lot of red tape, not everybody likes to share the playground. Believe me, it's a headache."

She picked up the stack of file folders and slid them across the table. Nathan and Carl divided them, began pouring over them, sifting through photographs, scanning reports.

"You said the pattern is the same," Nathan said. "It always starts with a girl in a mask." He held up a photograph of a nude woman, her face shrouded behind a mask. "The unknown woman of the Seine."

"Correct. *L 'Inconnue de la Seine.* Her body was pulled from the Seine River in the late eighteen hundreds. She was never identified. Suspected suicide."

"You think this guy is trying to recreate that event?"

"That's the logical assumption. The first victim is always a young female. He disposes of the body in water. Leaves them wearing the mask."

"That doesn't make sense," Carl said. "If the original case was ruled a suicide, why would he be trying to recreate it?"

"We don't know. As you said, he may be delusional. But he obviously has a knack for history."

"And folklore," Nathan said. "He seems to follow the traditional concept of vampires. Death by wooden stake, decapitation, burning. And garlic."

"Garlic?"

"We found a clove of garlic at one of the murder sites."

"That's interesting. And you're certain it was related to our unsub?"

"This is Iowa, Agent Trujillo. We grow corn. Soy beans, oats. Not garlic. I believe in coincidence as much as the next guy, but that would be pushing it."

Carl said, "So far, we've been able to identify all of the victims except the girl in the mask."

"Which means he's sticking to his pattern. In almost every case, the victims turn out to be locals. Except the first girl. We've never been able to identify them. They're not local to whatever area he happens to be operating in."

"Just like the unknown girl of the Seine."

"Yes, there appears to be a correlation. Prostitutes maybe. Hitchhikers. Girls that no one would miss."

"Doubtful," Nathan said. He stood up, carried his cup over to the coffeemaker, filled it, sat back down. He wanted a cigarette, but thought it would be unprofessional to light up in front of their new guest.

"How so?"

"Most prostitutes have a criminal record. Solicitation, drugs, theft. There's usually something. Meaning they would be in the system. If you haven't had any luck in identifying them, then the theory doesn't hold."

"I agree with you, but they didn't come from outer space. At some point, these women had families. Someone would have made a stink."

"Maybe. Or maybe you haven't put it together yet. You said these are all isolated cases, the guy moves around a lot, and if he randomly picks them up somewhere along the way..."

"I see where you're going with it. I'll be blunt. I'm not going to pretend I have all the answers, or even *most* of them. I can only tell you what I know. And what I know is this: our unsub is highly skilled, he's well-organized – the majority of the time at least – and he's constantly on the move. There doesn't seem to be a definitive pattern to his travels, meaning we don't believe that he's a long-distance truck driver, otherwise we think he would be hitting areas in a closer proximity, or following a particular route. But his work probably does involve travel. A salesman perhaps. He also has the ability to remain in one area for a length of time. He has flexibility. It's doubtful he's married. Most likely a loner, no serious relationships, and it's possible he's in control of his own schedule. Either he's built a reputation with his employer that allows him to come and go as he pleases, or he's self-employed."

"If he's employed at all."

"Staying mobile costs money, Sheriff. Gas, vehicle maintenance, food, lodgings."

"He has no qualms with killing innocent people. I doubt he'd have a problem stealing."

"You think he finances his endeavors by theft. I've entertained that theory myself. But from what we've learned about serial killers of our unsub's ilk, they're usually employed. They're chameleons. They fit in, they possess above average intelligence, they can carry on relationships, maintain employment, and, most importantly, no one suspects them. They're charming, oftentimes they're considered ladies' men. Take Ted Bundy. All the psychological testing came back clean. In school, he was a good student, popular with his teachers. He was accepted into several law schools. He was part of Daniel Evans's reelection campaign. No one suspected him. No one thought he was capable of committing the atrocities that he did."

Carl went on to explain how they had obtained client lists from both of the motels in town, how they had narrowed the lists down to a single man, Seymour Benton Jones, and how they were keeping round-the-clock surveillance on him. He had the faxed copy of Jones's driver's license ready, slid it over to Lindsay.

"We interviewed friends of Kathleen Black who were with her immediately prior to her disappearance. Witnesses said she went off with a stranger she met in the bar, described him as being tall and handsome." Carl pointed to the copy. "This guy Jones is six-three. I'd say that qualifies as tall in most places."

"I wouldn't describe him as handsome," Lindsay said, staring at the photograph.

"No, but it's hard to tell with the beard and the hair. Driver's license photos are notoriously bad – they can make anybody look like dog shit. But that license was issued two years ago. Plenty of time to have changed his appearance. He could have gotten rid of the beard, lost some weight, cleaned up a little."

"He's thirty-seven. That makes him a lot older than the victim."

Carl shrugged. "Some women prefer older men."

"It doesn't fit the timeline. If our unsub has been operating as far back as the eighties, this guy would have been a kid."

"*If* it's the same guy," Carl said. "And that's a pretty big *if*. We called in our reserve deputies to cover shifts while Nate, Iverson, and I keep watch on him."

"How long has he been under surveillance?"

"Less than twenty-four hours. Iverson's on him now. Nate's taking a shift tonight, and then I'll take over tomorrow morning."

Lindsay looked at the photograph again. She didn't look convinced.

"Lives in Des Moines."

"Rental house."

"You contact the property owner?"

"Not yet."

"Might be worth it. See how long he's been residing there. Our guy moves around a lot."

"He's bound to live somewhere."

"Think about it for a minute. He's been crossing the country for years. Then it turns out he lives an hour from here?"

"Could be."

"I'm thinking that's too close to home."

"We'll follow up with the property owner," Nathan said. "See how long he's been there. It makes sense though. You said he probably wouldn't have a family. It would be safer to rent, stay a little while, then move onto the next. Makes it hard to track."

"I'll say it again. He doesn't make mistakes unless it's on purpose. He may be crazy, delusional, or psychotic, but he's also smart. Smart enough to stay one step ahead of us. This is the closest we've ever been."

"We're going on a week," Nathan said. "Maybe it's over."

"No, Sheriff. It isn't over. He isn't finished yet."

"How do you know?"

"Because there haven't been enough dead bodies."

24

stakeout

To her credit, Lindsay Trujillo didn't once mention that the FBI had officially taken over the investigation. She could have easily flaunted her power, could have made it known in no uncertain terms that she was calling the shots. Nathan had reached a point where he didn't think he would have minded someone else taking the lead. He was willing to let someone else play quarterback for a while.

But Lindsay didn't take over, smart enough to know that it went without saying, and she seemed genuinely grateful for their cooperation. She offered information, guidance, and Nathan knew it had to be difficult for her, this being her baby and all, that she had spent countless hours in countless places trying to track down the killer. After a while, an unsolved case could turn into an obsession, and when that happened it was important to show a semblance of control. You got close to the thing, too close, and pretty soon it became a part of you, and just like a mother to a newborn, you could become possessive, determined not to let too many hands stir the pot. Your mind slowly narrowed, and soon you couldn't see the forest for the trees, couldn't step outside of it and take a gander at the bigger picture.

After the meeting, knowing he had to pull an overnight shift, Nathan had gone home and done his best to take a nap. Jess left him alone, ran errands, picked up some items from the grocery store. When she returned, he woke to the sound of cupboards being opened and closed, Jess a real whirlwind in the kitchen when it came to putting groceries away, acting like it was a timed event and she was trying to beat her previous score.

He tossed and turned, listening, and eventually gave up, came out to the kitchen and helped finish putting the groceries away.

Jess seemed anxious, agitated, and Nathan searched his mind for something he might have done wrong. Had she smelled smoke on his clothes? Her sense of smell was nearly superhuman at this point, and perhaps all the cheap deodorant in the world hadn't been enough to keep the scent of stale cigarette smoke from being detected.

He asked her what was wrong. She said it was nothing, nothing was wrong, and he could tell it was a lie, and the way she snatched up the empty plastic grocery sacks, smooshed them together, compacted them into a tiny ball, only supported his belief.

"Come on, I can tell when you're upset about something."

"What is there to be upset about, Nathan? What in the world? I'm only ready to pop any day now, any minute maybe, and there's a killer on the loose in town, *our* little town where nothing ever happens, and you're out there chasing him, hardly home anymore, but that's okay because I can do this by myself, thank you very much, I don't need any help."

Nathan listened, determined not to interject. Better to let her get it out of her system, even if that meant acting as her punching bag for a little while.

He hadn't had a chance to tell her about Lindsay Trujillo, that the FBI was now involved, or that Lindsay had mentioned participating in the surveillance tonight because she never had an easy time falling asleep in motels, so why bother, might as well do something productive. She wasn't sold on the idea that Seymour Jones was their man, and, truth be told, Nathan wasn't convinced either. It seemed too easy, and the killer they were looking for was smart, resourceful, and, according to Lindsay, only made mistakes deliberately.

Watching Jess now, in the middle of her rant as she expelled the bad feelings from her system, he didn't think mentioning the fact that he would be pulling night duty with another female, and a moderately attractive one at that, would be the best course of action. Jess had never been the jealous type, but she was pregnant, and that had wreaked havoc on her hormones, made her unpredictable and emotional.

No. Better to keep it to himself. It was another lie, but a small one, just like the cigarette smoking. He didn't like it, but he didn't want to deal with a blowout right now, not when his attention was needed elsewhere.

She went on for another minute or two, and then there was silence, Nathan finally speaking into it, saying, "You're right. I haven't been around. Believe me, it's not that I don't want to be. It's just…this thing…"

"I know. It's your job. You have to catch him. It's not your fault. It's just I didn't picture it being like this."

"That makes two of us."

"Just catch him. Okay?" She stepped closer to him. "Preferably, before we bring this child into the world. I would feel better knowing there was one less person like that around before she comes."

"*He.*"

"So hopeful."

They kissed. In the back of his mind, Nathan couldn't help thinking Jess would smell smoke on his breath, the taste of cigarettes in his mouth. But she didn't. She stepped back, opened her eyes, smiled at him.

"Better?" he asked.

"Maybe a little. You're leaving now?"

"Yeah. We might be onto something."

"When will you be back?"

"Morning probably."

"I hate you being gone at night. It's hard to sleep without you."

It's hard to sleep with *me,* he thought, not saying, rubbing her shoulders.

"You've got your Fruit Loops," he said.

She smiled again, swatted him playfully. As he was headed out the door, she said, "Nate…be careful."

He nodded and headed out into the night.

It was seven-thirty when he met Lindsay at the station. She had showered beforehand, changed into tight jeans and a gray hoodie a size too large for her. Somehow seeing her in civvies made her more attractive, and Nathan felt a pang of guilt for not having told Jess where he was going tonight, who he was spending time with.

Lindsay followed him out the station's back door, to the large garage that served as the Department's motor pool and storage area. The baby blue Chevy Caprice stared at them from the darkness, its front grille grinning at them with metal teeth.

Nathan opened the driver's side door, slid into the plush seat, sending up a small cloud of dust. He turned the key in the ignition and the car protested for a moment, coughed, came to life.

"You guys know how to ride in style," Lindsay said, getting in on the passenger side.

"It's less conspicuous."

"You think?"

"You sure about this?"

"What else am I going to do? Sit in my motel room and stare at the water stains on the ceiling?"

"Might be more exciting."

"Don't make me pull rank."

"Yes, ma'am."

"Drive, Sheriff."

He pulled out of the garage, the Chevy's engine rumbling. He radioed Iverson, met him a block away from the Candle-light, at the Pump N' Save.

Iverson was driving his personal vehicle, a newer Ford F-150. He recognized the blue Caprice as he pulled up to the gas station, parked next to it.

"Holy shit, you brought Old Blue out of retirement?"

"Her career isn't over yet."

Nathan introduced Iverson to Lindsay. They shook hands, Lindsay excused herself, going into the gas station to plunder the shelves for snacks – it was going to be a long night.

"Anything?" Nathan asked when he and Iverson were alone.

"Nada. His car hasn't moved all day. Which isn't surprising. If the guy thinks he's hunting vampires, then he wouldn't come out during the daylight hours. He'd hunt at night."

Why don't you go home. Spend some quality time with your girl, get some sleep."

"You won't get any argument from me."

Iverson got back into his truck. Before he could pull out, Nathan tapped on the window. After Iverson had rolled it down, Nathan said, "Another thing, when this thing is over, be sure to thank your uncle for me."

"Will do, boss."

He watched Iverson leave.

Nathan waited in the car. Lindsay came out several minutes later, carrying two plastic sacks, handed one of them to Nathan as she sat down in the passenger seat. "Here. Compliments of the FBI."

Nathan peered into the sack. There were energy drinks, bottles of soda, beef jerky, chocolate-covered peanuts, a bag of licorice. And buried beneath it all was a pack of Marlboros. He glanced up at Lindsay.

"I thought you might prefer those over donuts."

"You knew?"

"I've been around the block a time or two."

"What gave it away?"

"The smell of cheap deodorant. You're married, right?" Lindsay said, pointing at his wedding band. "No woman in her right mind would let her husband wear deodorant that smelled that bad."

Nathan smiled, backed out of the parking space, drove them to the Candlelight. He did a quick drive through the motel's lot until he spotted Jones's white Malibu.

He backed into one of the side spaces opposite the west side of the motel. From this position, they had an unobstructed view of the parking lot as well as the rear exit doors. According to the list that Cory Iverson had provided them, Jones was staying on the second floor, room 208, which would face the parking lot. There were tiny balconies with wrought-iron railings outside each of the rooms on the second floor.

"We should be able to catch him coming and going from here," Nathan said, rolling down his window and cutting the engine.

It wasn't long before they broke into the bags of snacks that Lindsay had bought earlier. She chewed on a licorice stick while Nathan smoked.

"Sure it doesn't bother you?"

"My father smoked all his life. Swisher Sweets. Remember those? He died in oh-seven, and whenever I try to picture him now, he's always got one of them stuck between his teeth. I wouldn't touch the things, but I like the smell. Brings back memories."

"How long you been with the Bureau?"

"Seven years. They recruited me straight out of college. Three in the BAU. What about you? You seem young to be sheriff."

"I've been with the Department for six, the last five months as sheriff."

"Ah, a malcontent no doubt."

"Pardon?"

"Well, I'm thinking not many people aspire to be the sheriff of a small town when they grow up, so I'm guessing you were discontent with your boss, decided to fight the establishment."

"Pretty much sums it up, I guess."

"Looks like the town saw something in you."

"My fan club isn't getting any bigger. Hand me one of those."

Lindsay peeled another licorice stick out of the bag, handed it to Nathan.

"Your father, how'd he pass? If you don't mind me asking."

"A few years before he died, he had a massive stroke. Left him paralyzed on one side, slurred speech. He couldn't move around much on his own. Lots of physical therapy, relearning the basics. Know what he taught himself to do over again first?"

"To smoke his sweet cigars."

"That's right. They probably were at least partly to blame for the stroke, but that didn't seem to matter to him. He always said if he was going to go out, he was going to go out doing the things he enjoyed. I guess that's exactly how it went in the end."

"Sounds like he was set in his ways."

"We're all set in our ways, Sheriff. Sometimes even if it kills us."

She seemed to draw inward for a moment, reflecting on something. Nathan thought about asking where her mind was, what memory had her in its grasp, but he refrained.

After a short silence, Lindsay said, "What does your wife think about all this?"

"She's like everyone else in town right now. Scared. She's due any day now."

"Congratulations."

"Thanks."

"What are you having? Boy or girl?"

"Undetermined."

"The two of you are waiting?"

"Me, at least. I want it to be a surprise."

"I'd never make it."

"Kids?"

"Not for the foreseeable future."

"Haven't found Mr. Right?"

"That's part of it maybe. The other part is being afraid that when they get old enough, I'll have to deal with the monster in the closet issue."

"Okay?"

"You know, when kids get to be a certain age, they're scared of the monster under the bed or hiding in the closet. And when that day comes, they come and they ask, 'Hey mom, are monsters real?' And, given what I do for a living, what am I supposed to tell them? Do I lie to them? Or do I tell them that yes, monsters are real, that they're walking around all over, only you don't know it because they look just like the rest of us?"

"I never thought about it like that."

"Yeah, well, men typically don't. It's usually the woman. How does your wife feel about you spending the night alone with another woman?"

Nathan was silent.

"You didn't tell her?"

"I didn't tell her."

"Shame on you."

"Things are already a little tense," Nathan said. "It seemed like a good time to keep my mouth shut."

"Which means it was the *ideal* time to open your mouth and tell your wife what it is you're up to."

They talked for a while. By the time the daylight faded and night descended, the bag of licorice was finished. Nathan helped himself to a Milky Way, ate half, started smoking again after that. Lindsay worked on a Red Bull.

They talked some more, their voices at whisper level now. Lindsay told him about college, about her first years in the Bureau, how it had taken her a while to be accepted into the BAU.

She told him about a serial killer they had apprehended in Louisiana, a black man, which was unusual, because the majority of serial killers turned out to be white males. They had caught the guy in Shreveport. They had found the body of a young boy in his trunk, which fit the profile, he was into boys,

Lindsay said, all of the victims had been between the ages of six and nine. He didn't molest them or anything, but what he did do was sacrifice them to a pagan deity he worshipped. Sliced them open, trapped their blood in a golden chalice, offered it up to his god. He was into some kind of voodoo, or hoodoo maybe it was, and later he agreed to show them his secret lair, which was nothing but a converted cellar, outfitted with a stone altar he used when he committed these ritualistic sacrifices.

"You should have seen this place," Lindsay said. "Bones all over the place. When he had enough of them, he liked to use them to make jewelry. Bone necklaces, bracelets, earrings. And he kept all these chickens, live ones, in these little cages that were stacked against one of the basement walls. I guess he would sacrifice those if he didn't have something better on hand."

"We don't see that kind of thing around here. Not until now at least. It has to eat at you."

"It does. Some of my colleagues live by what they call divorcing their emotions. They work on a case, they send their feelings on vacation. I've tried that. It doesn't work. Not for me. If it gets them by, more power to them, but I haven't had any luck with it. So I live with it. Maybe that has something to do with why I'm still single."

"Maybe," Nathan said, but he wasn't really listening now because the door at the rear of the motel opened and a man stepped out. Even in the semi-darkness, Nathan could see that the man was bearded, and he was big, a giant almost, and he pointed, Lindsay following his finger, both of them watching as the lumbering man crossed the parking lot until he reached the white Chevy Malibu.

"That's Jones," Lindsay said.

Nathan started the Caprice. Waited.

They watched as the Malibu backed out of its parking spot, creeped through the lot, turned onto the street.

Nathan followed.

"Don't get too close. You might spook him."

He felt himself getting nervous. The pain in his testicle was starting to come back, and it was only now that he remembered that he had left his pills in the glove compartment of his patrol car, and in the back of his brain he was hoping this wouldn't get ugly, wouldn't turn into a foot chase because the thought of running with the cursed pain caused his stomach to do somersaults.

The Malibu turned onto Main Street, followed it three blocks, turned left on Maple, went another four blocks, took another left, and soon they were in the nicer section of town, one of the new developments, most of the houses worth 170K or higher.

The Malibu went a little farther, slowed, pulled up to the curb at the intersection of Oak and Cottonwood. Its taillights blinked out.

"What's he doing?"

"Could be doing his homework."

"Homework?"

"Organized killers plan ahead. Once they've decided on their victim, they don't always act right away. They watch them for a while. Case the house, figure out their victim's patterns, like when they leave for work, when they come home, if they live alone. It's how they avoid making mistakes later. They do their homework."

"What do you want me to do."

"Keep going. He probably saw us behind him now. Go around the block so he thinks you're just passing by."

Nathan went by, focusing on the windshield, not looking over when they passed Jones's car. He turned at the intersection, drove several blocks down, then got back onto Oak.

"Go up another street and then park," Lindsay said. "That should put enough distance between us and him and we'll still have a good vantage point."

After he passed Evergreen, Nathan killed the headlights, slid up to the curb, killed the engine.

They sat and waited.

Hours passed.

It was past 11:30 P.M. when Jess texted him, asking how things were going.

"He's doing surveillance," Lindsay said. "That has to be it. You know anybody that lives in these houses?"

Nathan said he didn't, responded to Jess's text, saying he was still following up on a lead, that it might be a while yet.

"Your wife?"

Nathan nodded.

"If you need to go, you can. I can handle this. It doesn't take the both of us."

Nathan said he didn't like the idea of Lindsay doing it alone.

"Because I'm a woman?"

Nathan didn't say anything.

"I didn't peg you for a sexist."

"I'm not."

"Don't lie to me, Sheriff. You didn't seem to have a problem with your deputies doing this on their own."

"If we're right about this, I want to be around when we take this guy down. Why should you get all the glory?"

"Oh please. A lie buried in the truth doth still a lie make."

Nathan smiled at her.

"I suppose this is a lame attempt at being chivalrous. Perhaps I should be flattered. Next you'll start addressing me as 'm'lady.'"

"He's been at it for almost two hours now."

"Patience, grasshopper."

Midnight came and went. Lindsay searched the plastic bag of snacks, came out with a Butterfinger, offered Nathan half.

"No thanks." He cranked the window down, lit a cigarette.

Lindsay opened the Butterfinger's wrapper, bit off a piece. "I hate eating out of boredom. It all goes to my ass."

"I didn't notice anything wrong with your ass."

"You're moving on from chivalry to flirtation?"

"Just stating facts."

"If I was your wife, you'd be in the doghouse by now. But thank you. I'll be truly saddened when you die of cancer."

"Don't say that. I've got a thing about cancer."

"Said the man as he pounded another nail into his coffin."

"Jesus, how long is he going to take?"

"They're thorough. Our guy's down time is usually only a few days, a week tops. I've tracked several serial killers that spent weeks or longer researching their victims. These guys end up knowing more about their victim's than even the victim's friends do."

Up ahead, they watched the Malibu's taillights come on. The car pulled away from the curb.

"Here we go," Nathan said, started the Caprice, and followed.

25

gibson & daniels

IT WAS MIDNIGHT when Matt Gibson and Dan Daniels decided to drive up to the lake. Both had joined the Crater Lake Sheriff's Department two years ago when there had been a call out for reserve deputies. Neither of them possessed prior law enforcement experience. Gibson was in charge of marketing at Crater Lake Bank; Daniels sold insurance.

Typically, they were utilized when there was a local sporting event. They would act as added security at some of the high school football and basketball games. During his two years in the reserves, Gibson had written several speeding tickets. The most action Daniels had seen was when he had responded to a car accident on Highway 6 that had involved a drunk driver. The intoxicated driver had walked away free of injury, the man he hit had suffered extensive head trauma. That man was currently a permanent resident of Chickasaw Memorial. He had slipped into a coma and never woken up. There had been a lot of blood, and Daniels had thrown up most of the Big Mac and fries he had devoured earlier onto the asphalt several feet away from where the two vehicles involved in the crash sat entangled in a sculpture of twisted metal and shattered glass.

Both men led humdrum existences. Their day jobs taxed them neither mentally nor physically, so it was always a joy when they were called in for duty. Separately, they each dreamed of being action heroes, of making a huge bust or bringing down some high-level criminal kingpin.

In two years, action had been at a serious minimum. But a badge was a badge and a gun was a gun, and whenever the opportunity arose to don said badge and said gun, they jumped on it.

It had been slow, even for a Monday night. If people didn't normally take to locking their doors and shutting their windows, they did now. There was never much foot traffic at night in Crater Lake, but tonight the world seemed to be theirs and theirs alone.

Gibson was driving. Daniels rode shotgun. The car bumped over the dirt road as they approached the lake. A sea of blackness stretched out before them, still and silent. They were flanked on the right by the steep embankment and the woods beyond.

"Think about it," Daniels said. "What's it been? A week now? Guy's overdue. What if, man, just what *if* he decides to make an appearance tonight? We could be the heroes. You know how much pussy we could get after that?"

"Pussy? You're shackled to one pussy, same as me."

Daniels glanced down at his hand, at the gold band on his left ring finger. "What I was saying was it would be there for the taking, not that I'm going to partake of it."

Gibson didn't share his partner's enthusiasm. The glory he didn't mind, but he didn't like the thought of running into a man that was capable of cutting off someone's head. Sheriff Murphy had filled them in during briefing, had provided them the grisly details that had been kept out of the papers.

"You heard the Sheriff," Gibson said. "They've got a suspect. He's staking out the Candlelight where this guy is supposed to be staying."

"Yeah, but what if it's not the guy?"

Gibson turned the spot on, aimed the beam at the lake as they moved along at a crawl. His window was down, the cool air coming off the lake.

"Creepy up here at night."

"Why are we here again?"

"This is where they found the first girl. Pulled her out of the lake." Daniels stabbed a finger toward the embankment, the row of trees at the top. "That Struthers girl they found in the woods, right up there somewhere. That's two out of three that happened around here. This is like his hunting ground."

"Maybe."

"You think of anything better to do?"

"I could eat."

"Christ. We just ate."

"When I get bored, I eat."

"You're serious?"

"You ever had one of the dogs from the Pump N' Save?"

"No."

"They're huge. Too big for the regular-sized buns. They start them on the little rotisserie thing around eleven, but the trick is, you wait until later, like around dinner time, and that's the best time to get one. They look a little shriveled from cooking so long, but they taste fucking great. I could eat them every day. Little ketchup, some spicy mustard...let's swing by. You need to try one. I'm buying."

"I'm not hungry."

"Come on, partner. You won't regret it."

Daniels stared out the window, watching the spotlight's beam bob over the lake. "Okay, tell you what. Let's finish driving around the lake. Then we hit the woods, do a quick drive by, and *then* we'll get one of your fucking hotdogs."

"Deal. You'll thank me."

"I bet."

They kept going around the lake, Gibson feeling better about life now that he knew what the immediate future held. He hoped they weren't sold out. It was late, maybe too late. What time did the Pump N' Save shut the rotisserie down? Maybe all the dogs were sold out. That happened occasionally. Wouldn't that be a shame, get there and find out there weren't any left. Maybe if that was the case, he could talk whoever was working the store into firing up the rotisserie and throwing a couple of dogs on. If it was that pimply kid with the long hair that he had shot the breeze with last time, there was a good chance. It wouldn't be quite the same seeing as how they would have to eat them fresh, and he preferred it when they had been cooking for hours, the casings all leathery and wrinkled. But hell, it was still better than nothing. With a little extra luck, they would have the packets of mayo and relish, and he could really load the fucker up.

It took twenty minutes to complete their circuit around the lake. They came back the way they had come, turning off at the fork where the alternate road hugged the woods. Gibson trained the light on the trees.

"Slow down a little," Daniels said.

"It's quiet out, man. Satisfied?"

"Just keep going."

"Do you really expect to –"

And then they heard it: A piercing scream that echoed out from the darkness.

"Did you hear that?"

"Bird. Probably a loon."

"Bullshit."

"Coyote maybe."

Gibson thought it hadn't sounded like a loon or a coyote at all, but he didn't like to dwell on the alternative.

"Just shut up and listen."

Gibson stopped the car, listened.

The sound came again, unmistakably a scream this time, and neither man could fool himself into believing that it had been made by an animal.

They burst out of the patrol car as another scream sounded from the woods. Daniels unholstered his Beretta; Gibson followed suit, heart pounding, bringing the pump-action shotgun with him as he tried to catch up with Daniels.

Another scream.

Not a loon.

Not a coyote.

Oh my God, Daniels thought. *That's a person.*

26

wrong man

IN FRONT OF them, the white Malibu suddenly sped up, turned fast, and Nathan knew then that they had been made.

"He's onto us," Lindsay said.

"No shit. What do you want me to do?"

"We're blown. Pull him over."

Nathan jammed his foot down on the accelerator pedal. The Caprice's V8 roared, and they were barreling forward, catching up to the Malibu. Nathan went to turn the sirens on, remembered he wasn't in his patrol car.

"There should be a strobe in the back seat," Nathan said.

Lindsay unbuckled, turned, leaned over between the front seats, searching the back for the strobe light. She found it, plugged the cord into the cigarette lighter, reached her arm out the window and affixed the strobe light to the car's roof. Flashing red light flooded the darkness.

The Malibu took a right, doubled back. Nathan got up close, the grill of the Caprice inches from the Malibu's rear bumper.

"This is it, we've got him."

The Malibu slowed, started doing the speed limit.

"What's he doing?"

They followed the Malibu, doing twenty-five now, the brake lights flashing intermittently, and pretty soon they were in front of the Candlelight again, the Malibu pulling into the rear lot and coming to a stop.

"What the hell?"

"Strange."

Nathan and Lindsay got out of the car, guns drawn, pointing them at the idling Malibu, Nathan yelling, "Get out of the vehicle! Slowly!"

The driver's door opened, a leg came out, followed by hands, arms in the air, as the giant exited the vehicle. He towered over them, saying nothing, Nathan moving in, reaching up to grab one of the raised arms, spinning the man around against the car, bringing the giant's beefy arm back, twisting it behind the giant's back, holstering his Glock when he saw Lindsay had him covered, and got out his cuffs, fastened the one around the giant's wrist, brought the other arm around, repeated the process.

Nathan did a quick pat search, located a wallet in the giant's back pocket, stepped back. He tossed the wallet over to Lindsay.

Lindsay said, "I've got him. Search the car."

Nathan searched the Malibu, found a black bag in the front seat, brought it out, unzipped it, began rummaging through it. "You were right," he said, holding up a compact camcorder. "He was doing his homework. We've got you now, buddy."

Nathan's heart was racing, his testicle throbbing, ready to explode from the pain.

The giant stood silent, watched them.

Lindsay opened the wallet, found the driver's license, a few wrinkled bills, and then, hidden behind the wallet, a business card. She slipped it out, read it, squinted, read it again, her face changing.

"What?"

She handed the card to Nathan. Nathan read it, looked up at the giant, to the card, back to the giant. "You're a private investigator?"

The giant nodded.

"You aren't licensed. Would have come up when we ran the background."

For the first time, the giant spoke. "I filed my application a week ago. Hasn't gone through yet."

"Is this how you get your victims to go with you? Show them a bogus business card? Then you kill them?"

"I haven't killed anyone, Officer."

"*Sheriff.*"

"I haven't killed anyone, Sheriff."

"Then what are you doing in Crater Lake?"

"I'm on a job. A domestic gig. Cheating spouse. I've been here doing surveillance the last three weeks. You can check with the motel."

"We already have. If you're an investigator, you should have given us a courtesy call, let us know you were going to be on the job."

"It's a small town, Sheriff. People talk. Word gets around. Listen, if you don't believe me, I can take you up to my room. All my notes are up there. You can call my client. He lives here in town. I've been holed up in this dump for three weeks, haven't found a damn thing. Was planning on letting my client know tomorrow morning that it was a bust, his wife seems to be on the up and up, and then I was going to give him my bill and blow town."

"If you're legit, why did you run?"

"I didn't. I saw someone was tailing me, I took off. You were in an unmarked. It wasn't until you lit up the cherry that I figured you were a cop, and by that time I had made up my mind to get back to the motel."

Nathan stared up at him, studying the giant's face. Lindsay motioned him over.

"What do you think?"

"I think I never liked this lead to begin with."

"You want me to cut him loose?"

"I didn't say that. Bring him in. He'll have to stay in lock-up overnight. We can verify his story in the morning, see if he's got an application pending. See if it all checks out."

"This is all one big cluster fuck."

Lindsay shrugged. "It happens."

"I wanted this to be it."

"So did I."

"Damn it."

"Just calm down. We've all been wrong before. We played a hunch, and it turned out we were wrong. See if he'll let us take a look in his room, give us his client info. We call the client, see if he corroborates Jones's story. Without any other evidence, that's the best we can do. Go on, do it. We'll take him in, then we'll call it a night. You can go be with your wife."

Nathan nodded, doing nothing to mask his disappointment. He went back to Jones, explained things, told him it would take some time to corroborate his story. Jones came peacefully, shuffled over to the Caprice, got into the back seat.

Nathan's crotch was on fire. As soon as he had Jones in lock up, he was going to swallow a handful of pills, hope they got him through the night, and first thing Tuesday morning he would call Kobayashi's office and make an appointment. He couldn't deal with the pain any longer.

"You okay?" Lindsay asked.

"I'm fine."

"Then I don't ever want to be fine."

Weary and defeated, Nathan managed to smile.

He watches from the window, the drapes parted slightly, standing next to the table, gazing down on the scene below.

Wrong man, he thinks.

A light blue car, strobe flashing on top. He sees them cuff the giant, talk a while, and soon the giant is getting into the blue car and they drive away.

He lets out a long breath. He wants to be hunting tonight. It's time. He feels it.

But they're close. *Too* close.

They're smart. He wonders if he has underestimated them. Still, they went after the wrong man. Sooner or later, he knew they would begin searching the motels, but usually it was after he was long gone. This time, they're quicker than usual. The Sheriff he recognizes, young but clever.

His work is almost done, which is good because he can't stay much longer. They're too close now.

He's been playing this game long enough to know you don't check in anywhere alone. It draws less attention. They always look for a loner first. Better to bring someone with you, at least temporarily, write it down on the card, so when the sheep with guns came knocking, it was never on his door.

The urge is back. He feels it growing more and more powerful, almost irresistible. It's close to the end, and he is closer than ever to catching the Elusive One, and this time he won't let it get away. They will have their confrontation, their epic battle.

He doesn't feel fear. That doesn't fall within the narrow scope of his emotions. He knows it can't go on like this forever, this constant cat and mouse chase, the moving around, from one town to the next, always staying one step behind.

Sometimes he wonders if he couldn't have arrived at this point sooner. Has he purposely prolonged things? It is a hard truth to face, but part of him knows that it's true, that, whether he wants to admit it or not, he enjoys it. And he doesn't want to think about what life would be like without the game. Before this, further back than he cares to remember, he was lost. Mary's little lamb. Without the chase, what else is there?

It's late. He should be hunting, but instead he is confined to his room because they have gotten closer. They won't catch him. They've been close before, but they've never caught up to him.

He thinks about the girl, the pressure it took to push the stake through her chest, to pierce her heart, her eyes wide as he watches the surprise, and next the life slowly draining out of them. He remembers torching her body, watching it burn, the smell of the flames melting her flesh.

Soon. He needs another soon.

Down below, things are quiet. He closes the drapes, sits at the table, brings out his mirror, stares at his reflection. He stares at it for a long time, staring into his own eyes as they stare back at him.

27

escaped

THE SCREAMS WERE louder, closer now.

Daniels followed the sound. Things would go silent for a second, and he would stop, listen, hoping it would pick up again because the woods were vast and without the screams to guide him he would be lost.

His heart was beating fast and he realized he was afraid. He had hoped for this moment, but now that it was upon him, now that it was coming true, he was scared. He could hear Gibson coming up behind him, breathing heavy, and when he glanced around, Gibson was there, carrying the shotgun.

"Call it in," Daniels said.

Gibson gawked at him.

Daniels repeated himself. "Call it in."

Gibson brought his chin to his chest, turned his head, keyed the mic, said, "This is Charlie Thirty-six, requesting back up…" He paused, looked at Daniels. "…screams coming from the woods. Coldfall Woods…send back up."

Another scream sliced into the silence and Daniels was moving again, following the sound, shining his flashlight into the darkness, dodging trees, underbrush, low-hanging branches.

Out of breath, Gibson said, "Shouldn't we wait for back up?"

"No time."

Daniels spotted something up ahead.

Two things, actually:

A white pile on the ground, and something hovering over it, something tall and dark, almost a shadow.

It wasn't long before he was able to identify the white mass as a person, a woman, sprawled on the ground, blood coming from a gash in her forehead.

And the dark shape…

A man.

At least he thought it was a man, tall, impossibly tall, his back to Daniels.

Daniels yelled, "*Freeze!*"

That wasn't what they taught you to say at the academy. Didn't tell you to say *"freeze."*

Stop. Don't move. Hands in the air. Any of those things, but they never taught you to say freeze because that was for actors playing cops in bad movies.

The woman screamed again. At first glance, Daniels thought she was naked, her bare flesh impossibly white against the dark ground. But she wasn't naked. Mostly, but he saw she was wearing white underwear and a white tank top, both articles of clothing were soiled from crawling around in the dirt.

"It's okay," Daniels said to the girl, and then he turned his attention to the tall figure. "Turn around, slowly. Face me."

Daniels judged the distance between himself and the tall figure to be roughly twenty feet, give or take. The tall figure only stood there, back to him, hovering over the woman on the ground.

Daniels was scared, could feel his dick and balls shriveling as they retreated inward. This was their killer, had to be, no doubt about it. He remembered the description Sheriff Murphy had given them during briefing. The suspect was described as tall, handsome...but Daniels couldn't see the man's face, only his back, dressed in black clothing.

Yes, he was afraid, but he sensed Gibson close behind him, shotgun raised and pointed, and he mustered courage from that.

"I'm only going to say it one more time. Turn around. *Now.*"

Twenty feet.

The distance from them and the killer.

Give or take.

Gibson yelled, "He said to turn around, Mister!"

And then the man started to turn...

...but it all happened so fast. He was standing there, twenty feet away, and in an instant, in the span of an eye blink, something lifted him off the ground, and then he was flying through the air, landing on his back, the wind going out of him.

Gibson didn't hesitate. He didn't know what was happening exactly, but his instincts were there, his reflexes acting on their own, and he pointed the shotgun, fired into the tall figure coming toward him.

Nothing happened. The blast silenced the world, and there was only the ringing in his ears, but the figure was still coming, his hands locking onto the shotgun, yanking it from Gibson's grasp, tossing it aside, and Gibson felt something hard and small and incredibly powerful strike his chest, at first thinking he had fucked up, fired the gun wrong, shot himself.

He fell backward, clutching at the wave of pain radiating through his chest. Broken. He knew it. Ribs caved in. He couldn't breathe. He sucked at the air, but something obstructed its path.

Then the figure was on him, straddling him, leaning in close, and something putrid blasted his nostrils. His eyes tried to focus, and he was looking into a face, only it wasn't a face, couldn't be…it was something awful…and the eyes.

He felt himself being hauled up, flipped over, his face grinding against dirt and leaves, a heavy weight resting on his back.

Something touched his neck. It hurt, but only for a moment, and then it became gentle, pleasant almost, and he knew he should be afraid, terrified, but there was a warmth moving over his body, and he enjoyed it, didn't want it to end.

Ten feet away, Daniels pulled himself to his knees, Beretta in hand, brought it up, took aim, sucked in a breath, held it, fired. His finger squeezed the trigger, kept squeezing, round after round, until the magazine was empty and there was only a dry click when he pulled on the trigger.

A cloud of smoke hovered in front of his vision, the smell of gun powder, his hearing gone, except for the incessant ringing. He was staring at the figure, had emptied ten rounds.

I hit him. I know I did. No way I missed from this distance.

But the figure was still there, bent over Gibson, its face close to Gibson's neck.

Daniels screamed, "Get off of him!" He couldn't hear the sound of his voice. It sounded far off, distant, masked by the ceaseless ringing.

He ejected the magazine, reached for his belt, unsnapped the flap of his magazine holder, brought out a fresh magazine, slid it in, racked the slide, aimed again.

The figure rose.

For a moment, Daniels could see its mouth, something long retracting into it like a turtle pulling its head into its shell.

Gibson raised his head, spit out dirt, turned his head so that he was looking at Daniels. His mouth moved, nothing at first, then the words came through a crooked smile. "Don't worry, buddy…it's okay…it's A-okay…it doesn't hurt…it feels good…it…feels…so…nice."

The figure's hands came down on either side of Gibson's head, made a quick twisting motion, and Gibson's face did a one-eighty, and, literally, he had eyes in the back of his head because his face was facing the same direction as his back, still wearing the crooked smile as his body slumped forward, hit the ground, eyes staring.

Daniels fired. He wasn't thinking of the woman. She was in close proximity, but he had tunnel vision now, just had to hope that a stray round didn't miss its mark and hit the woman.

"Die!" Daniels screamed. "Why won't you die!"

Firing. One, two, three…eight, nine, ten…the dry click again.

The figure rose to its feet as Daniels scrambled for his remaining magazine.

The woman screamed, kicking out with her feet, trying to distance herself from the tall figure standing before her.

The figure approached him.

Daniels fumbled with the magazine. In his mind, he could see Gibson smiling, face caked in dirt, saying, *Don't worry, buddy…it feels good…it…feels…so…nice.*

Frantically, he jammed the magazine home, yelled, "Fuck you!" and was firing again.

But the figure was gone. Just like that. Gone. Vanished into thin air.

Daniels crawled over to Gibson, checked for a pulse, found none, brought the palm of his hand down over Gibson's staring eyes, brushed them closed. For the rest of his life he would remember those eyes and that smile.

He moved over to the woman, grabbed her. She screamed, fought, kicked at him with her feet. He holstered his weapon, put his arms around her, hugging her tightly, saying, "He's gone. It's okay. He's gone now. You're going to be okay." He didn't know if that was true, but it worked. She ceased her struggling, went limp in his arms. Later, he wouldn't precisely recall whether he had held onto the woman because he was trying to soothe her, or if he had held on because he was trying to soothe himself.

Nathan was sliding the cell door closed when his radio squawked.

...this is Charlie Thirty-six, requesting back up...screams coming from the woods. Coldfall Woods...send back up...

Gibson.

Nathan heard it, but it didn't register immediately. He stared at Seymour Benton Jones through the bars, the man pacing at first, then sitting on the metal bench, staring at the floor.

...send backup...

Lindsay was fast. She had heard Nathan's radio go off, Gibson's frantic voice, and she was already heading out the door, Nathan hurrying to catch up.

They were in the Caprice, Nathan flooring it.

It was a five minute drive. Coldfall Woods was large and Gibson hadn't given them an exact location, but as he was coming around the bend on the narrow dirt road that hugged the south side of the woods, they spotted the idling patrol car, the cherries flashing, and Nathan pulled up behind it, jumped out of the car, Lindsay joining him.

Nathan was running, headed into the woods, on his radio now, "Charlie Thirty-six, this is Eagle One, do you read me?"

Silence.

He tried again, something garbled came across, but deep in the woods he thought he saw light, and he moved toward it.

His Glock was drawn, flashlight out, beam piercing the darkness. Lindsay was beside him. It was all happening too fast.

"See it?" Nathan asked.

"I see it."

Lindsay kept pace with him, younger and obviously in better shape, she hadn't broken a sweat, wasn't struggling to breathe. Nathan's testicle felt like a ticking bomb ready to explode any second, and he winced as he ran, pumping his legs, ignoring the pain, trying again to get Gibson or Daniels on the radio.

The light was closer, a stationary glow. It would disappear and reappear as Nathan dodged around trees, and then the light of his flashlight caught something, not far now, closing in, and he saw the white against the ground, and then something small and shiny reflecting the light, Nathan realizing it was a badge, the gold star they all wore pinned to their left breast.

It was Daniels. He wasn't alone. A half-naked woman was sprawled in his lap. Young, milky white, blood flowing from a gash in her forehead.

Daniels was in bad shape. Even from a distance, his face was contorted in pain, Nathan hearing the sickly wheezing sound as Daniels breathed in and out.

Daniels's arm came up and his Beretta came with it, aiming it at Nathan.

Nathan yelled, "Wait! It's us, the good guys."

It took a moment to register, and briefly Nathan thought he was going to be shot by one of his own deputies, only then realizing he hadn't worn his bulletproof vest because lately temperatures had been climbing up into the nineties, a real heat wave, and the vest made him sweat, tended to chafe his skin after a while. Not once in the six years he had been in law enforcement had anyone taken a shot at him, let alone pulled a gun.

Slowly, Daniels lowered the Beretta, sank lower, said, "Oh God, Sheriff, I thought you were him, I thought he came back, and he was going to finish us off."

Nathan ran to them, fell to his knees, radioed dispatch, requested medical support.

"How bad is it?"

"Feels like I'm dying," Daniels said, but he slid out from under the woman, tried to get to his feet, faltered, Nathan grabbing his arm, helping him to stand. "Couple of broken ribs for sure. Maybe worse."

Nathan helped the woman next. She hadn't screamed again since Daniels had held her, but her eyes were wild when Nathan bent down, touched her, tried to help her up.

"She's in shock, and I don't blame her."

"It's okay," Nathan said, touching her arm gently. "We're here now."

She turned her face toward him, her eyes darting, the blood running down her forehead.

"She's got an injury on the back of her neck too," Daniels said. "Not sure from what, but it's gushing pretty good."

"Let me see," Lindsay said, stepping around. "Do you mind?"

The woman nodded.

Lindsay examined the back of the woman's neck, her eyes going to Nathan, telling him to come over, see for himself. Nathan did, saw the wound, the inverted Y enclosed by a circle, blood flowing freely now.

"It's our guy," Lindsay said softly.

"Gibson," Daniels said, pointing, and Nathan's eyes followed the man's pointing finger to the body that lay face down on the ground, the head cocked to the side at a strange angle, blood spreading out, staining the tan collared shirt. "Dead."

Nathan stared. He looked to the woman, then to Daniels. "Can you make it back to the road? I've got a first aid kit in the trunk."

"You can't leave him out here like an animal."

"I'll take care of it," Nathan said. "Head for the car."

The woman looked at Daniels, her savior, the only one she was willing to trust right now, and Daniels nodded, hooked an arm around her waist, and they hobbled toward the road like a pair of newlywed cripples.

Nathan approached the body, knelt down, Lindsay behind him.

"Same mark on the neck," Lindsay said.

Gibson's neck was swollen and discolored.

"We need to question her."

"We will. Daniels is right, we can't leave him here, not like this."

Sirens wailed in the distance.

Nathan slid his arms under Gibson's still form, lifted the dead weight, the pain in his testicle flaring to the point that he thought he might collapse, but he gritted his teeth, determined, carrying Gibson's body out of the woods.

By the time they reached the road, the ambulances had arrived. The paramedics tried tending to the woman, but she wouldn't let go of Daniels, they were inseparable, and he soothed her, told her it was okay, he'd go with her, and once she was loaded into the back of the ambulance, Daniels climbed in after her, and then one of the ambulances pulled away, leaving only the one, and the remaining paramedics brought out the gurney, Nathan depositing Gibson's body onto it as gently as he could.

The paramedics loaded the gurney onto the ambulance, departed, leaving only Nathan and Lindsay now.

"I'm sorry, Sheriff," she said. "I'm sure he was a good man."

Nathan watched the ambulances disappear into the distance, walked over to the Caprice, leaned in through the open window, grabbed his pack of cigarettes and lit one.

"Did he have a family?"

Nathan nodded.

The pain was bad. He let it envelope him, fold over him. He knew he should be feeling sorrow, guilt, but the only thing he felt now was anger. A crazy, unbridled rage that had him seething. He had always taken pride in being level-headed, not letting his emotions cloud his judgment, but things were different now. Not once had he acted outside the law, undermined his ethical obligations…

"When we catch this guy, and we *will* catch him, I promise you that, we're not going to take him alive. However it goes down, he doesn't make it out of Crater Lake still breathing."

For a while, Lindsay said nothing. She didn't doubt the sincerity of Nathan's words. It was personal for him now, she knew that, and although she didn't agree with him, she could understand.

"Come on," she said. "Get in the car. I'll drive."

28

the tall man

It was past three in the morning when they reached Alton, entered Chickasaw Memorial through the ER entrance.

They spoke to Daniels first. He had been fixed up, given Vicodin for the pain. Three busted ribs and a fractured collar bone. But he couldn't rest, not after what had happened to Gibson. He asked about Gibson, Nathan said he wasn't sure, but guessed that Gibson's body had been taken to the morgue.

The man was shaken. Who could blame him? Nathan said they could wait, come back later, but Daniels shook his head, said he was ready to talk, needed to talk, and things were starting to get blurry, better if he told them everything while he still remembered it.

Daniels started his story from the point he had suggested they drive up to the lake, look around, seeing as how two of the murders had happened around that area. He talked about he and Gibson's conversation, about how Gibson had been in love with these hot dogs from the Pump N' Save, had gone on and on about them. "We were going to stop by the Pump N' Save," Daniels said. "That was the plan anyway. Do a quick drive-by of the woods and then hit the Pump N' Save. Gibson thought maybe the kid working the store would be willing to throw some on the little rotisserie thing they cook them in. I'll have to try one. Gibson swore by them."

Daniels paused, shook his head again, picked up where he left off, telling them about driving up by the woods, following the curving dirt road, and how that was when they heard the woman scream.

"Like Jamie Lee Curtis," Daniels said. "You remember those old slasher flicks she used to be in when she was younger? They called her the Scream Queen. That was what we heard, only worse."

Then he was telling them about finding the woman, the tall figure standing over her, how he had told the guy to freeze. "That's what I said. *Freeze!* Can you believe that – like I was in a stupid cop movie. It took some time to get his attention, but then he was on us. So fast. I didn't even have time to blink. Twenty feet away, easy, and I didn't even see him coming. He knocked me down, and then he went after Gibson, did something *to* him, had some kind of weapon or something, and just kind of plunged it into the back of Gibson's neck. It looked like it hurt, but Gibson smiled about it, said he liked it. It was weird. Maybe I was hallucinating by that point – it's fuzzy, like I said."

"Take your time," Nathan said. "There's no rush."

Daniels nodded. "I unloaded on the guy. The whole magazine. I panicked, I'll admit that, but he wasn't far away, so I know I must have hit him at least a couple of times, but it was like throwing peanuts at an elephant. Didn't faze him at all. That's when he kind of lifted Gibson up, twisted his head around, broke his neck. Like it was nothing. He was strong, Sheriff. Damn strong."

Daniels told them how he had unloaded another magazine on the guy, loading a third, and then how the guy had just up and vanished like a magician, like Houdini, there one minute, gone the next.

"I was busted up, but I checked on Gibson. Dead. Then I crawled over to the woman. Is she all right? Do you know?"

Lindsay said, "She's stable. Resting now. Because of you, she's alive."

"I'm tired. Can I go home now?"

"Why don't you get some rest? Sounds like they want to keep you overnight," Nathan said. "If everything looks good, they'll let you go in the morning."

"My wife."

Nathan's eyes flicked to the phone on the small table next to the hospital bed. "Give her a call."

"She'll go nuts. I know it. Waking her up at this hour."

"You should call anyway," Lindsay said. "She'd want to know."

Daniels thought about it, eyes fluttering closed, opening again.

"You're going to be okay," Nathan said. "You saved that woman's life."

And what else was there to say? Nathan stood there, silent. Finally, it was Daniels who spoke. "I almost had him, Sheriff."

"Yeah, you did. And we're going to get him. I promise you that."

"I think I'll lie down now."

He sank back into the bed, closed his eyes. He was out within seconds, Lindsay saying, "The shock hasn't worn off yet. Probably won't for a while."

"He'll be okay." He recalled telling Carl the same thing about Iverson after Iverson had found what was left of Kathleen Black's body.

"We should interview the woman."

"Think she's in any shape?"

"If we leave it too long, she'll forget things."

Nathan nodded, and they went to the front desk, asked after the woman.

The nurse stared at them. "Now?"

Lindsay said, "Now, yes."

"She's delirious."

"She's conscious."

"Barely. We have her sedated."

"But she's awake?"

"She was last time I checked."

"Then we'd like to speak with her."

The nurse went on staring.

"Please. It's important."

The nurse sighed, showed them down the hall, entered a room.

The woman was lying on the bed with her eyes closed. She was hooked up to a monitor. The gash in her forehead had been stitched, looking like a child's drawing of a centipede.

The woman opened her eyes as they entered the room. She was calmer now, a sedate version of the frenzied woman he had first set eyes on in the woods. She turned her head without lifting it, gazed at them.

The nurse, the look on her face saying she still thought this was a terrible idea, left the room, but not before she warned them that she would personally throw them out of the hospital if they upset her patient.

Nathan and Lindsay approached the hospital bed.

On the ride over in the ambulance, after some of the initial shock had worn off, the woman had identified herself as Marla Waggener. She was twenty-five, single, and worked as a dental hygienist.

Nathan introduced himself, then Lindsay, asked if Marla felt up to answering a few questions. She was weak, tired, scared, but she said she would do her best. She knew they had given her sedatives, and the pain was mostly gone, but they were also making her sleepy.

"We'll make it as quick as we can," Lindsay said.

Nathan confirmed the information the woman had given to hospital staff. Name, age, address.

"Do you remember what happened?"

"Some of it. It's fuzzy."

Same thing Daniels said, Nathan thought.

"Do you remember how you ended up in the woods?"

She shook her head.

"That last thing I remember," she said, "was sitting in my living room, watching TV. I remember because there was nothing on, not that late on a Monday night."

"Do you remember around what time this was?"

"Ten maybe. A little later. Usually I'm in bed by ten-thirty or so, I have to be to work at eight in the morning, but I didn't feel tired. I heated up leftovers, ate them on the couch while I was looking for something to watch."

"All right. Do you remember what happened next?"

She was silent for a moment, closed her eyes, thought about it.

"Someone rang the doorbell."

"And this was a little after ten?"

"Yes. I had finished eating, was getting ready to go to bed. There was nothing on anyway. I had already showered and was in my pajamas. I remember the doorbell ringing and I panicked at first, because I was in my underwear, and I never get visitors that late at night, not unless I'm expecting them."

"The doorbell rings. You answer it?"

"Not right away. First, I ran to the bedroom and put on my robe. *Then* I answered the door."

"Who was it?"

"A man."

"Did you recognize him?"

"No. I'd never seen him before in my life."

"What did he look like?"

"He was tall. Really tall. I'm five-six and he towered over me, so I guess he must've been at least six-four, taller maybe."

"What about his features? Can you describe them?"

"Handsome. Not GQ handsome, not like some young punk. He was older."

"How old?"

"I'm not sure."

"Just approximately."

"I don't know. Forty? But a young forty. And he was thin. Not like puny thin, because he was big, wide shoulders, but he looked like he kept in shape. And his eyes…"

"What about his eyes?"

The handsome stranger, Nathan thought, remembering Kathleen Black, the stranger her friends claimed she had met in the bar.

"They were weird."

"Weird how?" Lindsay asked.

"It's hard to explain. They were dark, almost black. At least they looked black, but I only had the table lamp on, so it was kind of dark. But I couldn't take my eyes off them. It's like they drew you in and you had to keep looking into them."

"What did he want?"

"He said his car was broken down. Asked if he could use my phone."

"Did you let him?"

"Not at first. I'm not stupid. I know enough not to let a strange man into my home, especially not at that hour, but like I said, there was something about his eyes. They hypnotized me. And he didn't look dangerous. So I said sure, come on in."

"Then?"

"Then...nothing. I don't remember after that. Just that I woke up in the woods and he was there, doing something to me."

"Doing what?"

"He was on top of me."

"Were you raped?" Lindsay asked.

"No. Well, at least I don't think so. That's the funny thing. I wasn't afraid, at least not right away. For some reason I felt safe. But then he pinned me down, turned me onto my stomach, and that's when I started getting scared. I couldn't think straight, I think he might have drugged me or something, because my head was swimming. I struggled, tried to kick him off, but he was strong, very strong. I couldn't get away. That's when I screamed. I screamed at the top of my lungs, again and again. He pushed my face down, and I got dirt in my mouth, and then I felt something touch the back of my neck. It hurt at first, like when you go to get a shot and they stick you with the needle, but then it was okay again, and I felt warm all over. I could feel something on the back of my neck, and I remember thinking, 'What's he doing? Is he kissing me,' because it felt like that's what he was doing. And it felt nice. Like I didn't have a care in the world."

"Did he have a weapon?"

"Not that I saw. He didn't threaten me. He didn't talk after that either. After a minute – I don't know how long it was – he let me up, and that's when I remembered where I was, and that funny feeling went away and I screamed again. That's when the two cops showed up."

"What do you mean he let you up?"

"Just what I said."

Her eyes fluttered, closed, reopened.

"When he was finished, when that pleasant feeling wore off, he let me go."

"He told you to go?"

"Not in so many words. No words, actually. But he stood up, and he didn't act like he was going to stop me from getting away."

She was drifting off now, in and out, struggling to remain conscious. "They gave me stuff," she said apologetically, and then she mumbled something, Nathan glancing at Lindsay, nodding, deciding they were done, just in time as it turned out, because the overly protective nurse was back in the doorway, saying she needed to check on her patient.

Nathan thanked her. They excused themselves, exited the hospital, walked back to the blue Caprice.

"What did you make of that?"

"Which part?"

"About the killer letting her go?"

"Delusional maybe?"

Nathan said, "Maybe. But it fits."

"Fits how?"

"Carl explained his theory about this guy. That he's a split personality. Thinks he's both a vampire and a vampire hunter, or at least he plays the role of the vampire because it's one step toward fulfilling his fantasy that vampires are real and that he hunts them. This thing he does to them – whatever device he uses to drain their blood, maybe that's what he was doing to her, draining her blood, and once he was finished he was okay with letting her go because he wouldn't kill her immediately."

"I think I see where you're going," Lindsay said. "He let her live, would have let her escape so that he could fulfill the other half of his fantasy. The actual hunting of vampires."

"Yeah, makes sense, doesn't it?"

"I would agree that it fits the theory."

"You don't buy it?"

Lindsay opened the passenger door, got into the car. Nathan sat down in the driver's seat, brought out his smokes, lit one. His testicle throbbed. The pain was worse now, but he bit it back, reminding himself that in the morning (a few hours from now actually) he needed to call Kobayashi's office, schedule that appointment.

"It doesn't quite jive with everything we know about serial killers. Usually, they're organized, and they follow a strict set of rules. They can keep their fantasies in check enough to avoid being caught. But this would take the cake. This unsub, if he could stalk and capture his victims, and then release them – it shows a remarkable amount of self-control. When they're acting out the fantasy, that's when they have the greatest chance of slipping up, of letting their urges take over. If what you're saying is true, then our guy has a large degree of self-discipline. Almost too much to be believable."

"It's out there, but who's to say it isn't possible?"

"You're forgetting, it also puts them at risk. They're most vulnerable when they're attempting to snag their next victim. That's when they're in greatest jeopardy of being apprehended, or having someone witness the abduction. So taking the victim, letting them go, and then putting himself out there again…"

"I can't think of anything better."

"Maybe I'm missing something. I haven't slept in twenty-four hours. My brain is fried. Pretty soon I'll be seeing double."

"Come on, I'll take you back to the motel. You can catch up on your beauty rest. I'll even check to make sure there aren't any monsters hiding under the bed."

29

office visit

FUNNY, THE WAY things sometimes got stuck in your head and wouldn't let go.

Pretty soon, I'll be seeing double.

Nathan dropped Lindsay off at the motel. She said she'd try to get four hours of sleep and then check in. Nathan promised to notify her if anything came up in the meantime.

He was groggy, ready to pass out despite the pain in his testicle, but the thought remained in his head.

Pretty soon...

...I'll be seeing double.

Double. Two.

What if there were two of them? A team effort.

How likely was that?

Not very likely, Nathan thought as he pulled up in front of the station.

Historically, he knew there had been cases of killers working in pairs, but it was usually the exception rather than the rule. There was no indication that that was what they were dealing with here, two killers, each of them fulfilling one half of a larger fantasy.

Still…the idea had snagged itself in the net of his tired brain, wriggled and squirmed, tried to release itself, but remained trapped there.

Inside the Sheriff's Office, Carl was already waiting, standing in front of the holding cell, staring in at Seymour Benton Jones.

Carl looked at Nathan, took in the disheveled appearance, said, "You better start by filling me in. Looks like I might have missed something."

Nathan gestured for Carl to follow, and they went back to Nathan's office. Nathan told him about the events that had transpired the night before. About Seymour Benton Jones, about the woman in the woods, the handsome stranger, about Gibson and Daniels, ended the story with how he had only minutes ago dropped Lindsay Trujillo off at her motel.

At first, Carl didn't have any words. But he had a million questions. News of Gibson's death stunned him, made things real, and he could only imagine the earful he was going to get from Carol once word got around that an officer had been killed. Carol wasn't a huge fan of Carl's line of work, had been badgering him to find something else for a while now, something less dangerous and with better hours. Carl had always maintained that police work wasn't all that dangerous, at least not in towns like Crater Lake, just look at the data. Odds were more in favor of him dying in a plane crash on his way to Disneyland than being killed in the line of duty. So she had acquiesced, but the argument came up now and again, more frequently given recent events. And now that Gibson was dead, Carl thought she might stand all the taller on her soapbox.

"Jones isn't our guy?"

"Doesn't look like it, but I want to check him out anyway, see if what he's telling us holds up. If it does…"

"He can't be the guy, can he? Not if you had him under surveillance all night. Jesus, we were barking up the wrong tree."

"Do it this morning, first thing. I don't want to hold him any longer than we have to."

"You look like shit, buddy."

"I feel like it too."

"If you want to check out, go for it. I can hold down the fort."

Nathan nodded appreciatively, said he planned on doing exactly that, that maybe he'd get his report written before going home, and then there was the matter of telling Gibson's wife.

"I can handle it."

Nathan said no, he should be the one to do it, he was the captain of the ship, and if the ship was going down, he needed to go down with it.

But the truth was, he didn't want to handle it, didn't even want to contemplate it at the moment. Only it needed to be done, and, after all, hadn't he gotten enough practice lately? In his mind, he saw the faces of Rick and Cheryl Struthers, of Jack and Audra Black. And soon he would have to face Patricia Gibson, Matt's wife, probably on her doorstep, not wanting to make eye contact as she broke down. But this time there would be no support, no one to catch her if she fell. Gibson was young, and he and Patricia could still have been considered newlyweds.

"You look like shit," Carl repeated.

"I'm going home."

"Might wanna freshen up first."

Nathan stared at him, confused.

"You smell like an ashtray."

By the time he left the station, it was five after seven, a little under an hour until he could ring Kobayashi's office.

Jess was in the baby's room when he got home, seated in the glider, a book open in her lap. She hadn't slept well the night before, but she didn't dwell on that, instead appraised her husband's appearance, immediately sensing that things weren't entirely right in the world.

"Rough night?"

"The roughest."

"Want to talk about it?"

He didn't want to talk about it and shook his head to say so, but then he was talking, telling Jess about the surveillance, how it had been a bust, and then about Marla Waggener and, finally, about Gibson being dead.

"*Matt* Gibson?"

She had worked with Matt Gibson at the bank. Gibson had been in charge of marketing, so their paths hadn't crossed often, but Crater Lake Bank was small, and she had seen him on a routine basis, at least until she had cut her hours down to part-time.

"How?"

Nathan didn't want to give her the nasty details, just said that they had an altercation with the killer, that Gibson and Daniels had been heroes, had saved a woman's life. He omitted the part about Marla Waggener telling them that the killer had, inexplicably, set her free.

Jess came to him then, tears in her eyes, hugging him, burying her face in his chest, and his first thought was that she would smell the cigarette smoke on his clothes and would confront him with it. But if she noticed, she didn't say, just continued to hug him, sobbing.

When she pulled away, she stared at him and said, "Are you all right? You didn't get hurt?"

"I'm fine. Physically, anyway."

"Sleep. No argument."

She led him to their bedroom, began unbutton his shirt, undoing his belt, undressing him until he was down to his boxer briefs, and then she took his hand, led him to the bed, put her hands against his chest, applied pressure.

Nathan obeyed, but then the pain in his testicle flared and he grimaced, and Jess asked him what was wrong, was she sure he wasn't hurt, and that was when he came clean, at least about the pain, told her it hadn't gone away after all this time, was getting worse, and he had finally come to the conclusion that she had been right, he needed to see Kobayashi.

"His office opens in half an hour. I should stay awake until then."

"Nonsense," Jess said, forcing him down, shoving the pillow under his head. "I'm perfectly capable of making a phone call. I'll see if he can get you in today. I'll bypass the receptionist and talk directly to his nurse. She's good about squeezing people in at the last minute."

He listened to her go on, but he was fading fast. She kissed his forehead, pulled the comforter over him. For Nathan those details were already part of a dream that he wouldn't remember later.

He woke, startled, covered in sweat.

1:45 P.M., according to the clock on the nightstand next to the bed.

Nathan wiped sweat from his forehead. It had been a nightmare, but already he couldn't remember much of it. Jess had been there. The two of them in the woods. And Gibson, he remembered Gibson, talking to them about something, but then the handsome stranger had interrupted them, coming out of the shadows, tall, tall as a giant from a fairy tale, and the stranger's eyes burned red, and when he smiled, his mouth had been lined with rows of pointed teeth, thin needles made for extracting blood.

Upon seeing the stranger, Gibson had fallen dead. As far as Nathan could remember, the stranger hadn't touched him, but Gibson's eyes had gone wide, and he had pitched forward face first into the ground. He raised his head a few inches and it was covered in dirt, but he was smiling, saying, "It feels good. It feels so nice."

Then the stranger had approached them, ignoring Nathan, it was Jess he was after, and Nathan had stood in front of her, shielding her, going for his weapon, but discovering that his Glock wasn't in its holster. In its place, his hand brushed sanded wood, a narrow cylinder at least a foot long, and when he pulled it from the holster, he saw that the tip had been fashioned into a fine point.

"What am I supposed to do?"

"Stab him," Jess had said. "Stake him through the heart. That's how you stop him. That's how you kill a vampire. Aim for the heart, straight through the heart."

And Nathan had tried. Had raised the stake above his head, brought it down at an angle, going for the stranger's chest, but the stranger had batted him aside and come after Jess. Jess had screamed, hands on her stomach, protecting it, as the stranger came closer. "Not my baby," she had screamed. Do something, Nathan. *Please!* Don't let him hurt the baby!"

There had been an audience; hovering on the fuzzy border of the nightmare, standing in a semi-circle. Nathan recognized them. Rebecca Struthers, Kathleen Black, and, finally, the girl in the mask. She was thin and nude and still wearing the mask.

Nathan came forward with the wooden stake again, plunging downward with it, and again he was batted aside like he was nothing.

And now the stranger was on Jess, had her pinned to the ground, and Jess was screaming as the stranger raked long fingers over her exposed stomach.

Behind him, Gibson was still smiling, saying, "Don't worry, Sheriff. It only stings in the beginning. After that, it's smooth sailing. Doesn't hurt at all. In fact, it feels nice, like you're riding on the ocean."

Nathan glanced at Jess. The stranger's fingers were gliding down her stomach, heading over the curve and then down it, but now they were drawing blood and then it was Nathan's turn to scream. Jess ceased her screaming, and was smiling now. "He's right," she said. "It isn't that bad at all. It only tickles a little. Why can't *you* make me feel like this?" The blood was pouring out of her stomach now, the stranger's fingers making deep grooves in her flesh, like prison bars, and then they expanded, and he heard crying, the choked wails of a child.

It was at this point that he had woken up.

Next to the clock, was a small square of paper. A note from Jess, explaining how she had gone out for groceries, and that she had managed to get him in to see Kobayashi. The appointment was at two-thirty.

P.S. – I'll be back before that in case you want me to go with you.

He sat up in bed, stayed that way for a while. For a second, he thought he was pain free, that maybe it had gone away on its own, but once he stood up and was headed for the bathroom, the pain started to come back.

Nathan heard the front door open; Jess arriving home from her trip to the grocery store. She was struggling with several plastic bags of groceries, and Nathan took them from her, carried them to the kitchen, went outside for the rest as Jess worked at putting them away.

"Did you see my note?"

"I saw."

"And?"

"And what?"

"Did you want me to come with you?"

"You don't have to."

"I don't mind."

"I think I'm going to go solo on this one."

"So you don't want me to come?"

"It'll be embarrassing."

"I've seen your junk before."

"But you haven't ever seen another man play with my junk before. It's awkward enough to have a grown man play with my balls, you being there would only make it weirder."

"And my recent office visits have been any better? You've come to all of those."

"I know. I'd just like to do this on my own."

"You better get going then."

Silence after that. He helped her to finish putting away the groceries, knowing that she wasn't thrilled with his decision to go alone, but it wasn't enough to make him change his mind.

On the way to Kobayashi's office, he phoned Carl, and Carl gave him an update on what they had come up with on Seymour Benton Jones.

Jones's story checked out. He had submitted an application, along with the necessary fees, to the Iowa Department of Public Safety. The application was still pending. Jones had also given them the name of his client, and Carl had followed up on that as well.

"Cut him loose," Nathan said.

"Did it an hour ago. I also talked to Gibson's wife."

"I said I'd handle it."

"I didn't have much of a choice. They released Daniels earlier this morning and, seeing how he and Gibson were great friends and all, he went straight to Patricia, gave her the news. I know it isn't what you wanted, but since he's close with the family, probably didn't hurt for him to be the one to tell her."

"What about the girl?"

"As far as I know, Chickasaw Memorial's holding onto her for the time being."

"Back to square one."

"Shit, I know."

"Lindsay been in?"

"Haven't heard from her. You comin' in soon?"

"Give me an hour. I've got an appointment."

"Finally bit the bullet. I just thought of a good pun, but I'll save it."

"Thanks."

"Hey Nate?"

"Yeah?"

"I hope it isn't cancer."

Carl was still laughing when Nathan hung up on him.

After he checked in, Nathan sat down, grabbed the copy of Men's Health from one of the waiting room tables, got a third of the way through it before a nurse called him to the back, where she weighed him, showed him to an examination room, confirmed a few details, listened as he explained his symptoms.

Kobayashi arrived five minutes later, a thin Asian man with neatly combed dark hair and glasses. His English was decent, but he had an accent, and occasionally he would stumble while searching for the correct word. He pulled his stool up close to Nathan, attentive as Nathan explained his symptoms again. Kobayashi nodded, thought about it, politely asked if Nathan would mind him taking a look.

Earlier, the pain had been fierce, but, as was usual when an illness became serious enough to warrant an office visit, it had started to subside by the time he had arrived at the clinic. It often worked that way. Nathan thought maybe it was the fear that always caused him to start feeling a bit better when he actually went through with it. Adrenaline or the work of some other pain-killing chemical reaction kicking in at the last minute, causing him to question the necessity of his visit.

The pain was tolerable now as he unbuttoned his pants and slid them down to his knees. His underwear followed, and it wasn't a moment before Kobayashi was feeling him up with his cold, small hands, fondling the dangling part of his manhood.

Nathan had expected pain, but there wasn't any. Kobayashi asked Nathan to turn his head and cough, repeated the request, checking for hernias. Finally, he nodded and scooted back on the stool.

"I do feel something there. A mass of some kind."

"A lump?"

"A mass."

"Cancer?"

"I don't think it's cancer."

Nathan asked again, thinking he had heard wrong.

"Your testicles appear normal. The left one is slightly enlarged. I'll be right back."

Nathan was left standing there with his pants at his ankles. He pulled them up, sat back down. Kobayashi returned holding a sheet of paper, which he handed to Nathan, explaining how he thought what Nathan had was something called a varicocele.

"This is when veins in your scrotum become enlarged. You can think of it like a varicose vein."

Nathan listened as Kobayashi explained how usually when a varicocele occurred, it occurred in the left testicle. How it could cause tremendous pain, but usually resolved on its own.

Kobayashi listed off the associated symptoms: aching pain in the scrotum, feeling of heaviness in the testicle, palpitation of the area can feel like you're holding onto a bag of worms.

"Is it serious?"

Kobayashi shook his head. "Worst case, surgery."

Outpatient. Minimally Invasive. *If* it came down to that.

Kobayashi told him to monitor it for another week. If it didn't go away, Nathan should come back and be referred to a urologist. He prescribed eight hundred milligram ibuprofen. "As needed for pain."

Nathan left Kobayashi's office feeling relieved. The pain started to come back the second he walked out to his car, but he drove to the pharmacy, picked up his prescription, called Jess, tried to explain as best he could, and then headed to the station.

part

III

the elusive one

30

new recruit

"HE GAVE US high praise on our biscuits and gravy," Carl said. "Said it beat the motel's complimentary breakfast any day."

This was the message Seymour Jones had asked to be passed onto Nathan at the time of his release.

"Doesn't look like he's gonna hold a grudge. Not that he's gonna join your fan club anytime soon."

Nathan said he could live with that.

"And another thing. A favor, actually. If you're gonna smoke, do it in the locker room, would ya? I spent part of the morning Lysoling the entire damn place because it smelled like one of those hookah bars they've got in the city."

"Carol's really rubbing off on you."

Carl rolled his eyes, followed Nathan back to his office where a stack of papers waited.

"That's all of it," Carl said. "Once I sent Jones packing, it was quiet, so I caught up on some of the reports."

"What would I do without you?"

"Probably go begging Talley to take his job back."

"I'd attempt seppuku first."

"Might not be such a bad idea."

"Thanks for the vote of confidence."

"What I mean is, maybe recruiting Talley wouldn't be such a bad idea. We're low on manpower, and with Gibson gone… maybe we could use the help."

Nathan glanced up from the stack of papers.

"Listen, I know the thought alone leaves a bad taste in your mouth, but think about it. He's got the experience, knows the area. Could draw you a map in his sleep. Still knows how to handle himself. It might be a good thing, you reaching out to him, see if you two can bury the hatchet. You don't have to like him, but this might be a good time to swallow your pride."

"And it could just as easily blow up in my face."

Carl nodded.

"Say I did. What makes you think he'd agree to it? He'd rather see me squirm."

"I didn't say it'd be pretty. I wouldn't have brought it up if we weren't facing a worst case scenario."

"Suicide might better."

Carl sat down in one of the chairs, leaned forward, rested his elbows on Nathan's desk. "Before you do that," he said. "I wanna pass an idea by you."

He still thought it was a bad idea as he took the muddy road that curved around to the far side of the lake.

Nathan had driven to Talley's house first, and when no one answered, he decided to check the cabin Talley owned out by the lake. It was a modest place, small, set back in the woods. About a hundred yards separated the cabin's front door from the rocky beach.

Arriving there, Nathan could understand why Talley had fallen in love with the place. It was quiet, secluded, and the scenery wasn't bad either.

Talley had purchased the rundown property years ago, not long after he had first been elected sheriff, a kind of celebratory gift to himself. Word around town was that Talley had spent the interim paying the mortgage down and now he owned the place outright.

Nathan parked his cruiser at the base of the dirt driveway, walked the rest of the way on foot. Talley had sunk a small fortune into renovating the place; had done a lot of the work with his own two hands. He had added an addition to the side of the house, built a deck in the back, and there was a large aluminum shed next to the garage where he stored his boat during the winter months.

Nathan tried the door first. Knocked and waited.

Talley was still active in the community, always busy networking, and Nathan had little doubt that come next election, he would be again throwing his hat into the ring. But on a day like this there was a better chance that Talley would be out fishing.

Nathan descended the steps, took the meandering path through the woods, walking the hundred yards until he reached the small outcrop of rock and mud that served as a poor excuse for a beach. His boots made sucking sounds as he moved close to the water, shading his eyes with his forearm as he scanned the lake.

He spotted a boat at about the halfway point between the north and south edges of the lake. It bobbed gently, and he could see a man wearing a wide-brimmed hat slouched down in one of the two chairs, a fishing pole sprouting at a forty-five degree angle from between his legs.

The hat was tilted forward, hiding the man's face. Maybe the fish weren't biting and he was dozing while he waited for a nibble.

Nathan raised his arms, waved them back and forth. It didn't do any good. Talley wasn't paying attention.

He cupped his hands around his mouth, yelled "Talley," and when that didn't work, he shouted again, louder this time.

The man in the boat stirred, hand reaching up to the remove the hat. Nathan took the opportunity to shout again, and this time Talley sat up, cocked his head, and Nathan yelled a final time. Talley's face swiveled in his direction, and Nathan waved his arms back and forth in the air. Nathan heard the faraway sound of the boat's engine whining to life. It began to move, slicing forward and curving around until it was headed toward land.

Talley cut the boat's engine when he was a few feet out, coasted to shore, and Nathan helped him drag it onto the beach and anchor it.

"Sheriff Murphy," Talley said in an overly jovial voice. "This is quite a surprise, quite a surprise. What brings you here?"

Talley's tone grated on Nathan's nerves. Nathan told him, stumbling a bit, not sure how to put it into words. This was Carl's idea, not his, and his stomach churned as he asked Talley if there would be any chance that he would be interested in coming on board, nothing big, just to beef up their man power until this thing was over.

When he finished, Talley stared at him for a while. Then he was moving, trudging toward the house, the mud sucking at his shoes. He reached the front steps, climbed them, turned, sat down. His face was lined and wrinkled, his skin like leather from too much time in the sun, but he still looked lean and powerful.

Nathan stood there in front of him, wondering if he should take Talley's unresponsiveness as an answer.

Talley looked up and said, "It's a funny thing about pride. You'd think it would be harder when you're on top, but that just isn't the case. It's when you're down, near rock bottom, that's when it swells. I don't like it, Murphy, not one bit. The thought of working for you…"

"This was a mistake," Nathan said. He started toward the car.

"Hold on, hold on. Let me finish for Christ's sake, you owe me that much at least. Where was I now? Oh yeah, I was trying to explain to you about pride. I've always had an abundance of it, and maybe that's why I'm sitting here and you're standing there, because we all suffer that burden. And the two of us, let's face it, we've never seen eye to eye. You aren't a follower. I'll give you that. Stubborn maybe. I can ponder a guess as to how bad it must be for you to seek me out like this. That's a big drink to swallow. I'm inclined to send you on your way, but that would be the sin of a prideful old man, wouldn't it?"

"You talk too much, Abe," Nathan said. "That's always been your problem."

Talley nodded. "I'm talkin' to a man of action, is that it? Get to the point, he says. All right, Sheriff. I'll help, in whatever capacity you need me. Can I tell you something?"

Nathan waited.

"The damn fish weren't biting anyway."

31

the turning

HE FEELS HIMSELF spiraling out of control.

The bottle of Wild Turkey sits empty on the table as he stares into his square of mirror, gazing at his reflection, his eyes wild with uncertainty.

How could this have happened?

It isn't his fault. He tells himself this repeatedly, but it doesn't make him feel any better. He needs to think, organize his thoughts…his mind races, and he feels himself going into a dangerous tailspin. A rapid nosedive toward defeat.

The woman.

The morning newspaper lies open in front of him, an article on the front page telling him about the attack, about the noble actions of two reserve deputies and how they had rescued the woman in the woods. She was in the hospital. Recovering.

She has been bitten. Without knowing it, she is slowly turning. The Elusive One's seed is in her, a parasite, a virus, coursing through her veins, taking her over, turning her into something that isn't human.

It's only a matter of time.

How long?

Days.

Three at the most.

Time has already passed. They don't understand the signs, the symptoms. There is a wolf in their midst and they have no idea. They tend to her, *heal* her, but they are harboring a monster.

A matter of time.

Think!

He looks in the mirror and sees failure. A once handsome face turned sunken and sour.

His instinct is to act, but he stifles the urge. Times like these, it's important to keep his temper in check.

What to do…what to do…

He needs time, doesn't have it.

Come on, think now.

He could go to the hospital. Could pose as a doctor or a nurse. He isn't good with disguises, doesn't have the experience.

Too dangerous. They might have the woman under guard, police protection. Then what?

No good.

But if he waited…

He's seen something like this once before, during his time in North Dakota. Not quite like this, but close. He hadn't gotten to a woman as fast as he should have and she had had time to start turning. It was the opposite of what he had expected. Disoriented at first, sickly, but then a miraculous recovery, almost back to normal. Then the cravings would start. They would get worse and worse until they couldn't be ignored.

He understands cravings, how they could eventually overpower a person. We are all slaves to our desires. We can resist for a while, but in the end, we give in to them. It's nature. Biology.

He picks up the bottle of Wild Turkey, remembers it is empty, hurls it across the room where it collides with the wall, shatters, leaves broken glass on the floor and the bed.

Why did I do that?

Easy now. Stay calm.

People that make mistakes get caught. Remember that. Always, if anything, remember that. That's what they are counting on. That he will make a mistake. It only takes one. He's been careful so far, maybe even lucky to a certain extent.

He slides his hand over the sharp edge of the mirror, draws blood, watches as crimson droplets splatter the glass.

He breathes. In and out, in and out. Holds a breath, releases it slowly. He feels himself start to regain some control.

Taking her at the hospital would mean an unacceptable level of risk.

Alternatives? Think.

They can't keep her, not forever. She will appear to be in excellent health, at which time they would have no choice but to discharge her.

That will be the time, his opportunity to strike. When she's vulnerable.

It will be close. Three days, *tops.*

Close but doable.

He starts to feel slightly better. Things could work out.

He goes to the bathroom, winds toilet paper around his hand, carries it back to the table and cleans the blood from the mirror. He watches his reflection smiling back at him.

32

lore

THE IBUPROFEN THAT Kobayashi had prescribed did wonders, carrying him through five hours without pain, and when the dull ache started to come back it was manageable, far removed from the almost incapacitating torture he had experienced for the past week.

If Kobayashi was to be believed, there was hope now; hope that he didn't have cancer, but a not uncommon condition that should, according to Kobayashi, rectify on its own. Failing that, treatment entailed minor outpatient surgery. Nathan feared the thought of surgery, but it beat months and months of chemo.

When he had arrived at the station, Lindsay had returned and was chatting with Carl in the conference room.

"You look like shit," she said.

"Everybody keeps saying that."

"I've been conferring with your colleague, and he was explaining this far out idea of his."

"Listening," Nathan said.

Carl pulled out one of the chairs and sat down. "She's right, it's far out there, but just listen all the way through before you judge. I think Marla Waggener is our ace in the hole."

"Go on."

Nathan tried to give it his full attention. He wanted a cigarette, badly, and he brought out his pack of Marlboros, held it up, getting permission from the others in the room, and when no one objected, he lit one, watched the gray smoke snake its way around his head.

"So this guy thinks he's a vampire, right? Or at least that's our operating theory, and I'd say the theory's pretty sound at this point. Case in point – the Waggener woman. He did something to her neck, drained some of her blood with whatever contraption he uses, and then he backed off. According to her, she was under the impression that he was letting her go. With me?"

Nathan nodded.

"That fits the theory, because on the other side of the coin, he *also* thinks he's this big shot vampire hunter. But in order to hunt vampires, you have to have one to hunt. Attacking Marla Waggener – that's him creating a vampire. Once he finishes doing that, he has to let her go. Gives him something to hunt."

"Told you it was far out," Lindsay said.

"And I said to let me finish," Carl said.

"Sorry. Continue."

"Thanks. Anyway, he never got to finish. He only completed half of his fantasy. I don't know what his timeline is like…if he lets them go and then starts the chase, or if he picks it up the next night, but he didn't get a chance to finish this time because Daniels and Gibson interrupted him. Rescued Marla Waggener, and now she's in the hospital."

"The job's unfinished," Nathan said.

"Exactly. In his mind, there's still a vampire out there."

Lindsay said, "You want to use Waggener as bait."

"Way to spoil the climax."

"A little predictable."

"Bite me."

"You think he'll come after her?" Nathan asked.

"I do."

"It just might work," Lindsay said.

"I thought you weren't buying this whole vampire theory?"

"I still don't. Not entirely. But I'm out of ideas, and we're close, really close, this time. If far out is what it takes, I'm willing to try it."

"You want me to put added security on her at the hospital?"

"Too dangerous. He's organized, and that would present an unacceptable level of risk."

"Unless he's losing control. Precipitating factors. Unfulfilled fantasy."

"If it was me, I'd wait it out. Come after her once she's released."

"When are they letting her out?"

"Tomorrow," Carl said.

"Doesn't give us much time."

"We'll have to fill her in."

"She was scared shitless. You think she'll agree to acting as bait for the same guy that already tried killing her once?"

"We can appeal to her better nature. Tell her it'll save lives."

"And that'll work?"

"I'll talk to her," Lindsay said. "Woman to woman. Might have a better chance."

"You really think he's going to go for this, don't you?"

Lindsay shrugged, leaned forward in her chair. She glanced at the crime scene photos that were tacked to the corkboard on the opposite side of the room. "I hope so. We might just have a chance to catch him this time."

Nathan was silent for a while. And what if they did catch the killer? The real question was: what were they going to do with him.

Peter "Hashbrown" Hornick agreed to come down to the station. It was late evening by the time he arrived.

Carl and Lindsay had made the trip into Alton to visit Marla Waggener at Chickasaw Memorial. It had taken some convincing, quite a lot of it in fact, but she had reluctantly agreed to go along with their plan. She didn't like it. But if it meant saving lives, it was hard to say no.

Nathan was in the conference room with Peter when Carl and Lindsay got back. Peter was smoking one of the cigarettes Nathan had given him. It smelled like an old-fashioned British Gentlemen's Club.

Carl spotted Peter when he entered the conference room, eyes widening, the surprise on Peter's face saying he couldn't have felt guiltier if he had been caught in the act of dumping a body.

Carl's gaze went from Peter to Nathan. "You gave him a fucking cigarette?"

"It's *okay*, Carl," Peter said.

"I wasn't talking to you. And like hell it's okay. You know how your mother feels about that."

"Relax."

"What's he doing here?"

"I asked him to come down."

"Oh right, he's the vampire *expert*. How could I forget? Are you trying to put my ass in a sling, Nate?"

"The cigarette was a lapse in judgment."

"No shit. A big one."

Nathan turned to Peter. "You're on your own here on out."

Peter took a drag off his cigarette, mashed it out in the coffee mug on the table. He put up his hands, said, "Okay, okay, fingers off the triggers, I surrender." He smiled crookedly at Carl. "Happy now, Carl?"

"Blended families in the wild," Lindsay said, taking a seat.

"You think it's funny too?" Carl asked.

"I find it interesting."

"Guess the joke's on me."

"Let's get to it," Nathan said. "Peter, why don't you fill us in."

"Where do I start?"

Nathan looked at the faces in the room. "At the beginning I guess."

"You probably already know the basics. Vampires can't come out in the daylight. Sunlight kills them. You can also stake them through the heart, decapitate them, burn them. The Romani people drove spikes through a body to pin it to the ground and then placed bits of steel in the mouth. They also had stones called *dolmens* that they would place over fresh graves to keep the dead from rising. Supposedly, to hasten the departure of the soul. In the old days, they identified a vampire's grave by leading a virgin boy through a graveyard on a white stallion. Though some accounts say it's a *black* stallion."

"What about protection?"

"You're talking about apotropaics. Crucifix, mirrors – they don't cast a reflection, sprinkling mustard seeds on the roof of a house, hawthorn plant, branch of wild rose, and, of course, there's garlic. That's the popular one.

"As far as origins, those go way back. Every culture has some version of the vampire myth. In the Philippines, they believe in mandurugo. It's a spirit that takes the form of an attractive girl during the day, but at night it sucks the blood from sleeping victims. The Norse had the draugr. Ancient Babylonians called it Lilitu, which in Hebrew becomes Lilith, who sustained herself on the blood of babies. In ancient times, Lilith was believed to be Adam's first wife before Eve came along. In the Egyptian Book of the Dead, they cite something about a part of the soul called 'ka.' If it didn't receive adequate offerings, it would leave the tomb to drink blood. I mean, this goes back four thousand years, when the Sumerian's had *Ekimmu*...spirits that weren't buried properly.

"Old people did some pretty fucked up shit. They thought someone was a vampire if they were born with birth defects, or if a baby had teeth too early, or even something as simple as having a full head of hair. Nowadays, they think maybe some of the myths could have been loosely based on uknown diseases. You know how things get embellished over time. There's a thing called porphyria, which is a rare blood disorder that causes sensitivity to light. Then there's rabies. That might be how they linked the use of garlic and light as weapons against the undead. One of the symptoms of rabies is hypersensitivity. Could be related.

"The Romani believed that there was something known as the dhampir, which was basically the offspring of a male vampire and a human woman. This dhampir child was supposedly really good at hunting vampires, but didn't suffer from the usual weaknesses that vampires have."

"Maybe that's what this guy thinks he is," Carl said. "Makes sense. A *damper* or whatever."

"*Dhampir*."

"Guy thinks he's the bastard of a vampire. So he hunts them."

Nathan lit another cigarette. Peter eyed it, craving one, but he was also aware that Carl's gaze had settled upon him, and he didn't risk asking.

"That's possible," Peter said. "From what you've told me, it sounds like he's well versed on the folklore."

"Is there anything that would help facilitate capturing one?" Lindsay asked.

Peter thought about it for a while. He had chosen on this occasion to go sans make-up; no white face paint or black lipstick. His dyed hair was pulled back into a ponytail. He almost looked normal. "Well, about all I can think of is something called arithmomania. It's a mental disorder linked to OCD. The literature talks about it a lot. Not about the disorder, I don't think they associated it with a mental thing back then, but it comes up again and again, so there might be something to it. People with arithmomania get hung up on counting objects. Like steps, letters in words, or touching something a certain number of times. Supposedly, vampires suffer from a similar disorder. If you wanted to stop one in its tracks, you scatter poppy seeds or rice on the ground. You or I, we'd just laugh and keep going, but a vampire has to stop and count them."

"So we could throw a bunch of Cheerios on the ground and he would have to stop everything and count the damn things?"

Peter shrugged. "If you believe the folklore."

Lindsay said, "We don't know how powerful his fantasy is. If he believes he's a vampire strongly enough, he might obey the rules. But in the end, we're dealing with a person. He might deviate from his beliefs based on the situation or his personal needs."

"Anything else?"

"That was Vampires 101, the condensed version."

"I think that should do it."

"That's it?"

"That's it."

"You're kicking me out?"

"What are you asking?"

"If you're trying to capture a vampire, I want to be there."

"Like hell," Carl said, glancing at Nathan.

Looking at Nathan, Peter said, "Hey, you came to me for help. I didn't volunteer. You need me."

"Since when do you care?"

"Since now."

"Nate…"

"Come on, Sheriff. You asked for my help and I helped. But you could still use me. I didn't tell you everything, and if something comes up, you might benefit from having my…*expertise.*"

"The only thing you're expert at is getting high."

"High praise coming from you."

"Don't tell me you're seriously considering this?" Carl said.

"He's got a point."

"I don't give a shit what he has. We're not going LARPing. This isn't for kids."

"I'm not a child, Carl. More importantly, I'm not *your* child."

"What's that supposed to mean?"

"Exactly what it sounds like."

"Knock it off," Nathan said, "the both of you. This isn't a pissing contest."

"He started it," Peter said.

Carl was quiet, tight-lipped, stewing. Finally, he said, "What if he gets hurt? What are you gonna do then?"

Nathan weighed it out, thinking that Carl had a fair argument, but Peter might not have outlived his usefulness yet.

Strategically, Nathan thought they could use all the help they could get.

"The three of us will be there," Nathan said. "I'll bring Talley in, and Daniels, if he's feeling up to it. That's some decent manpower."

"You're seriously doing this?"

"This was your idea."

Carl pointed to Peter. "Involving *him* wasn't my idea. That was all you."

Both Carl and Peter stared at Nathan, awaiting a decision.

"You guys figure it out."

"What?"

"You heard me. Fight it out between the two of you and come to a decision."

"That's easy," Carl said. "He's not going."

Peter stood up, knocked his chair back. "Asshole," he said and stormed out of the room.

"Wonderful," Carl said.

Peter had hoofed it out of the station on foot. He had gotten three blocks by the time Carl caught up to him, keeping pace with his patrol car.

Carl rolled down the window, said, "Wanna ride?"

Peter ignored him, kept walking.

"Being sour won't solve anything," Carl said. "Just get in. We need to talk."

Peter stopped, stood there and debated his options.

"Get in."

Reluctantly, Peter came around, got in on the passenger side.

Carl drove, taking the long way home.

"Why do you want this so bad?"

"What?"

"You know what."

"I don't know."

"You're gonna have to do better than that. You know your mother. She'd send me packin' if she knew I was even considering letting you do something like this. So, *convince* me."

"Your mind's already made up."

"Are you thick? I'm giving you a chance to make me change my mind. Don't ask me why because I don't have the slightest. But you're gonna have to give me something more than the cold shoulder."

"What do you want me to say?"

"You're a smart kid. Think of something. This isn't make-believe. You understand that, right? This guy we're after, he's killed a lot of people. Not just in Crater Lake either. He's been all over. He's dangerous. That's well established. Probably deranged." Carl tapped his temple with a crooked index finger. "All fucked up. He might think he's a vampire, but he isn't."

"I know vampires aren't real, Carl, if that's what you're getting at."

"I know you know that. That's not what I'm saying. What I'm saying is, most people don't *volunteer* to be put into a bad situation. That's what I'm questioning. Why do you want it?"

"Because I'm a fuck up."

"For once, I whole-heartedly agree with you."

Peter half-smiled, said, "Fuck you."

"Look, I know I'm not your favorite person in the world. You hate my guts, I get that, and I can live with it. I think what you're so eloquently trying to get at is that you want to prove something. Maybe to others, but probably to yourself. Am I right or am I right?"

"You're not completely wrong."

"Which in Peter-speak means yes."

"Maybe you aren't as dumb as you look."

"Knock it off with the compliments. Flattery will get you nowhere. If this is something you really want, then I won't stand in your way. You're an adult, and you can make your own decisions in life. But I'll tell you this: if your mom catches wind of this, I'm going to vehemently deny it. I'll take it to my grave."

"Fair enough."

"So it's settled then."

There was silence for a while as they pulled up in front of the house.

"Thanks," Peter whispered.

"What was that? I don't think I heard your right."

"You heard me. And for the record, I don't hate your guts. Not all the way anyway."

33

release

HE PHONES THE hospital impersonating a relative of Marla Waggener. He's calm, voice smooth, friendly but authoritative. He's done this many times, knows how to get the information he's looking for.

It isn't all that difficult. The nurse asks for personal info and he supplies it. He has access to several databases that he pays for on an annual basis. He has done his homework on the Waggener woman, knows pertinent details like address, phone number, birth date.

The nurse, a woman with a deep voice, answers his questions readily. How is she doing? When will she be released?

Good. Bouncing back, the nurse explains to him. *She'll be out tomorrow.*

In his head, he does the math. How many days have passed? Two? Three?

If the woman was acting strangely, he is confident the nurse would have mentioned something. There's still time. Not much, but enough. He thanks the nurse for her time and hangs up the phone.

Mysterious ways. That's what they say, and, for once, he almost believes it. Maybe patience was the key all along.

After all, won't the Elusive One want to claim its prize?

He has thwarted the Elusive One time and time again, performing his work, moving swiftly. He thinks maybe he has the inside track to how the Elusive One operates. He feels like he knows him. *Predictable* isn't the word for it. This isn't about routine. His target has been around for a long time, and maybe it isn't human, but doesn't everyone get lonely from time to time? He knows loneliness, lives with it, but he also knows himself. He's no good at relationships, never has been, has made his peace with this fact.

Under cover of darkness, he exits the phone booth and walks the two blocks back to his motel in long strides. When he isn't hunting, he feels exposed, as though he's wearing a sign and everyone is staring at him. But the streets are mostly void of pedestrians at this hour. The occasional car or two, but otherwise the night is quiet and peaceful. The sky is partially overcast, clouds coasting in to blot out the stars.

He hasn't felt this good in a long time. There is hope. Yet... it scares him. What if his plan works? What if, finally, he confronts the Elusive One? What then? And, scarier, what if he succeeds in his mission?

Cross the bridge when you come to it. One thing at a time.

Best not to let hope cloud his judgment.

He moves faster, reaches the motel's rear entrance, uses the access card to gain entry. He enters the stairwell, takes the stairs two at a time, reaches his floor, pads lightly down the hallway, lets himself into his room. The door closes behind him. He throws the deadbolt, leans against the door for a moment, takes a deep breath.

He reaches into his pocket, brings out the wedge of mirror, stares into it briefly, puts it away.

A new bottle of Wild Turkey rests at the center of the round table. He crosses the room, picks it up, unscrews the cap, pours some into a plastic cup.

He parts the drapes, takes a drink. Feels good. Afraid, but good.

The urge is strong, rising up in him, but the anticipation of tomorrow is enough to satiate his appetite for now.

Hope. Fear. Change.

He sits, stares out the window, drinks, pondering what the future might bring.

34

the morning of

NATHAN WAS ASLEEP when he felt something touch his shoulder, and then he felt Jess's weight leaning on him, her hair falling into his face as she said, "Howdy stranger."

He rubbed sleep from his eyes, checked the time. Early yet. "Stranger huh?"

"That's what it feels like. You've been missing in action lately."

"I know. But it won't last forever. I think we're getting somewhere."

He had given Jess some of the details last night. Not all of them, but he had told her they had a plan and that he was hopeful. She told him she was worried about him, but left it at that, didn't ask for more. She wanted it done and over with, wanted to know that the town where they would be raising their child was safe again.

Before going to sleep, they had tried making love, but it had been awkward and uncomfortable, especially for Jess, who couldn't seem to find a suitable position. In the end, she had finished him. He had fallen asleep feeling guilty about that, but he heard her get up and return several minutes later, the sound of the spoon clanking against the ceramic bowl as she slurped up her Fruit Loops and vegged out on another mindless program.

His sleep had been fitful, but nightmare free. A cloud of darkness had been hanging over him, following him since the dream about being in the woods, the one where the handsome stranger with burning eyes and long teeth had clawed its way into Jess's stomach. If he concentrated, he could still hear the cries of the baby, the screams of memory.

"I know you'll make it safe again."

"Or die trying."

"Poor choice of words. I know it'll be dangerous."

He shifted, turned to face her. "Can't get around that."

"But Carl will be there?"

"Everybody. Carl, Talley, Lindsay. I'll have plenty of back-up."

"Lindsay? Who's Lindsay?"

He'd let it slip and there was no taking it back. Thank God he'd had the forethought not to mention that Carol's son, Peter, would likely be there as well.

"The Special Agent from the FBI. I told you about her."

"You certainly didn't."

"I did."

"You said you were working with the FBI. You didn't say anything about it being a woman."

"I thought I did."

"You didn't."

"Well, she's a woman. What difference does that make?"

"None, I guess."

She shifted away from him.

"What? Are you mad?"

"Of course I'm not mad. Why would I be?"

"Upset?"

"Not that."

"Jealous then?"

There was a long pause; Jess deciding how to word her response. "No. Not jealous. Or maybe a little bit. It's my self-esteem, babe. It's completely shot. I look like a damn hippo."

"I would have gone with elephant."

"You tell me I'm beautiful."

"I wasn't lying."

"No. I know you weren't. But you aren't being entirely truthful either. I know what I am. I see myself in the mirror every day."

"It's temporary."

"Would you still love me if I let myself go?"

"There's a fifty-fifty chance."

He could tell she wasn't interested in humor. This was serious coming off as playful. He didn't know what to say, all the soothing in the world wouldn't make her feel better, but it didn't matter, she changed the subject on her own.

"Do me one favor, it's all I ask."

"Anything."

"When this thing happens, whenever it is, this dangerous thing…think of our child. Think about how she –"

"He," Nathan corrected.

"He, she, whatever…think about how it would be for our child to grow up without a father. Think about that before you do anything heroic."

"Don't do anything stupid is what you're saying."

"More or less."

"In that case, you have nothing to worry about. I've never done a single stupid thing in my life."

That made her smile.

35

final prey

IT IS EARLY afternoon and his few belongings are packed away, bags ready, his tools of the trade laid out on the table neatly before him. He has spent a great deal of time visualizing the way things will be, and he has himself more or less under control, has tried to plan for every possible contingency, but beneath this organization lies a restless beast eager to be let out of its prison.

Several hours pass as he sits and stares out the window, not really seeing the scene outside, but instead spending this time lost in his own fantasies.

As daylight begins to fade, he carries his bags down to the lobby, checks out, pays in cash. He carries his things to his car, which is parked two blocks away, in the lot of another motel.

His patience is thinning.

Easy now.

This is the day. He *knows* it.

Wishful thinking? Perhaps. But his gut says otherwise. He wonders why he hasn't thought of this sooner, of letting the Elusive One think he's won, of letting one of its creations live.

The perfect trap, he thinks. What else would lure the Elusive One better than one of its own kind? It will come to her, or her to it.

He drives across town, stays within the residential speed limit as he passes Marla Waggener's house. He scans the area, driving around the block and past the house again, looking for anything out of the ordinary, for anyone that might be waiting. It hasn't escaped his attention that this could be a trap. That they might be waiting for him.

It's a quiet summer night. The sky clear, but clouds are gathering in the distance. The neighborhood is serene. Birds chirping, dogs barking, the sounds of children playing at a nearby park.

He feels at ease. There's nothing to see. He parks the car a few houses down, on the opposite side of the street, still has a clear view of Marla Waggener's modest yellow house.

His hunting bag is on the passenger seat. Among the items in the bag is a bottle of Wild Turkey. He wouldn't mind a drink. After all, it is tough to say how long he might be waiting, but he stifles the urge, reprimands himself. He needs to keep his mind clear. Anything else would be an unnecessary risk.

He watches and waits.

After a while, he starts to pull the mirror from his pocket, but puts it away without looking into it. He doesn't need reassurance. He knows who he is; knows *what* he is. He is ready for the hunt to start. Tonight, he will claim his victory.

36

the trap

MARLA WAGGENER WAS released from Chickasaw Memorial Hospital at 5:21 P.M. Her older sister, Diedre, was there to pick her up.

On the short drive back to Crater Lake, they gabbed and gossiped, Diedre fussing over her as only an older sibling can, but not once did Marla mention that she had business to attend to tonight.

It was quarter to six when they turned into Marla's driveway. Diedre said she was coming in, Marla said it wasn't necessary, but Diedre insisted.

They went inside. Diedre fixed a pot of coffee, carried a steaming cup over to the table, handed it to her sister. They chatted some more, Marla surreptitiously stealing glances at the clock on the kitchen wall, growing more agitated, drumming her fingers, listening to Diedre drone on and on about all the drama that was happening at work. She wouldn't have traded Diedre for the world, family was family after all, but even she had to admit that her sister had a tendency toward being self-absorbed, as if the world had fallen into orbit around her.

Six-thirty.

"Don't you think?" Diedre asked.

"Huh?"

"Aren't you listening?"

Marla stared at her blankly, glanced at the clock again, feigned an exaggerated yawn. "I'm sorry. I'm just exhausted, I guess. I must not be all the way over it."

This wasn't entirely a lie. Earlier, she had felt on top of the world, but the energy had dissipated quickly. She felt lightheaded, like maybe she would faint if she moved too quickly. She scratched at the sore on the back of her neck. The tips of her fingers came away wet with clear pus. She looked at it in disgust.

And another thing: her teeth had started to bother her. The pain wasn't bad yet, but it was getting worse. It reminded her of when she was in junior high and had just gotten braces. For the first week, the pain had been nearly unbearable, and the thought of eating solid food had been unfathomable. She had taken her calories through a straw, and even that hadn't been painless.

She yawned again.

"What's wrong with your eyes?"

"What?"

"Your eyes. They're really bloodshot."

"Sleep deprivation maybe," Marla said, yawning. "I'm so sleepy all of a sudden."

"You want me to go?"

"You don't have to."

"That didn't sound very convincing."

"Sorry, I don't know what's wrong with me."

Diedre, skeptical at first, surrendered to a moment of tenderness. She said, "Okay, I'll go, but not before I make you something to eat," as she stood up from the table, disappeared into the pantry and came back with a can of chicken noodle soup. She took a bowl from the cupboard, poured the soup in, covered it with a paper towel, placed it in the microwave.

"I'm really not hungry."

"Nonsense. It'll help you get your strength back."

"You sound like mom."

"Sick or not sick, I won't tolerate your insults."

They both giggled at the inside joke.

The bowl of soup came out steaming. Diedre grabbed a spoon from the drawer, carried everything over to the table and placed it in front of her sister and said, "Eat."

The smell of the soup repulsed her, but Marla diligently shoveled a spoonful into her mouth, ignoring the wave of nausea that passed over her. If she wanted to expedite Diedre's departure, it was better to comply with her sister's demands.

"There? Satisfied?"

"You're sure you don't want me to stay? I hate leaving you like this. Bill has T-ball practice at seven, but I can see if Mark will take him."

"No. I'm okay. Really. *Go.*"

"You're sure?"

"You're becoming a pest."

For good measure, Marla spooned another bit of soup into her mouth. She nearly gagged, but, chewing the squishy noodles slowly and deliberately, she managed to choke it down.

"Well, all right then. But if you need me, just call. Promise?"

"I promise. Now go. I officially banish you."

Diedre nodded, picked up her purse, paused at the door. "Call if you need anything."

Marla said she would, waited until she heard the sound of the door opening and then closing again. She stood up from the table, black splotches dancing in front of her vision, waited for them to clear, and then moved to the living room window, parted the blinds ever so slightly, watched Diedre back out of the driveway.

Finally. Alone at last.

She didn't want to admit it, but being alone in the house scared her. She glanced out the window again, scanning the street, left, then right, searching for anything out of the ordinary.

She hadn't been lying to Diedre. She *did* feel tired. Only she couldn't sleep. Not now. She had work to do. She had promised to help, and although the dread was overwhelming, she would keep her promise.

The empty house scared her, but the thought of going back into the woods *terrified* her.

I must be nuts, she thought, taking little consolation in the fact that law enforcement would be there.

The sore on her neck burned. She touched it again, her fingers dipping into the sticky pus. She felt dirty, decided a shower might do her good. She went into the bathroom, started the water going, nice and hot, and as she stepped under the steaming spray, she tried not to think about what the next few hours would bring.

They had assembled in the conference room at six-thirty. Nathan, Carl, Lindsay, Talley and Peter. Talley was the only one among them that looked chipper. Small wonder. Nathan thought Talley looked smug, but put it out of his mind. He couldn't afford to let his personal feelings get in the way. Talley was an extra body, nothing more, simple as that. A hired gun.

Peter looked nervous, slouched in the chair, a black backpack resting in front of him.

"What's in the bag?" Nathan asked.

"Toys."

"He thinks he's a vampire hunter now," Carl said.

"Blow me, Carl," Peter said without animosity.

Lindsay was fidgeting, shifting around a lot, her eyes continually drawn to the crime scene photos plastered to the corkboard wall. After so many years, she had grown used to disappointment, of arriving days, hours, minutes too late, but this time it felt like they really had a chance, could finally close the books on this one. She had been tracking this serial killer for years and she knew little about him, save that he was tall, relatively handsome, and something about his eyes could make a woman swoon, force them to suddenly lose their inhibitions. She was thinking of Ted Bundy, who had been described as intelligent and charming, but behind that handsome demeanor a monster had been lurking just below the surface. She had called the SAC at her local field office, apprised him of the situation. He had suggested sending reinforcements, but Lindsay had declined. Too many hands on deck increased the chance that things would get fudged up.

A phone rested in the center of the table. They stared at it, waiting for it to ring.

"Maybe she got cold feet," Carl said. "God knows I wouldn't blame her."

"She'll come through."

They were all aware that Marla Waggener had been released from the hospital a little after five that afternoon. Nathan had had one of the guys from the Alton PD stationed in an unmarked car outside the hospital. He had phoned Nathan around five-twenty to let him know that Marla Waggener had just been released, was being driven home by her sister in a gray Ford Escape.

"What if he got to her?"

Lindsay shook her head. "Nobody panic. Our guy doesn't take chances remember? He'll be careful. He might even suspect that we've got eyes on Waggener, so he'll be extra cautious. Probably scope out her house, make sure the coast is clear. He's going to look before he leaps. Trust me."

So they waited.

"Anybody having second thoughts?" Nathan asked, eyes going to Peter.

"What are you looking at me for? Are you questioning my resolve?"

"I'm giving you the chance to back out. Once this thing gets going, you won't get another chance."

"I'm in."

Carl said, "I told Carol we were going out to a movie."

"And she bought it?"

"She bought it because I corroborated the story," Peter said.

Carl shrugged.

At 7:45, the phone rang.

Nathan picked up the handset, listened, cupped a hand over the mouthpiece and whispered, "It's her." Into the phone he said, "You're sure about this?" Waited. "And you know the drill…okay…give us twenty minutes, then get going. Don't stop for anything."

Nathan hung up the phone.

"We're on. Let's get going."

They took two vehicles to the Coldwater Woods. Nathan drove his patrol car, Carl rode shotgun, Peter in the backseat. Lindsay rode with Talley in the blue Caprice.

"I'm pretty sure my balls have gone missing in action," Carl said, trying to lighten the mood.

"That would mean you expect us to believe you had balls to begin with," Peter said. His backpack rested on his lap. He clutched the nylon handle at the top in a deathgrip with both hands. He would never admit it, but he was close to pissing himself. He felt giddy as well, excited, but those feelings didn't dampen the undercurrent of fear that had adrenaline pumping through his veins.

"You think this is going to work, Nate?"

"It was your idea."

"I know, which is why I'm asking."

Nathan concentrated on driving. Letting his thoughts get out of control wouldn't help. The pain in his testicle had remained at bay for longer than usual, but had started to creep back as a dull ache. He had lived with it for as long as he thought he could before taking one of the horse pills Kobayashi had prescribed him.

He thought about Jess at home, alone, probably worried sick. About how she might go into labor any minute, who could tell, and wouldn't it be just his luck if that happened now, when they were in the middle of trying to catch a serial killer. He had also reminded her of the 9mm he kept in a hide-ride holster on the top shelf of the closet. The magazine was loaded, a round waiting in the chamber. She didn't care for guns, and she hadn't been especially receptive when he had taken the time to show her how to use it. But there really wasn't much to it. Grab it, unholster, aim, squeeze the trigger. Jess had maintained that she would never have a need to use it. It had been gathering dust on the closet shelf for over a year now, untouched. And she was probably right; she would probably never have to so much as touch it, but he wanted her to remember that it was there if the time ever came. If nothing else, it was for *his* peace of mind as much as hers. He figured if someone ever tried breaking into the house, the first thing she would do was call him, and if that happened, he would calmly instruct her to go to the closet, reach up, feel around with her fingers until she felt the smooth leather of the holster or the cool metal of the 9mm, pull it down, undo the snap, gently remove the gun from the holster, and then hole up in a corner of the bedroom. He would keep her on the phone, trying to keep her calm, and if he couldn't get there in time, he would walk her though shooting the intruder if he had to.

When they reached the woods, Nathan took a right at the curving fork, following the dirt road around to the far side where the woods separated them from town. He chose a spot where the surrounding land was relatively level with the road, veered off, mowed through waist-high grass for twenty feet, knowing it would be a bitch to trek through, but hoping it would make their presence more inconspicuous. He didn't want the killer coming around the backside and spotting the patrol car.

He waited for Talley to pull up next to him, and then they exited the vehicles. Carl had a pump-action shotgun cradled in his arms. They trekked through the tall grass, crossed the dirt roads, and entered the woods. Nathan allowed Carl to lead the way. He was the most familiar with the labyrinth, and they had instructed Marla Waggener on where to go, and Nathan wanted to make sure they got it right. If they made a mistake now...

Talley trampled over the underbrush, keeping pace with the rest of them.

"This doesn't work out the way you planned, you're going to have egg on your face," Tally said in a quiet voice as he came up next to Nathan.

"Something you can use against me in the next election."

"That's what you think, isn't it? That I'm out to get you?"

"Doesn't take much of a stretch of the imagination."

"It's your imagination that's gotten out of control, Murphy. You imagine there's bad blood between us, but the simple truth is that there isn't. You winning, well, I won't lie, that was a chink in the armor of my pride, but I've moved on from that misery, and it hasn't turned out half bad. I'm not carrying any baggage, and my best advice is that you don't either."

"What is it you're trying to say, Abe?"

"It's water under the bridge as far as I'm concerned. On my end, at least."

"You picked a hell of a time to go soft."

"Maybe. Figured if things go sideways, it's best to have a clear conscience."

"Glad you're thinking ahead. Listen, I appreciate you coming out. It's good having your help on this."

Nathan thought maybe Talley was on to something: maybe a clear conscience was the way to go.

Carl stopped, looked around, nodded. "This is the spot."

"Everybody take cover," Nathan said. "Stay down and keep it quiet."

They each took positions behind the surrounding trees, hunkering down, trying to keep low profiles.

A light wind rustled the leaves.

Marla Waggener was out the door, backing her Ford Escort out of the driveway, by eight o'clock. She had felt slightly better after her shower, not great, but better, and some of the wooziness had gone away by the time she slipped into blue jeans and a ragged white t-shirt. Her teeth were still giving her trouble, nearly making her wish for a swift death when she downed a glass of cold tap water and the pain flared. She wasn't certain of all the drugs they had loaded her up with during her hospital stay, but now she wondered if she was having an allergic reaction to something they had given her. Either that, or she had developed a nasty cavity. Only that didn't seem right since it wasn't just a single tooth that was bothering her.

She was hungry now, suddenly starving, but a quick appraisal of the contents in the fridge only made her feel sick again. She didn't think much of it. After days of Jello-O and other semi-solid hospital food, her stomach had yet to adjust to the normal world.

There wasn't time anyway.

Before she left the house, she had stopped in the living room, parted the blinds discreetly, looked up and down the street again.

She tried to keep her focus on her car, not looking around, making straight for it, opening the door, scooting into the driver's seat, turning the key in the ignition.

Sheriff Murphy had talked to her about this, had told her not to spend too much time looking over her shoulder. The trick was trying to look (even if in truth she wasn't) oblivious.

As she drove down the street, she couldn't resist stealing a glance into the rearview mirror. Was someone following her? It was almost full dark now, and she saw headlights far behind her, but that didn't mean anything. No reason to start getting paranoid.

When she reached the lake, she followed Sheriff Murphy's instructions, taking a right at the fork, which took her away from the lake and along the wood's edge. She drove slowly as pavement ended and gave way to a dirt road. She drove until she thought she had reached the spot they had talked about, pulled over as far as she could, and then parked.

Marla sat in the car for a long moment. She gazed into the woods, into that impenetrable darkness, and debated turning around.

What have you gotten yourself into, Marla? What have you agreed to?

She wanted to go home. In fact, that sounded like the best idea in the world. But her hand found the door's handle, pulled, and then she was stepping out of the car into a cool gentle breeze, and her skin went instantly cold.

You could turn back. You don't have to do it. It's not like they can arrest you for not going through with it.

But the time to flee had passed. Inherently, she was aware of this.

She felt sick again as she gazed at the woods, the narrow dirt road the only thing separating her from the unknown.

Such silence. Hard to believe that a few blocks to the east lay the town, houses, people, *safety*.

Slowly, her reluctance faded, and was replaced by something else. Instead of fear, there was something soothing about the woods, they almost called to her now, almost beckoned to her. It was an unspoken invitation, and she was drawn to it. Her fear melted away. The wound on the back of her neck tingled. The pain in her mouth subsided.

She crossed the dirt road and disappeared into the woods.

37

last hunt

HE FOLLOWS HER, keeping his distance, wary that this might yet be a trap. He expects her to stop at the grocery store or the gas station, surprised that she has left the house already, but she keeps going, leaving town, heading in the direction of the lake.

She leads him to the woods, watches as she takes the right fork, kills his lights as her car disappears around the curve.

What is she up to?

But he knows the answer. The Elusive One, he thinks. It calls to her, has beckoned her.

The knowledge is bittersweet. He has waited for the moment for so long that he can scarcely believe it is happening.

Is he being foolish?

No. Only his nerves talking. He is armed, prepared, eager.

He stops and parks before the curve in the road ends. He exits the car, cocks his head to listen, hears the sound of a car door closing. The gentle breeze carries sound in his direction.

His pack is slung over his shoulder. He moves into the tall grass, makes his way forward, the dirt road to his left. As the curve ends, he sees her standing in the road.

What is she doing?

He realizes that she is listening. He watches her disappear into the woods. He digs into his pack, brings out one of the sharpened wooden dowels, and follows her into the woods.

They had been waiting for half an hour and Nathan could feel the burn in his thighs from crouching in one spot for too long.

Radio silence.

To his left, he could see Carl squatted down behind a neighboring tree, Peter close beside him. Lindsay to his right, prone, her weapon already drawn. Talley was nowhere in sight.

Don't let this be a bust.

He glanced over, looked at Carl, a white form against the darkness. Carl held up his hands, shrugged. *Maybe she backed out?*

Nathan heard the rustle of leaves, and when he glanced up he saw the woman coming into the woods. Her white t-shirt was loud against the darkness, and as she came closer, Nathan could see that it was Marla Waggener.

A voice seemed to call to her. It was only in her head, but as she moved forward through the darkness, careful of low-hanging branches, the voice seemed to grow louder and louder.

Marla obeyed the voice. She didn't know why, but she couldn't help herself. It was soothing, and somehow she knew the voice would lead her to safety.

It was almost as though she was hypnotized, but not in a scary way. This was pleasant. She felt warm and at peace.

Something else: she was hungry again. Famished.

The voice persisted. Promised her things, promised to feed her hunger, quench her thirst.

Thirst for what…

…doesn't matter.

She reached a small clearing in the woods. She might have recognized it as the very place where she had had her encounter several days ago, but her mind was elsewhere.

The voice in her head commanded her to stop. She stopped.

And that was when the handsome stranger appeared.

Nathan glanced in Carl's direction again, then in Lindsay's. Quietly, he drew his Glock.

Marla Waggener stood thirty feet away, maybe a little more, and one second she was walking in their direction, the next she came to a sudden halt, doing nothing, just standing there, arms at her sides.

Then another figure materialized. Tall and dressed in black. The black clothes made the man's body blend in with the darkness, and for a moment it looked like a ghostly disembodied head was gliding six feet above the ground.

The handsome stranger approached Marla Waggener. Nathan was sure that Marla would run, but she stood her ground, staring at the man coming toward her. It was like she was hypnotized.

His eyes, Nathan thought. *Something about his eyes.*

"Come to me, child," the handsome stranger said.

His voice was low, quiet, but in the otherwise silence, the words drifted on the breeze.

Marla took a step closer to the stranger.

"Do not be afraid. No harm will come to you."

Nathan looked to his left, Carl looking back, mouthing the words, "What the fuck?"

On the other side of him, Lindsay had her gun up, thrusting her head forward impatiently. "Let's go, let's go," she gestured. She had waited for too long to miss her opportunity. It was now or never.

When Marla was closer, the handsome stranger brought up his arm, his pale wrist moving to his mouth, and he bit into it. Blood was gushing from the self-inflicted wound, and he held his arm out toward Marla, said, "Drink. Quench your thirst."

And Marla was going to do just that. Without hesitation, she moved closer, her hands wrapping around the stranger's forearm, pulling the bleeding wrist toward her own mouth.

Nathan gave the signal, popped out from behind the tree, pointing his weapon, yelling, "Stop!" as he approached. The others followed. Carl coming in on his left, Lindsay on his right, Talley to the right of Lindsay. Peter remained behind the tree, watching.

Nathan yelled, "Hands up. *Now!*"

Marla screamed then. "*No!*"

The handsome stranger turned slowly to face them.

Nathan was close now, within ten feet, and he could see the stranger's face, pale and narrow, but none of that mattered, because it was the eyes that registered, the eyes that drew him in. Suddenly, the eyes changed from black to glowing red embers and Nathan knew this was the face of a killer. Those other faces, Robert Trenton Chase, Peter Kürten – those had been the faces of seemingly ordinary men, the monsters inside of them hidden. But this creature that stood before him, he knew with certainty that this was a monster, both inside and out, no question about it.

Fear gripped him. He steeled himself, transfixed and appalled by those burning red eyes, steadying his gun. "Don't move! Hands in the air."

The others were coming around, trying to flank the handsome stranger.

"I said, hands in the air!" Nathan shouted, stepping forward.

Marla screamed again. "No!" Moved herself in front of her master, shielding him.

Nathan shouted, "Get out of the way!"

She stood her ground, arms held out at her sides, protecting the monster behind her.

"I can't get a shot!"

Carl moved fast. Hunched over and threw himself, tackling Marla to the ground. She screamed and squirmed, raked at him with her nails. Carl pinned her down, brought up his gun, and then brought it down on the back of her skull. She went limp under him.

Nathan said, "Last chance."

The crimson eyes blazed at him, and then the handsome stranger was moving toward him. Nathan didn't stop to think, he aimed, fired, but in an instant he was propelled back, hitting the ground hard, rolling, coming up, scrambling to get his gun up, but a powerful hand caught his wrist, bent it back with in credible force. The gun fell from his hand, and the stranger's face was inches from his own, the mouth yawning open, impossibly wide, and Nathan saw something moving from within its depths, thinking at first it was the stranger's tongue, but the way it moved, leapt out like it had a life of its own. He was staring at something otherworldly; a long gray protuberance slithered out, cylindrical, opening and closing to reveal three long teeth that formed an inverted Y.

The protuberance undulated up and down, a sentient thing, reminding Nathan of a miniature elephant's trunk. Saliva dripped from its gaping mouth, the three teeth glistening.

Nathan pulled away, but the hand that gripped his wrist wouldn't budge. An iron hand found his crotch and squeezed. Sudden fire erupted from his genitals and a high-pitched scream escaped his lips. His vision swam and all that was left in the world was agony. The feeling was absolute. He had been under the assumption that he was familiar with pain, but what he experienced now shattered his beliefs. In that moment, he nearly prayed for cancer; it would have been tame compared to this.

The undulating proboscis stiffened, shot forward toward Nathan's face. Clinging to consciousness, Nathan let himself fall, became deadweight, kicked out with his legs, striking the stranger in the torso.

Suddenly, his wrist and his balls were free. He scrambled away, his manhood screeching at him, feeling as though his testicles had transformed into lead weights. Frantically, he searched through the leaves for his gun, not finding it, and he sensed the stranger moving toward him...

...but the sound of gunfire saved him.

Gunshots rang out, a barrage of them; Carl, Lindsay, and Talley all firing now that they had a clear line of sight and weren't in danger of hitting Nathan by accident.

Bullets ripped into the handsome stranger, but they didn't seem to faze it. It turned, was gone in a flash, reappearing next to Lindsay, the prosboscis darting in and out of its mouth.

Nathan found his weapon, staggered to his feet, turned in time to see Lindsay thrown to the ground, crawling through the underbrush on her stomach as the handsome stranger moved in, straddled her, the trunk flashing toward her exposed neck.

He fired. Unloaded his magazine, ejected, rammed home another. The handsome stranger's head turned toward him, eyes on fire. The face changed in an instant. It became wrinkled and elongated, the nose tilting upward, the face of a giant bat.

Nathan aimed for its face, fired again and again, saw a chunk of protruding forehead explode outward as one of the rounds struck its target.

The handsome stranger screeched. Lindsay scrambled away, rolled over, began firing. The stranger disappeared momentarily, reappeared behind Carl, its proboscis darting out, making contact with the back of Carl's neck. Carl screamed, fell to his knees, scared at first, but slowly his expression changed, a smile spread across his face. "Hey, Nate, it doesn't feel so bad."

Then Peter jumped out from behind the tree, hollering a war cry, his arm extended outward as he ran at the stranger. There was a cross in his hand.

The stranger glanced up, its proboscis retracting. The thing hissed as it caught sight of the metal cross, threw an arm across its face to shield itself.

Carl squirmed on the ground, back in control of himself, whispering, "Peter...don't..."

The creature lashed out, grabbed the cross, foul-smelling smoke coiling up from its hand. The cross melted, disintegrated, and Peter was staring into its fiery eyes. There was something else in his hands, and he thrust it forward now, smashing it against the bat-like creature's snout.

The creature recoiled as the bulb of garlic exploded in its face. Talley closed in and fired, his revolver jerking in his hands. "It won't go down!"

Peter fumbled for his backpack, reached in, found one of the wooden stakes. "It's a vampire!" he shouted, a phrase he hadn't expected to use even if he had somehow lived to be a hundred. It sounded odd and juvenile saying it now, his voice a faltering croak. He gripped the stake, glanced at the creature, thrust the stake forward, but the thing was fast, impossibly fast, and it was gone, Peter thrusting at empty space, and then he was picked up from behind, a single cold hand gripping the back of his neck, lifting upward until his feet left the ground, and he felt himself hurled through space, crashing into a nearby tree. His shoulder struck first, absorbing most of the impact, but something snapped, and the sudden burst of pain informed him that something was broken.

"My bag!" he yelled. "I've got rice in my bag!"

It sounded ridiculous to his own ears as he said it, an absurd thing to say if one was to consider the possibility that they were seconds away from death.

But Carl listened, and whether he registered the absurdity of it all or not, he dove for the backpack, landed on it, hand digging into it, bringing out a Ziplock baggie full of grains of white rice. Carl held it up, stared at it, wondered what the hell he was supposed to do with it.

"The ground! Scatter it on the ground!"

The creature was approaching him, hunched over, its fingers having grown, seeming to go on forever and ever until they ended in curved talons. A razor-sharp talon swiped at him. Carl jumped back, tripped, fell to his ass, but managed to open the baggie, dumping the contents to the ground, scattering grains of rice everywhere.

The creature paused, glanced at the ground, at the scattered rice.

Holy shit, it worked, Peter thought, but too soon, because the creature stared for only a moment, and then turned its misshapen head toward Carl, mouth spreading open wider into a grotesque smile revealing rows of crooked fangs.

Carl drew his gun, began unloading the magazine, knowing it wouldn't do any good.

Holes appeared in the creature's flesh, blood the color of crude oil spilled out of the wounds, but the creature kept coming.

Carl knew he was a goner. Knew, without a doubt, that this was the end of the line. He couldn't believe what he was seeing, this creature, this *vampire,* was coming at him, and there was nowhere to go. His weapon was empty. He squeezed the trigger, heard nothing but the weak click of a dry fire, stared at the monster that hovered over him now, thick drool streaming from its flickering proboscis, dripping onto Carl's face.

He did the only thing he could: closed his eyes, lips moving, saying a prayer, the only one he remembered these days, whispering the words, "Our Father, who art in Heaven, hallowed be Thy name…"

Even with his eyes closed, he could sense the thing moving closer, could smell the stink of its foul breath. He prayed for saving, or, at the very least, for the minor miracle of a swift and painless death.

Shots rang out. Nathan was down on one knee, squeezing off round after round until his final magazine was empty.

Maybe it won't hurt, Carl thought. It hadn't felt terrible when the thing's second mouth had attached itself to the back of his neck. In fact, he had experienced exactly the opposite. The feeling had been almost euphoric. Give him that again and maybe he could die thinking pleasant thoughts. Or like Gibson, his neck broken, snapped, snuffed out instantly.

For a moment, nothing happened. All was silent.

Carl opened his eyes in time to see the strange man appear out of nowhere, launching himself, landing on the creature's back, locking his arms around the thing's neck, his legs wrapping around its torso.

The creature whirled around, trying to free itself of this wild man, but the man's grip was strong, one arm squeezing against the creature's throat, his feet interlocked at the ankles at the front of the thing's torso, his right hand coming up, holding a sharpened stake, and his arm came up, then down, the tip of the stake sinking into the creature's left breast, and it screeched then, ear-piercing, blood-curdling, a scream that Carl, for the remainder of his days, would never erase from his memory.

The creature continued to thrash frenziedly, clawing at its back, a taloned-hand reaching for the stake, trying to remove it, but the man held on for dear life, kept it planted deep in the thing's chest.

The horrific dance went on for what seemed like hours. The creature spiraling, thrashing, trying to buck the man off.

Maybe it was only minutes, maybe less, but slowly the creature began to lose momentum, the fight draining out of it. It collapsed, taking the man down with it. They both thudded to the ground, the man rolling away, coming up fast, throwing himself on top of the creature, gripping the protruding stake with both hands, plunging it downward with all he had, twisting it until it sank deeper, until the others thought it must have gone clean through.

The proboscis blasted out from between its open jaws, searching for something to strike, but the man managed to dodge it deftly, until it, too, lost its fight, slithered back into the creature's mouth and disappeared down its throat.

Finally, after the creature had been still for several long minutes, he stood, reached into his jacket and produced a knife with a serrated blade. He crouched down, slid his fingers through the creature's hair, pulled back, exposing its throat, and then he began carving away.

Nathan stood stupefied, doing nothing. He merely watched. His heart was racing, pounding so fiercely that he worried it would explode.

The man worked quickly, sawing back and forth, the blade disappearing into the creature's wrinkled flesh, black blood gushing, until finally the task was finished, and the head was removed. The man held it up in front of his face.

Linsday, Peter, Talley and Carl all gathered close to Nathan, spectators now, silent and watching as the man completed his work.

When he was through, the man placed the severed head on the creature's still body, stepped away.

Carl was the first to speak. "What is it?"

"It's a vampire," Peter said. "Or something that inspired the folklore."

"It's a fucking nightmare," Carl said.

Nathan didn't know what it was, and in that moment he didn't care. "Is everyone okay?"

They nodded, grimly, in turn.

"What do we do with it?"

But the question was answered almost immediately as the man dug into an olive-colored bag, brought out a red plastic container, unscrewed the cap, began pouring the liquid over the creature, dousing it thoroughly, and Nathan identified the smell as it blasted his nostrils. *Gasoline.*

The man took a box of wooden matches from his pocket, struck one, and let the flame grow before tossing it onto the creature's body. It burst into flames.

They stood there and watched it burn.

38

masks

Days passed.

At least that's what it felt like.

But it took only minutes. They watched the flames eat at the flesh, blacken it, until it became nothing but ash. Eventually, the flames died out.

The man's name was Daniel Florescu. He offered that and nothing else. Nathan regarded the man with a kind of awe. This entire night felt like a fairy tale. No, not a fairly tale. Carl had been on the money when, minutes earlier, he had referred to it as a nightmare.

"I was wrong," Carl said. "It wasn't one man. It was two all along. Nate…there's something that's got me freaked. That thing… it bit me. I don't want to turn into whatever the hell it was."

It was Peter who answered. "I don't think so. I think you're safe. Based on everything I've read, you kill the master vampire, and the infection won't take hold. Either that, or a transformation doesn't take place unless you drink the vampire's blood."

Nathan glanced over at Lindsay. She was staring at Florescu, couldn't take her eyes off of him. He moved over to her, whispered, "What's wrong?"

"A better question would be 'what isn't?' There's nothing right about any of this." She nodded subtly at Florescu. "He's a killer, Nathan. All those girls. He's responsible for that."

"What are you saying? I'm not sure exactly how to handle this."

Peter was close enough to eavesdrop on the conversation. He said, "They were vampires. That's what it did to them. He turned them. Made them like him."

Talley interrupted, asking Nathan if it was all right to leave. Marla stood next to him. He had draped his jacket over her shoulders. She appeared dazed, badly shaken. "I'll take the young lady home. She's had a rough night. I guess we all have."

Nathan didn't know what to say. All he came up with was, "Thanks."

"You're welcome. And it's all yours. The job, I mean. You can keep it. I'm going to the cabin. I'm going to grab a bottle of Jack and take the boat out and I'm going to do some fishing. And I'm going to drink until I'm properly skunked. When I wake up, I'm going to pretend this was all a bad dream. You got that? You handle it however you see fit, you're the Sheriff of Crater Lake after all, but in the future, should our paths cross, as far as I'm concerned, that's all it was – one bad fucking dream."

Nathan nodded and watched them leave.

"What's the play?" Carl asked.

They watched as Florescu stood over the pile of ashes. His hand went to his pocket, brought out a small wedge of mirror. He stared into it for a long time.

"What's he doing?" Nathan whispered.

"Checking for a reflection," Peter said.

Nathan looked at Carl. "Get your kid home."

Carl nodded.

"I'll see you tomorrow?"

"Why wouldn't you?"

"Something like this," Nathan said. "Well, I wouldn't fault you for looking for another line of work."

"Hell of thing. But you aren't gonna get rid of me that easy. Who knows, maybe next election I'll get a wild hair and run against you."

"By then, I might just let you have it. And thanks."

"Just doin' my job, Sheriff."

That left only him and Lindsay now – and Florescu.

Florescu was gazing into the mirror, still as a statue. Nathan could spot an odd duck when he saw one, and Florescu definitely fell within that category.

"What do you want to do?" he whispered to Lindsay. "Your call."

Lindsay was thinking about it. She was right, he was a killer, had picked up the trash. It didn't take a stretch of the imagination to understand how the relationship had worked. The handsome stranger had made the mess, Florescu had spent however long cleaning it up. Criss-crossing the country, cat and mouse, a game that may have lasted for decades.

Nathan watched her, could almost read her thoughts.

"I'm torn," Lindsay said. "There's something about him that's a little *off*, wouldn't you say?"

"Everything about this is off."

"Call it a gut feeling."

He knew where she was coming from. The exhaustion was on him now, and all he really wanted to do was get home to his wife, let her know that the monster had been slain. The town was safe again.

"Do you believe in vampires?" he asked.

"You're asking me like I have a choice. I saw it with my own two eyes, but I'm having trouble believing it."

Her eyes went to the pile of charred remains. Even now things were starting to blur, and her mind was clinging to the reality she had known all her life, trying to wipe away what had happened in an effort to rid itself of the night's incongruous events. "Thinking about it logically, what exactly am I supposed to put in my report? I've always been strong on the truth, regardless whether it aligns with my own personal beliefs, but now...if I tell the truth, I'll be out of a job. Or, at the very least, I'll be laughed out of the Bureau."

Nathan had been struggling with what he would put in his own report, but whatever that was, he had already come to the decision that the word 'vampire' would be absent from it. He was going to have a long chat with Carl, and Carl would have to have a heart to heart with Peter, and then there was Talley to consider, but Talley had already made it clear that tonight was better off forgotten.

Finally, Nathan said, "I think this time maybe it's okay to fib a little. I don't see any other way."

Lindsay nodded, letting it go for now.

"Mr. Florescu," Nathan said.

Florescu turned and looked at them, pocketing his mirror. "What am I going to do now?"

He looked deeply saddened. Nathan almost felt sorry for him. Lindsay didn't share in his sympathy. She said, "For starters, we'll need you to come with us. We have some questions for you. Lots of them."

Daniel Florescu accompanied them back to the station willingly. When Nathan opened the rear door of his patrol car and gestured for Florescu to get in, Florescu asked about his own car, and Nathan said they would drive him back to pick it up when they were finished with him.

They rode in silence. Once they were inside the station, Nathan asked Florescu if he needed anything. Florescu declined. Nathan led them back to the conference room, took out his cigarettes, asked was it all right if he smoked, and when no one objected, he lit one, knowing it was his last. The three of them looked haggard, as though they had just come away from a long and vicious war, soldiers returning from battle.

Lindsay left the room, returned five minutes later with her laptop tucked under her arm. She produced a digital recorder, placed it on the table, asked Florescu if he was opposed to her recording their conversation. He didn't care. She started the recorder going.

LT: Your name is Daniel Florescu?

DF: Yes.

LT: Where are you from?

DF: Originally?

LT: Sure.

DF: I grew up in Michigan. My grandparents came over from Bucharest in the 1950s. My parents died when I was twelve, so I ended up living with them until I graduated from high school. My grandmother was very superstitious. Believed in all the folklore, and she used to sit in her chair at night and tell me about it.

LT: Are you currently employed?

DF: No. My calling makes it difficult to keep a job.

LT: Your calling?

DF: Yes, what I was born to do.

LT: And what is that?

DF: To protect the innocent.

LT: And when you say you 'protect the innocent,' what does that entail exactly?

DF: Killing vampires.

LT: You believe that vampires exist?

DF: You saw one with your own eyes tonight.

LT: Is that what you think happened tonight?

DF: Without question.

LT: Have you killed vampires before?

DF: Yes.

LT: How many have you killed?

DF: Real vampires?

LT: I don't understand.

DF: The Elusive One was the first true vampire I have killed.

LT: The Elusive One?

DF: It's this story my grandmother used to tell me about an ancient king that used to set out on nightly quests to capture what they called the Elusive One.

LT: The Elusive One was a vampire?

DF: That is my belief, yes.

LT: How long have you been tracking this Elusive One, as you call him?

DF: A long time.

LT: Can you be more specific?

DF: Eight years.

Lindsay paused to open the screen of her laptop, studied what was on the screen for a moment.

LT: Mr. Florescu, have you ever been arrested before?

DF: When I was younger.

LT: For aggravated assault, correct?

DF: Yes.

LT: And you were found guilty?

DF: Yes.

LT: And sentenced to a psychiatric institution?

DF: That's correct.

LT: How long did you spend there?

DF: Two years.

LT: While you were there, you were diagnosed with ASPD with psychopathic features.

DF: They didn't believe me. I told them vampires were real, but they didn't believe. Didn't *want* to. But I proved them all wrong, didn't I? I can't be insane if something actually exists, can I?

LT: Let's go back to the original crime of assault. You tried to sexually assault a seventeen-year-old female. Correct?

DF: Correct.

LT: Was she a vampire? Is that why you attempted to assault her?

DF: Of course not.

LT: If she wasn't a vampire, why did you attempt to rape her?

DF: I don't care for that word.

LT: Rape?

DF: It's a filthy word.

Lindsay glanced at Nathan without saying anything.

LT: Why did you attempt to *assault* her?

DF: I used to have problems.

LT: Problems?

DF: I had these...*urges*, I guess you'd call them. I wasn't able to control them.

LT: But now you can.

DF: Yes.

LT: You said you've only killed one vampire.

Lindsay pointed to the crime scene photos tacked to the corkboard behind her.

LT: What about them? Were they vampires?

DF: Yes and no.

LT: Please explain.

DF: They weren't true vampires, but if I hadn't stopped them, they would have become real vampires. They were in the process of turning.

LT: You know this how?

DF: They bore the mark. The Elusive One had marked them. *Infected* them. I don't know how it works, but something happens to their blood. The Elusive One drains the blood and leaves some kind of parasite inside of them. Before I disposed of any of them, I would check for the mark on the back of their neck. If they had it, I would put them at peace.

LT: And by 'put them at peace' you mean you would murder them?

DF: They were no longer innocent. They weren't sheep anymore.

LT: Sheep?

DF: I protect the sheep.

LT: Sheep are anyone that isn't a vampire?

Florescu nodded.

DF: The rest are wolves.

LT: Vampires?

DF: Or the infected that will become vampires.

LT: So you're saying you've made it your mission in life to protect all of us from vampires?

DF: You're welcome.

LT: If I understand correctly, all the women in those photos were vampires or on their way to becoming one?

DF: That's right.

LT: You're sure about that?

Nathan had been listening to all of this in silence, taking it in, not sure exactly where Lindsay was going with it, other than maybe trying to satisfy her own curiosity. But, suddenly, he thought he understood. He had a hunch where Lindsay was leading Florescu, and the thought of it disturbed him. He didn't know how he could have missed it. It was all there. Lindsay had seen it first, and she was trapping her man now.

He watched as Lindsay stood up, moved over to the corkboard. She began to remove thumbtacks from several of the photos, taking them down, making a neat pile, and when she was finished, she sat back down and handed them to Florescu.

"Do me a favor, look through those would you."

Florescu glanced at her and then at the stack of photos. He began sifting through them, and Nathan noticed something now. Florescu was slowing down, spending a lengthier amount of time on each photo, almost staring at them longingly. A normal person would have had a different reaction when presented with something as grotesque as a series of young girls, nude except for the mask covering each of their faces, all of them becoming the Unknown Girl of the Seine.

Florescu gazed at the photos, lost, captivated, the touch of a smile forming at the corners of his mouth.

Nathan had respected Lindsay, but now he thought she was something close to brilliant. She glanced at him, and when she did, Nathan nodded, a gesture that said, "I understand now."

"Mr. Florescu, do you recognize the women in those photographs?"

When Florescu glanced up, he looked as though he was in a daze.

"You said your victims were only vampires, or people that were in the process of turning. You also said that you confirmed that they were infected by checking for the distinctive inverted Y mark on the backs of their necks. But none of the girls in those photographs had the mark. None of them were butchered like the rest. They all died by strangulation. You used your hands. So I'm extremely curious, why did you murder them?"

Daniel Florescu was placed under arrest at 1:57 A.M. for the murder of over a dozen women, a series of heinous crimes that spanned a course of years and numerous towns across the United States. Lindsay read him his rights. Florescu waived them, and confessed to all of it.

Lindsay called in a favor, and the US Marshals arrived to transport Florescu to a more secure facility that same morning.

By the time Nathan and Lindsay had finished listening to the recording of Florescu's confession a final time, it was nearly six, and the darkness outside was giving way to lighter shades of blue.

"You're a savant. I missed it at first."

"Thanks."

"He didn't have the 'urges' under control at all."

"Guys like him typically don't. It's overpowering to them. You can't do something like that once and then just stop. I didn't remember it right away, not when we were still in the woods, but it was right there, and I knew something was off. It didn't hit me until we came back and I ran his name through the database. That's when I put it together."

"The girls with the masks. Those were *his* victims."

"Yeah," Lindsay said. "I think his mission, the *calling* as he describes it, helped him stay smart. It gave him an outlet for killing women. It was still sexual for him, but for a lot of his kind, the act of penetration isn't the factor that gets them off. It's the power. The domination and control. He's a sexual sadist, and what he was after was making them suffer."

"But there were stretches when he was traveling."

"Right. Sometimes weeks, maybe a month, and that's when fantasizing wasn't enough to carry him through. So he found easy prey along the way."

During questioning, Florescu had admitted to killing the young girls. They were all victims of opportunity. Most of them prostitutes or hitchhikers.

He had a certain preference: females, between sixteen and twenty-five, long hair, slender and athletically built. It wasn't difficult. Usually, circumstances had already isolated them, and because the majority of them were runaways or hookers, no one was looking very hard. They wouldn't be missed.

"It was the masks that had me curious," Lindsay said. "He wasn't afraid of killing, none of them were his first, so it couldn't have been because he felt guilt or shame."

"It was because they were sheep," Nathan said.

"A case of fucked up thinking. To him, there were only two kinds of people: sheep and wolves. Vampires were wolves, everyone else were sheep. So the girls he picked up along the way were sheep. Basically, meaning *innocents*. To him, they weren't vampires, so he used his hands. The masks were like him leaving his own kind of mark, like the handsome stranger marked his victims' necks. The mask represented the Unknown Girl of the Seine. He considered those girls to be innocent. He marked them with the mask, maybe so there wouldn't be confusion, to symbolize that they hadn't done anything wrong. Did you catch how he tried to justify it?"

"By using them to check into the motel to draw less attention to himself. He said people tend to notice loners, give them more scrutiny."

"Yeah, that was a load of shit. Maybe he used them for that, but it's still a load of shit. He killed them because he wanted to."

"Do you think he enjoyed it?"

"I *know* he did. Every minute of it. It's not even a question of which he liked better. If it wasn't for his delusion, he probably would have always used his hands. The only reason we linked the strangulated victims with the ones he butchered was due to proximity. The pattern formed and showed it to be more than coincidence. Otherwise, we probably would have assumed it was the work of two separate killers."

"In the end, he was right. Vampires *do* exist."

"But it didn't take a vampire to make Florescu a killer. He became that all on his own, long before he started hunting mythical creatures. For him, the vampire angle was just extenuating circumstances. Something to rationalize his fantasies."

"Where do you think it came from?"

"I don't know. It was old, that's one thing. The timeline we put together, the connections to Europe, that many years – kind of makes sense now. Not that anyone will ever know."

"People are going to listen to his confession and think he's insane."

"I'm okay with that."

"Are you? It isn't the truth, at least not the whole one, and I know that rubs you the wrong way."

"There's no way around it. He'll pay for what he did, and that's all that matters. We took care of the rest."

"You think there are others out there?"

"Who knows. Maybe they're an endangered species. Maybe they're mostly extinct. It could have been the last of its kind.

Scientists are always discovering species they thought were long dead. Personally, I hope to God it was the last."

"At least we'll know what to look for."

Lindsay nodded solemnly. She tried a smile. "So, what's next for you?"

"I've got a wife at home that's ready to burst. That's where I need to be."

"Are you going to tell her?"

"About all this?"

"I gather you've already made up your mind."

"Didn't take much thought. I'll tell her the monster is gone. That's all she'll care about. The rest is details."

"This one anyway," Lindsay said. "A sad and troubling fact of life on this planet is that no matter how many we catch, there will always be monsters out there. All we can do is be ready."

epilogue

rest the innocents

A LITTLE OVER two weeks later, Amelia Marie Murphy was born. It was a Friday. Labor lasted for sixteen hours, and for most of that, Nathan held his wife's hand. She had squeezed his hand until all the feeling had gone out of it. It was 4:52 A.M. when he heard his daughter's voice for the first time, screaming and crying her way into the world, and a minute later he was staring at her face, her eyes pinched tightly shut, her mouth open as she cried at the top of her lungs. For Nathan, it was love at first sight.

They brought her home a day later.

Saturday night, it was Nathan's turn with the bottle. He held Amelia in his arms, still worried that she was so fragile he might break her. He tried to feed her, but she refused, just cried and cried, until Jess came into the room and took Amelia into her arms and the cries went away.

"Guess you're off the hook."

"All she wants is mommy."

"That'll change. She'll be a daddy's girl. Wait and see."

After Amelia was asleep in her crib, Nathan and Jess went to bed, watched TV, talked for a while. Jess confessed that if she never saw a bowl of Fruit Loops again it would be too soon.

Hours later, still unable to sleep, Nathan slid out of bed, careful not to wake Jess. He padded down to the basement to the makeshift office and sat in front of the desk, laptop open, doing research. Since the night in the woods, he had found himself obsessed with vampires. Perhaps it wasn't healthy, and maybe he should have put the events of that night behind him, but the memory persisted, the burning red eyes, the enlarged snout, the bat-like visage, and the long flickering proboscis. It haunted him. The nightmares he suffered were vivid and terrifying, mostly, he thought, because they had been inspired by reality.

He hoped they would fade over time. He hadn't told Jess, not the details, and she hadn't pried. He had emailed Lindsay at the Bureau last week, and he couldn't help himself when he asked if she was having nightmares. She had responded in the affirmative, that in their line of work, nightmares were simply par for the course. She had also suggested that perhaps confronting his fears might lead to him conquering them. So he had begun researching vampires. He had scoured the Internet, checked out books from the local library, and had spent many nights after Jess had gone to bed, reading about them, pouring over the folklore, learning as much as he could.

Another thing Lindsay had told him: "Watch them." Meaning Carl and Marla Waggener. They had both been bitten by the creature, and despite what Peter had told them, Lindsay was cautious. Maybe she didn't trust the lore; it was hard to put faith in a myth, even if you had stared that myth in the face. He had been placing weekly phone calls to Marla under the guise of checking in, Nathan telling her that he owed her a debt of gratitude, that in a small town you took care of your own, but beneath it all he was doing his job, making sure they had gotten rid of the monsters for good.

He knew Carl was still having a tough time of dealing with it. Occasionally, Carl would phone him late at night saying, "Listen, don't get the wrong idea, I'm not a pussy, and I'm not reaching out here, but that shit is stuck in my head, Nate. Why can't I get rid of it?"

What Nathan didn't know was that Carl had stopped by the hospital on the day Jess had gone into labor, that he had planned on poking his head in to see how things were going, but that he hadn't quite made it that far. He had checked in with one of the nurses, had been walking down the hallway, when a scent had caught his attention. He had glanced over to see a door slightly ajar, had gone to it and peeked in, had seen a woman in a chair donating blood. He lingered longer than he should have, had shaken his head as if trying to dismiss an unpleasant thought, and had turned around and left.

Two days later, he had dropped by Nathan's house, had presented the baby with a brand new stuffed doll.

Nathan told himself that Crater Lake was safe and sound again. It had been a quiet town for a long time, and in a single month it had seen not one monster but two, and, as far as Nathan was concerned, that was enough to last a lifetime.

He read until his eyes were tired. He closed the laptop screen and sat in the darkness until from upstairs he heard Amelia's high-pitched whine.

He waited, thinking that she would fall back to sleep on her own, or that he would hear the sound of Jess's footsteps above him as she went to the kitchen to warm up a bottle.

When neither of those things happened, Nathan headed upstairs, took a full bottle from the fridge, nuked it for a few seconds, squirted a few drops onto his arm, and then went to Amelia's room. He picked her up from the crib, held her close to him, gently rubbed her back.

He sat down in the glider, soothed her, whispered to her calmly, brought the bottle's nipple to her lips and she quieted down and began to drink. Her eyes were open, gazing up at him as she polished off the bottle. When she was finished, he lifted her up, patted her back until she issued an impressive burp, and then held her. Slowly, her eyes fluttered closed, and she fell back to sleep.

Nathan sat with her for a long while before he placed her back into the crib. He stared at his daughter, peaceful and innocent. He knew that Lindsay had been right when she said that there would always be monsters in the world. But he also knew something else: staring at his daughter's face, this tiny miracle that he had played a small part in bringing into the world, he knew that as long as monsters existed, it was his job to protect her from them.

acknowledgments

THERE ARE TWO of them this time around. The first goes out to my longtime friend from across the pond, Keith Thomas, who spent a good deal of time on the phone with me, offering his wisdom and insight without pulling any punches. The second is for Sara Smith, who is the founder and book blogger over at The Loaded Shelf. Her advice also contributed to making this a better book. What else can I say? Both of them provided criticism in such a way as to not be overly damaging to my fragile ego. Because of them, the whole is greater than the sum of its parts.

about the author

J.W. BOUCHARD IS a horror, crime, science fiction, and children's fantasy author best known for his novels *Last Summer* and *The Z Club*. When he isn't writing, he enjoys surveying unexplored parts of Wind Cave in South Dakota, traveling to exotic locales, and teaching his kids bad habits. He lives in Iowa.

You can sign up for the newsletter he rarely ever sends here: http://eepurl.com/z7gGb

more books by j.w. bouchard

Made in the USA
Lexington, KY
17 November 2017